# Lost Enchantment

*by*

Barbara Cartland

**Dales Large Print Books**
Long Preston, North Yorkshire,
BD23 4ND, England.

British Library Cataloguing in Publication Data.

Cartland, Barbara
    Lost enchantment

    A catalogue record of this book is
    available from the British Library

    ISBN   978-1-84262-761-7 pbk

First published in Great Britain in 1972
by Hutchinson & Co. (Publishers) Ltd.

Copyright © Barbara Cartland 1972

Cover illustration by arrangement with
Rupert Crew Ltd.

Published in Large Print 2010 by arrangement with
Cartland Promotions, care of Rupert Crew Limited

Dales Large Print is an imprint of Library Magna Books Ltd.

Printed and bound in Great Britain by
T.J. (International) Ltd., Cornwall, PL28 8RW

# OST ENCHANTMENT

thought of Leone, the toast of the ice Regent's Carlton House set, the irqu brow clouded. Beautiful, ir ie, desirable Leone was trying to oeuvre him into marriage, that he w... he could not know was that st e girl was also trapped – trapped a of deceit and treachery that was to ol n both...

# LOST ENCHANTMENT

The author would like her readers to know that the background of this story set in the year 1803 is as accurate as research can make it. The details of Napoleon's invasion fleet, the spy fever gripping England and the personages in the Government are all part of history.

# 1

The Marquis of Alton was blue-devilled, which meant that everyone in the whole of Alton Park, from his personal valet, who had come down with him from London, to the lowest scullion was affected by His Lordship's temper.

He had arrived unexpectedly long after midnight, and because he was in one of his black moods it seemed that nothing was to his satisfaction.

The Chef, shaken into wakefulness, performed miracles in providing a cold collation in under fifty minutes, but even so His Lordship looked disdainfully at it, and having nibbled at a few dishes left the rest untouched, which cast a shadow of despondency over the whole kitchen staff.

Also, on entering the huge baronial Dining Room and glancing in a disparaging way at the shining array of silver which had with unprecedented speed been taken from its shrouds of green baize to ornament the table, His Lordship had remarked sourly:

'Short of footmen, are we, Westham?'

The old butler, who had been at Alton Park since he had started as pantry boy to

9

His Lordship's father, replied apologetically:

'As I was not aware that Your Lordship was honouring us with a visit, I allowed four of the younger men to repair to the village to drill with the Volunteers. They were keen, M'Lord, and I felt it was my patriotic duty to encourage their enthusiasm.'

There was nothing His Lordship could reply to this, and after a moment Westham ventured:

'What news is there of the war, M'Lord? We hear little here, but what we do learn sounds extremely ominous.'

His Lordship remained silent, and the butler continued:

'They are saying, M'Lord, that this year of 1803 will be known for ever as the Year of Invasion.'

'If we are invaded,' His Lordship said in his most uncompromising voice, 'then I can assure you, Westham, that we shall repel Bonaparte with every weapon at our command.'

There was a moment's silence, but as His Lordship glanced with no show of interest at a succulent Boar's Head garnished with fresh peaches, the butler said:

'The Volunteers are most dissatisfied at the idea of carrying pikes, M'Lord.'

His Lordship had pushed back his plate with an angry gesture.

'There are not enough flint-locks for

10

everyone, Westham, and pikes can be an intimidating weapon if used with intelligence.'

His Lordship did not sound very convincing even to himself, and it made him even more angry that his own men who had joined the Volunteers should be treated in such a shoddy fashion.

However, it was not policy to say so, and the Marquis could only curse the Addington administration silently as he had cursed it so often before. Refusing the rest of the dishes which were awaiting his approval he walked from the Dining Room.

'A glass of port, M'Lord?' Westham cried in despair.

His Lordship did not deign to answer, but he would have been honest if he had admitted that he had already consumed enough wine that evening, which was in part the cause of his ill temper.

It must have been the unusual amount of wine, he told himself the following morning after spending a restless night, that he had drunk at dinner with the Prince of Wales which had been the cause of all his troubles.

One always ate and drank too much at Carlton House, but this had been an exceptional occasion when the Prince was entertaining on an even grander scale than usual, and a large number of his guests were extremely unsteady on their feet by the time they left the Dining Room.

The Marquis had not been unsteady, but he had certainly been in a receptive mood, and it must have been for that reason he had listened to Lady Leone Harlington when she had sought him out as the gentlemen joined the ladies and looked at him provocatively from under her eyelashes.

'It is a long time since Your Lordship honoured me with a visit,' she said in her soft seductive voice which had enticed more men into committing indiscretions than anyone could possibly count.

'You have missed me?' the Marquis asked.

Lady Leone turned her face towards his with a gesture which adoring swains poetically compared with the beauty of a swan arching its long white neck.

'You know that I have missed you,' she replied softly. 'Justin, what has gone awry between us?'

'Nothing of which I am aware,' the Marquis replied, and though he spoke with an effort of sincerity they both knew that he lied.

'Are you not running away from the inevitable?' she enquired.

'The inevitable?' he questioned.

'You know that I intend to marry you,' she answered.

Even in his slightly befuddled state the Marquis sensed the iron determination beneath the gentleness of her voice. Yet, because he had dined too well, her presumption had only amused him.

It was later, much later, that he found himself seated on a comfortable sofa in the Countess of Harlington's Salon with Leone beside him.

At the reception which had followed the dinner at Carlton House she had never left his side, and he realised that she had flaunted him as her escort as a man might flaunt a trophy he had won in battle.

There had been more to drink, more to eat, and while caution told him that he was putting his head into a noose, some cynical part of his mind told him that Leone was right – it was inevitable.

They had known each other since childhood, and while the Marquis had grown up to become the most elegant, the most handsome and the most sought-after Corinthian in the whole of the *Beau Ton,* Leone, when she emerged from the schoolroom, had become overnight the toast of St James's, the 'Incomparable of Incomparables', and without exception the most talked-about young woman in London.

Even while the Marquis was away fighting in the war he heard of her escapades, her daring, her adventures, and a thousand ways in which she contrived to get herself criticised by the older generation.

He had returned to London when an armistice was declared between France and

Great Britain to find Leone at the peak of her beauty.

He had found it amusing to flirt with her when they met, but he did not make any push to become one of the circle of infatuated Bucks who followed her adoringly.

The Marquis already had the reputation of a gay Lothario, and there were countless ladies of fashion ready to fall into his arms, ready, if he as much as looked in their direction, to make open for him a way to their hearts and their bedchambers.

In a very short time the Marquis's love-affairs were the talk of every club. Society, ever eager for succulent titbits of gossip, exaggerated the number of husbands he had cuckolded and his many *affaires de cœur*, but there was, in fact, little room for exaggeration.

The Marquis, refusing no feminine favours, at the same time grew increasingly more cynical. He had enjoyed the cut and thrust of war, he had gloried in having to fight to win.

It was in contrast almost banal to find how easy a different sort of conquest could be and how inevitably boring it was to be the pursued rather than the pursuer.

He also became aware that most people thought a match between Leone and himself would not only furnish a respectable ending to her somewhat flamboyant escapades, but would also be an advantage to them both.

It was time Leone settled down, it was time she married; and while she had everything to gain with regard to rank and wealth by becoming the Marchioness of Alton, she was also not averse to winning for herself the most sought-after bachelor in the length and breadth of the country.

From the Marquis's point of view the situation was even simpler. It was important he should be married. His relations continued to tell him so until he avoided them because the subject made him yawn; but when Mr Pitt had started on the same track he was astonished.

'What you want, Alton,' the former Prime Minister said almost aggressively, 'is a wife.'

'A wife?' the Marquis queried in surprise.

'Yes, a wife,' Mr Pitt repeated. 'It has been over a month now since on my return to the House of Commons I asked you to ferret out the Napoleonic spies in our midst – and one in particular. But you have got no further in discovering who this traitor may be. It is always the women who have secrets whispered to them on the pillow and repeat them to their bosom friends the following morn.'

'I assure you, Sir,' the Marquis said with a little twist of his lips, 'that I hear a deal of female chatter.'

'That I can well believe,' Mr Pitt assented, 'but I still think you would learn more if you had a wife constantly by your side, a wife who perhaps would not spend so much time prattling of love as your present fair charmers do.'

The Marquis put back his head and laughed. Then he said quite seriously:

'I am prepared to oblige you, Sir, by devoting my time, my wealth and anything else you may ask of me in trying to solve your immediate problems, but even for the sake of my country I am not prepared to shackle myself to some empty-headed chatterbox, whose conversation when the war is over I would have to endure for what would seem an eternity of time.'

Mr Pitt had smiled and then said:

'I understand only too well your devotion to bachelorhood, but at the same time, Alton, this is damned serious. I am absolutely convinced that the traitor is someone close to the Government, someone in one of our most vital Ministries. But God knows whether it is the Admiralty, the War Office or the Foreign Office.'

'Then you do admit, Sir, that you have given me a difficult assignment,' the Marquis smiled.

'I know no one who could do it better,' Mr Pitt declared, 'but I still think you need a wife to help you.'

It was with Mr Pitt's words ringing in his ears that the Marquis had looked down at

16

Leone seated beside him on the sofa, her dark seductive eyes half closed with a passionate intensity which he knew was not all pretence.

He was well aware that she was trying with every womanly wile she had ever known to entice him into declaring himself.

'Oh, Justin,' she said softly, 'you know we would deal well together. We could give the most sought-after parties in London, we could entertain at Alton Park. We would be, if it is not conceited to say so, the best-looking couple the *Ton* has ever seen. And besides all that, I have a decided partiality for you, as you well know.'

There was a feline sensuality in the manner in which her eyes slanted at him from beneath her dark lashes; there was an open invitation in the pouting red lips raised towards his.

'You are very lovely, Leone,' the Marquis said thickly, and put out his hand to touch the rounded whiteness of her long neck.

There was no telling which had made the first move, but the Marquis found himself kissing her passionately and with a certain brutality which she somehow evoked in him by her very compliance.

It was the sophisticated kiss of two people easily aroused to passion, and as the Marquis drew her closer and closer he could not help wondering in some detached part of his

17

mind how many men had kissed her in just this way before, how many men had held the soft warm seductiveness of her body in their arms and found their breath come quicker at the fiery response of her lips.

Leone's arms were round his neck, and as he crushed her almost breathless with the violence of his desire, he might at that moment have said the words she was longing to hear had they not been interrupted.

There was a sudden noise in the Hall outside the Salon, and a male voice called:

'Leone, are you there?'

It was the Viscount Thatford returning home from a party, and Leone had drawn herself reluctantly from the Marquis's arms.

'It is Peregrine,' she said with a note of anger in her voice.

Then as her brother came into the room she whispered so that only the Marquis could hear her:

'Come and talk to Father tomorrow – I shall be waiting for you.'

It was this last sentence which sent the Marquis blue-devilled to the country. It was too well planned, too obvious! It gave him a sense of being trapped, of being forced into a declaration before he had finally made up his mind.

Granted he had kissed Leone, but she had deliberately enticed him into doing so. She had seduced his kisses from him, and then taken it for granted that he would say the words that he had never in his life said to any woman.

Reaching his house in Berkeley Square, the Marquis had ordered his fastest Phaeton, changed his clothes and set off for Alton Park.

He had a sudden yearning to be free of London, to be away from the scented softness of women, to breathe instead the fresh air of the country, to smell the fresh fragrance of flowers and know that he was alone – alone and content with his own company.

By the time he reached Alton Park he was too angry to enjoy what he sought. His brain was beginning to clear, and he knew it was wine which had undoubtedly blunted his better judgment.

It was all those damned toasts he had had to honour: 'To Victory' – 'The annihilation of our enemies' – 'The downfall of Napoleon' – 'The Navy' – 'The Army' – 'The Volunteers'. There had been dozens of them and, because the Prince proposed each one of them, none of his guests could refuse to empty his glass.

The Marquis's constitution was strong and when he woke in the morning his head did not ache, but he was still oppressed by the thought of Leone waiting for him in London, the Earl of Harlington calculating how large a marriage settlement he could extort, the knowing smiles on the faces of their friends who would assert it was exactly what they had expected from the very beginning.

'Curse William Pitt! It is all his fault!' the Marquis tried to tell himself as he emerged from his bedchamber and slowly descended the magnificent carved staircase with its heraldic murals standing like sentinels at every turn.

However, he was fair-minded enough to admit that it was really no one's fault but his own. No outsider, however important he might be, could coerce a man into marriage; no man, unless he was cork-brained, would allow himself to be coerced.

Leone was by no means the first woman who had aspired to snare him into making her an offer of marriage; nevertheless he had been stupid enough to let her manœuvre him into the very position he had tried to avoid.

He had been well aware that she was determined to capture him, and that was why he had deliberately avoided being with her in any compromising circumstances.

Then yesterday he had dropped his guard and now she was waiting for him. There had been a look of satisfaction on Lord Thatford's somewhat inane face when he had come into the Salon and found them alone together.

From what the Marquis had heard Thatford was well under the hatches, and the thought of a wealthy brother-in-law would undoubtedly lift his depression.

The duns who were after him would be only too willing to give him time before they pressed their bills further once it was known that his sister was to marry one of the wealthiest noblemen in England. If his brother-in-law did not cough up, Thatford would see that his sister did, the Marquis was convinced of that.

There was no doubt that Leone was beautiful and, from all he had heard, her whole family had been gambling on her beauty.

'Why was I such a fool?' the Marquis asked himself aloud, and Westham, who was hovering at the back of his chair, enquired:

'You spoke, M'Lord?'

'Only to myself,' the Marquis said disagreeably.

The old butler sighed. He had known the Marquis too long not to realise that a fit of the sullens which lasted all through the night must have arisen through some real problem. It was unlike Mister Justin, as he still thought of his master. He could be mad as fire on occasions, but it invariably lasted but a short time.

As a boy he was noted for his sunny nature; as a man he had become difficult and at times overbearing. But one thing he had always been and that was just.

21

Old Westham knew that for the Marquis to be disagreeable for more than a few hours to those who served him meant that something untoward had occurred.

He was wise enough not to attempt to converse further with his master, merely bringing food to the table which was summarily waved away, and noting somewhat apprehensively that the Marquis drank a large brandy before walking through the open window out onto the Terrace. It was not His Lordship's habit to partake at breakfast.

'Something must be wrong – very wrong indeed!' old Westham told himself.

Bareheaded in the sunshine, the Marquis sauntered through the rose garden, not seeing the beds of flowers which had been planned so exquisitely by his mother some years before she died, not noticing the wide herbaceous borders with their budding promise of colour to come or the flaring flame of the azaleas against the mauve, purple and white of the fragrant lilacs.

The gardens at Alton Park were famous, but the Marquis walked through them with unseeing eyes, intent on his own thoughts, confused and apprehensive, and in a despondency which he had not known since going back to Eton at the end of the holidays.

'Damn! Damn! Damn!' he muttered to himself.

He timed his curses to the movement of

his feet, yet found the oaths brought him little relief.

He walked on and on, deep in his thoughts, too intent to notice where he was going, until he was startled by a sudden cry.

Almost automatically he stood still to listen. The cry came again, and then as he became aware that he had wandered far from the house and into the woods a girl came running from between the trees.

'Help, help!' she was crying. Then she saw him standing in the path and ran to him.

Surprised at the swiftness of her arrival, he became conscious of a small pointed face on which the tears were running down as they overflowed from two large frightened eyes.

'Help me ... oh help me!' she begged breathlessly. 'My dog ... he is caught in ... a trap... I cannot release him ... please ... please come!'

'Of course,' the Marquis said quickly.

He felt a very small hand slipped into his and found she was compelling him to run through the trees quicker than he had ever attempted to move since he had left school.

'He is ... here,' she panted as they turned into a clearing, and there was no need to say more.

A small black and white King Charles spaniel was caught by the leg in a rusty gin-trap. The dog was frenzied with fear, yelping and whining and tugging at his leg, which was bleeding profusely.

The girl ran towards the dog, but the Marquis, grasping her hand, restrained her.

'Do not touch him,' he said in a voice of authority. 'He is frightened and may bite you. At this moment he cannot recognise friend or foe.'

'Release him ... please set him ... free,' the girl pleaded.

The Marquis, grasping the dog in an expert fashion, held him firmly, and with his foot released the gin-trap so that the rusty iron teeth sprang open.

'Thank you ... thank you,' the girl breathed, and reached out her arms towards the dog.

The Marquis did not hand the little animal over; instead he carefully inspected the torn and bleeding leg. As if the dog had understood who had rescued him, he turned his head and tried to lick the hand which held him.

'Is his leg broken?' the girl asked.

'I am not certain,' the Marquis replied. 'What we must do is take him at once to someone who is experienced in the care of animals. The wound must be washed because, as you see, the trap was old and rusty.'

'How can people be so cruel – so wicked – as to put such things in the wood?' the girl asked. 'No animal should be trapped in such a manner.'

'I do not think there are many traps in these woods,' the Marquis answered.

He remembered he had given the order over five years ago that no traps were to be used on his land.

'I hope not,' the girl said. 'I was so happy ... and so was Columbus until this ... happened.'

'Columbus?' the Marquis questioned, looking down at the little dog in his arms.

'I called him that because he was so curious,' his owner explained. 'Now see to what a state his curiosity has ... brought him.'

She gave a tiny sob as she spoke, and taking a handkerchief from the waist of her pale green dress she started to wipe away the tears from her cheeks.

'Do you read Greek?' the Marquis asked in an amused voice. 'Or did somebody tell you that Columbus meant curious?'

'I know a little Greek,' she answered simply, 'but how can I thank you, Sir, for saving Columbus?'

'We have not saved him completely as yet,' the Marquis replied. 'As I have said, he must be taken to someone who understands dogs, who will treat the wound.'

'Oh dear,' the girl exclaimed helplessly, 'I wonder if there is someone like that in the village! I could ask.'

'I have a better idea,' the Marquis answered. 'A man I know who is really experienced lives not far from here. Shall we take Columbus to him?'

'I do not like to inconvenience you, Sir,' the girl answered. 'You have been so kind already.'

'You will not inconvenience me,' the Marquis answered.

Looking down at her he realised how pretty she was in a strange kind of elfin way. She had a little pointed face, huge eyes which he now realised were unexpectedly green, and very fair hair curling in the most unfashionable manner over her tiny head.

She had a bonnet, but she had obviously thrown it to the ground in an effort to release her dog. Now she picked it up and said:

'Can I carry Columbus?'

'I think it would be easier with me,' the Marquis answered. 'See, he is no longer afraid, and perhaps in my arms he would be less jolted than in yours.'

'You are so kind,' she said. 'If you had not been there I do not know what I would have done. I never expected there would be someone in the woods to help me.'

'You might have come across a keeper,' the Marquis said, 'but he undoubtedly would have accused you of trespassing.'

Her eyes were wide with apprehension.

'Am I trespassing?' she asked. 'I never thought of that. You see, when I used to walk with my father in the Vienna woods they were free to everyone. I forgot that in England woods would be in the possession of an autocratic owner.'

'Perhaps not always autocratic,' the Marquis demurred, 'but in England every man's home is his castle, and every man's property is private.'

'If he is lucky enough to own a property,' his companion said.

'So you were happy in the woods until this happened?' the Marquis asked.

'So very, very happy,' she said with a little sigh. 'You can have no idea what it is like for me to be among trees again, to forget...' – she paused and substituted– '...to remember the stories my mother told me when I was a little girl. Then the woods to me were peopled with nymphs, dragons and Knights-Errant.'

She stopped as they moved along the woodland path.

'Of course, that is what you are,' she exclaimed, 'a Knight-Errant come to save me – or rather Columbus! How wonderful, it is just like a story!'

'I am honoured that you should think so,' the Marquis said with a smile on his lips.

'But do you not understand?' she said. 'It is indeed one of the tales my mother used to tell me at bedtime. I have thought of them so often lately. I was desperately frightened for Columbus, and then suddenly you were there! A Knight to the rescue, but you should have been on a horse!'

'I regret the omission,' the Marquis replied. 'My horse was er – indisposed.'

'And being in search of fame and fortune you could not afford another one!' She sighed. 'But you ran to the rescue – that would have been difficult in armour!'

'And indisputably noisy!' the Marquis remarked drily.

They were both laughing. He realised she had an entrancing dimple in each cheek, and her eyes had when she was amused a Puckish mischievousness.

'I forbid you, Sir, to spoil my story!' she challenged him.

'I promise you not to do that,' the Marquis answered. 'But tell me why do you have such a partiality for woods?'

She put her head a little on one side as though she was considering his question.

'I think it is because we all have special places in the world to which we feel we belong,' she said. 'Some people feel fulfilled in themselves when they are beside the sea; some people wish to climb mountains: which give them something they cannot explain, something I suppose which is spiritual.'

She paused, then continued. 'But I have

always felt at home and happy in a wood. I seem to belong to the trees, and this is a very lovely wood.'

The Marquis looked round. Most of the trees were silver birch. The pale green of their spring leaves made an arch over their heads so that the sunshine only flickered through fitfully, casting tiny gleams of gold on the mossy path.

'You look like a wood-nymph yourself,' he said. 'In that green dress, without your bonnet, you might indeed be part of the forest.'

She smiled, and he saw that her smile illuminated her face and made it almost breath-takingly beautiful.

'I think my parents must have known that,' she said, 'when they christened me.'

'And what is your name?' the Marquis enquired.

'My name is Sylvina,' she said. 'Do you know what that means?'

The Marquis wrinkled his brow.

'It is not Greek?'

'No.'

'Latin?' he enquired.

She nodded.

'That is clever of you. Now can you guess the rest?'

'It is not very difficult,' he smiled. 'A forest maid?'

She laughed like a child.

'I believe you knew,' she said accusingly,

'or else you are too good at guessing.'

'What is your other name?' he enquired.

To his surprise she turned her head away, and for a moment there was silence. Then she said a little hesitatingly:

'Could you please not ask me that question? Just for today I want to forget everything but the woods. I do not want to remember why I am here and where I have come from, I just want to be – Sylvina.'

'Of course, that is as it should be,' the Marquis said. 'Here in the magic of the wood we have no identity outside. And in case you are interested, my name is Justin.'

She turned to him again with a light in her eyes.

'That is perfect!' she cried. 'Only a true Knight-Errant would be called Justin. And now I can say once again: Thank you, Sir Justin, for rescuing Columbus.'

They walked for some little way, the trees thinning, until the path ended and they came out at the side of a field. Ahead of them and a little below lay Alton Park.

The morning sunshine was glittering on its diamond-paned windows. Encircled by lakes which were linked by arched bridges, it had an almost unearthly beauty, the grey stone of the great mansion blending with the flower-filled gardens and the deep green of the woods which guarded it like protecting arms.

As the Marquis glanced at his home with satisfaction, he heard a small frightened voice beside him say:

'Surely ... that is ... Alton Park.'

'Yes indeed,' he answered. 'It is beautiful, is it not?'

'It is where ... the Marquis of Alton ... lives.'

'It is,' the Marquis replied.

There was a little pause and then she said:

'I cannot go there ... you do not ... understand, I cannot ... go to ... Alton Park.'

'I was only taking you to someone who lives in the precinct of the house,' the Marquis said drily. Then he added: 'But why would you not wish to visit such an attractive place?'

'I know ... the Marquis is not at ... home,' Sylvina replied. 'Indeed, I believe he seldom comes ... here, but I would not wish... Oh, I cannot explain ... but please give me Columbus and show me the way to the village.'

The Marquis was intrigued.

'Listen, Sylvina,' he said, 'there is nothing to hurt you at Alton Park, of that I am sure. And as for the Marquis, why have you such a dislike of him? Do you know him?'

'No indeed, I have not His Lordship's acquaintance,' Sylvina replied stiffly.

'Then it must be something you have heard about him,' the Marquis insisted.

He wondered a little wryly which of his

indiscretions had been repeated to this small, exquisite creature who certainly appeared to have no direct connection with the *Beau Ton*...

Her dress was pretty but cheap. There was nothing fashionable about the arrangement of her hair or of the straw bonnet she carried by its ribbons.

'What can you have heard about the Marquis?' he asked.

For a moment there was silence.

'I have ... heard,' Sylvina said at length, speaking in a low voice, almost as though she spoke to herself, 'that he is ... tenacious ... uncannily perceptive and ... merciless.'

The Marquis was astonished.

'Who can have told you that?' he asked.

'Oh, I should not have said such things!' she exclaimed. 'It was indeed presumptuous of me to speak in such a manner of the Marquis, but I believe he is old and ... frightening, and therefore ... for reasons I cannot explain I must go back ... to the village.'

'Is that not somewhat unkind to Columbus?' the Marquis asked.

She turned to look up at him and he was astonished at the fear in her eyes.

'I do not want to be unkind to Columbus,' she said, and her lips trembled, 'but I cannot go to ... Alton Park.'

'Then I have a solution,' the Marquis sug-

32

gested, 'that is, if you will trust me.'

'Trust you?' Sylvina asked. 'But of course I do. You rescued Columbus.'

'Then what I suggest is this,' the Marquis said. 'You go back into the wood. I will show you a place a little way from here where there is a fallen tree. Sit there and wait. I will take Columbus, have his leg treated and then bring him back to you.'

He saw that she was hesitating and added:

'If we do not do something quickly, the poor little dog may get blood poisoning.'

'Yes, yes, of course, I understand,' Sylvina said. 'But would you really do that for me? Is it not too much to ask?'

'No indeed,' the Marquis replied. 'Have I not vowed myself to your service? Is not that what Knights-Errant do when they come to the rescue?'

As if his tone had been a little too intimate, he saw a lovely flush of colour creep up her cheeks and her eyes fell before his.

'If you promise that I am not imposing on your kindness, Sir,' she said with a dignity which had something childlike about it, 'then I shall wait as you suggest.'

The Marquis showed her the fallen tree he had mentioned. It was very old and half covered with ivy, and he remembered sitting on it when he had been a boy playing truant from his tutors, escaping into the woods when he should have been poring over his books.

'I will not be longer than I can help,' he promised.

He saw the trust in her face, as she said:

'I will wait and think how lucky I am to have found you Sir Justin, just when I needed you most.'

The Marquis strode away from her, the dog lying peacefully in his arms save for an occasional little whimper when his torn leg hurt.

It was nearly three-quarters of an hour before the Marquis returned. As he came back towards the fallen tree he half wondered whether the forest maid would still be there waiting for him.

Had he perhaps been dreaming? If it had not been for a spot of blood on the cuff of his new whipcord coat, he would have thought he might have been.

He came almost silently through the trees and saw her.

She was sitting looking into the heart of the wood, her face in profile to him, her straight little nose etched against the trees, her eyes wide, her lips parted as though she felt a sudden ecstasy at being alone in the woods and a part of them.

Looking at her the Marquis realised how tiny she was. As she had walked beside him the top of her head had been about level with his heart.

Now she moved her hands and he thought that her slim little fingers were as exquisite as the flight of the kingfisher.

As if she knew someone was watching her, she turned her face, and he saw her eyes light up as though the sunshine had become imprisoned in them.

'You are back!'

She scrambled down from the tree and ran towards him, only when she reached him did she realise he was alone.

'Columbus!' she exclaimed. 'What has happened to Columbus?'

'He is all right,' the Marquis said soothingly. 'The man to whom I took him said that the muscles of his leg are torn, but he thinks there are no bones broken. He has bandaged his wounds and given the dog something to ease any pain he might be feeling. So he wants Columbus to remain quiet for an hour or so. After that I have arranged that you should take him home.'

'He will get well, will he not?' Sylvina asked.

'I promise you there is nothing really wrong. Columbus has been very lucky. The trap might have really injured him, but in two or three weeks he will be perfectly fit again.'

'That is beyond words marvellous!' Sylvina cried. 'How can I thank you for your kindness?'

'You can thank me,' the Marquis answered, 'by letting me entertain you until Columbus has had his rest. Would you like me to show you a pool in the middle of the wood where the deer drink in the evening and where I am certain Pan plays his pipes to those who can hear such music.'

Sylvina clasped her hands together.

'Oh, could you really take me there?' she asked. 'How lovely that would be. And have you ever heard Pan playing his pipes? It is something I have longed for more than anything else, except perhaps to see a bluebird.'

'A bluebird!' the Marquis exclaimed.

'Yes. My mother used to tell me that when people are really happy, the gods send a bluebird to sing to them of joy, to tell them of the heavenly things which no one can tell us here on earth. Only a bluebird has the right song for those who truly love each other.'

'And you think perhaps we could hear one today?' the Marquis asked.

She blushed in confusion.

'No, of course I did not mean that,' she said. 'I was only relating to you what I feel would be a wonderful and unforgettable experience. Now you have made me feel that I am saying all the wrong things. It is something I often seem to do these days.'

'It was not the wrong thing,' the Marquis said quickly. 'I was only teasing you. Do you mind being teased?'

'No indeed,' Sylvina answered, 'my brother often does it. It is just that having been so much alone these past years, I have the habit of saying without thinking just what comes into my head. I know that it is unconventional and very foolish, because people misunderstand me and then I feel ashamed.'

'I think it is exceeding pleasant,' the Marquis said, 'to find someone who is natural, who says what they think is the truth rather than things they think they ought to say.'

'I wish I could believe you,' Sylvina replied, 'but Mr Cu...' She stopped. 'There are ... p ... people who say I must curb my thoughts and try to be a fashionable lady. But I hate the fashionable world, I do not want to be a fashionable lady, I do not want to have anything to do with society.'

She spoke so passionately that her voice seemed to ring out in the woodland.

'You would be a great success in fashionable society,' the Marquis said. 'You are beautiful, and the social world loves beautiful women.'

'Now you are teasing me again,' Sylvina complained. 'You know I am not beautiful, and you can see how unfashionable I am. I made this gown myself, and when I look at the ladies in London I know they would laugh and sneer at me if I went amongst them looking like this. Besides, I have no desire to go to parties or to be dressed up like some … people want me to be.'

There was so much unhappiness in her voice that the Marquis was startled.

'Why should anyone want you to do things you do not want to do?' he asked.

There was silence, and then she said:

'We agreed we would forget today … all the unhappy and … frightening things and … think only of the woods.'

'That is what we agreed,' the Marquis smiled.

'Then let us forget,' Sylvina begged, 'please, please, Sir Justin, let us forget just for a little while that we have to go back. Let us pretend that there is nothing outside the woods and that we could stay here for ever.'

'For ever?' the Marquis repeated with raised eyebrows.

'For ever,' Sylvina repeated almost passionately. 'If only I could lie down on the moss beneath the trees and never go back. If time could pass me by and I could awake to find myself old and grey, then I would be utterly content.'

'There must be a less drastic way of solving your problems,' the Marquis suggested quietly.

She shook her head.

'There is no other solution!'

'At times we all feel we are like Columbus caught in a trap, but invariably if we try hard enough, there is a way out,' the Marquis said, and wondered if it was the truth.

'No,' Sylvina answered dully, 'for me – there is no way out.'

'How do you know?' the Marquis asked.

'I have thought and thought,' she said simply, 'and I cannot find one.'

'Then suppose you let me think for you,' the Marquis suggested. 'I am considered rather adept at solving puzzles.'

She looked up at him and he thought she had the sweetest face he had ever seen. She smiled at him as one might smile at a clever child, and then she said, her voice infinitely sad:

'I would like to let you try to solve my puzzle, Sir Justin, but it is not mine alone. And so I can only attempt to solve it myself, and unfortunately there is no solution.'

'Let me...' he began to plead, but she interrupted him.

'Oh, look! Look!' she whispered.

He saw that by leading her down a woodland path while they had been talking they had reached the pool in the centre of the wood of which he had told her.

Surrounded by trees, it had a strange, almost eerie mystery about it.

With the sun throwing shimmering rays through the darkness of the trees, the water glimmering and the kingcups glowing in golden profusion on the banks, it really did seem an enchanted place.

Then the Marquis felt a small eager hand slipped into his and a soft, breathless little voice said:

'Thank you, thank you, dear kind Sir Justin, for bringing me here.'

# 2

There was a mossy bank sloping down to the forest pool, and Sylvina sat down on it and pulled her skirt over her ankles.

She looked up at the Marquis.

'Let us sit here for a short while,' she suggested. 'Perhaps we shall see the deer come down to drink.'

He stretched himself at her side, his highly polished Hessian boots glinting in the sunshine.

After a brief glance at him she sat looking into the shadows of the trees, her small fingers clasped in her lap, her eyes wide and excited like a child who was being taken to a playhouse for the first time.

The Marquis watched her with an expression on his face that his friends would have found hard to recognise. For once he was not looking cynical, there was no hard line to his lips and his eyes were no longer bored.

The wind rustling the leaves in the treetops sounded like the whisper of a tune, in the distance there was the cry of the cuckoo, and near at hand the wood-pigeons were courting.

Then, just as Sylvina had hoped it might happen, a small speckled deer came stepping delicately between the silver-birch trees.

He stood for a moment on the edge of the pool as if he sensed their proximity. There was something exquisitely beautiful in his stance, in the grace of his neck and in his soft liquid brown eyes.

He bent his head and drank, until as suddenly as he had come he scampered away, leaping over a fallen tree-trunk with the effortless ease of a racehorse.

Sylvina gave a cry of sheer delight and turned to the Marquis.

'Was not that lovely?' she asked.

'Lovely,' he agreed.

But he was looking at the sunlight through the trees touching her fair hair with gold and making a halo for her little heart-shaped face.

There was something in his eyes which made her turn away again.

'I think we should be returning,' she said in a shy voice, as if suddenly she had become conscious of him as a man.

'There is no hurry,' he replied. 'The longer Columbus can rest before he is moved the better it will be for his leg.'

Sylvina rose to her feet.

'All the same, I think I should … go back,' she said a little hesitantly.

'Are you afraid?' the Marquis enquired.

Her chin rose as if she felt that the question was an insult to her pride, and then she answered honestly:

'Not afraid to be here with you, but merely of what people would say if they knew.'

'Why should they ever know?' the Marquis asked. 'Have we not agreed that this is a few hours of enchantment snatched from eternity? We are anonymous to each other and to everyone else. Perhaps – who knows? – we may even be invisible.'

She laughed at that, and he saw that she was no longer tense, no longer on the defensive.

'Come,' he said authoritatively, 'there are other things I want to show you.'

He felt she would have protested, but somehow the words died on her lips, and she let him lead her further down the wood, twisting and turning along the moss-grown path which seemed never to have known the pressure of human feet.

After a while the trees thinned and instead there were great high banks of rhodo-dendrons, purple and white, their colours against the blue sky almost breath-taking.

Sylvina did not speak, but the Marquis knew that her eyes took in the beauty of every blossom. As he led her on, walking between the bushes, she asked:

'Where are you taking me?'

'Could anything be more beautiful than this?' he asked.

She shook her head.

'I could not imagine anything so wonderful,' she answered. 'I can only think that I am dreaming and this is Heaven.'

'I forgot to tell you,' the Marquis said in a matter-of-fact tone, 'that I am a magician, and so I have cast a spell which I hope will meet with your approval. Shut your eyes for a moment and give me your hand.'

'What kind of spell?' she asked delightedly, at the same time obeying him.

She shut her eyes so that her long dark lashes lay against the pale transparency of her skin. He took her hand in his, feeling the cool slimness of her fingers, and knowing they quivered a little in the warmth and strength of his own.

He drew her forward.

'Do not open your eyes until I tell you to do so,' he admonished her.

He led her a few paces, then he turned her a little to the left and let go of her hand.

'Abracadabra!' he exclaimed. 'You may open your eyes.'

She opened them wonderingly and saw in front of them a Grecian temple, white as a pearl against the flaming beauty of crimson rhododendrons.

She clasped her hands together and was silent, her expression rapturous.

Then she asked in awed tones:

'Did it really come from Greece?'

'Yes, really,' the Marquis replied. 'It was brought to England over a hundred years ago by my grandfather. Do you not think it looks a suitable place for the gods and goddesses of Olympus to meet and enjoy themselves?'

'It is perfect,' she answered.

'My spell is not yet finished,' the Marquis continued, 'come and look inside.'

They passed through the white pillars and into the coolness of the temple itself.

There in the centre was a table laid with a white cloth and laden with every sort of delicacy. There were crystal glasses and bottles of wine in a silver cooler filled with ice.

Sylvina looked at it wonderingly and turned to the Marquis with a question in her eyes.

'I felt we were both in need of sustenance,' he explained. 'Let us pray that the food is worthy of its surroundings. The wine at least should taste like nectar.

'But how could it be here?' she asked.

'I have told you I was a magician,' the Marquis replied.

'You must have ordered it when you took Columbus!' she said almost beneath her breath.

'I did not expect you to be so practical,' the Marquis said reproachfully. 'Can you not accept gifts of the gods without question?'

Two dimples appeared in her cheeks.

'Do you really think I am so ungrateful?' she asked. 'Perhaps it is distressingly human, but I am indeed extremely hungry.'

'Then shall we not be seated?' the Marquis suggested. She moved towards the table, when a sudden thought struck her.

'This temple … this food – it does not … belong to the … Marquis of Alton?'

The Marquis paused a moment as if he chose his words carefully.

'They both belong to me,' he answered truthfully.

The expression of anxiety on her face disappeared.

'Oh, I am glad, Sir Justin!' she cried. 'It was perhaps wrong of me to ask, but I would not become involved in any way with the Marquis.'

'Why have you such a dislike of him?' the Marquis enquired. 'I understood you to say you had not met him.'

'No indeed,' Sylvina replied, 'and I would not wish to do so. Please do not let us discuss His Lordship. Even the very thought of him makes me … afraid.'

'Afraid of what?' the Marquis asked.

She made a little gesture with her hands that was somehow pathetic.

'I cannot tell you,' she answered. 'I pray you, Sir Justin, let me forget my fears for just a little longer. I have been so happy this past hour, happier than I have been ... for a long time. I have felt free and unafraid, just as though you had in fact killed the dragon that was ... th ... threatening ... m ... me.'

She stammered over the words and he saw a sudden darkness in her eyes, a fear in her face that he had seen before only in the eyes of men going out to battle.

He bent forward and put his hand over hers as it lay on the table.

'Let me help you, Sylvina,' he said.

There was a deep note in his voice which made her glance up at him enquiringly. Then suddenly her eyes were held by his and for a moment both of them were very still.

It seemed to the Marquis as though something magical passed between them, something quite unexplainable in words, and yet somehow quiveringly alive.

Then with what was almost a little cry Sylvina turned her head away and broke the spell.

'I ... cannot,' she said almost beneath her breath, 'I cannot ... tell you. And even if I did so you could not help me ... no one can.'

There was such depth of despair in her voice that the Marquis was startled.

Then realising that she was not far from tears, he drew the silver ice-bucket towards him and took out a bottle of wine. He wrapped it in a cloth of white damask and poured the golden liquid into her glass.

'We are both hungry,' he said. 'Let us eat, and I can only hope this poor collation will meet with your approval.'

'Meet with my ... approval?'

Sylvina's voice was breathless and he knew that she was making a tremendous effort to return to the commonplace.

'There is enough food here for a dozen hungry people,' she said.

'Then what may I offer you?' he enquired. 'Shall we start with this *pâté* of goose livers? Yet that hardly sounds exotic enough for Olympus. It should be at least peacock's tongues or a heart of an osprey.'

'I do not believe the gods and goddesses are so cruel,' Sylvina answered.

Allowing the Marquis to help her from various dishes, she was unaware of what she was actually consuming.

She only knew every mouthful was delicious, and though she only sipped at the wine she felt that it must have a very strong effect because everything seemed so golden.

It was not only the beauty of the flowers outside, the exquisite perfections of the temple itself, or that their meal was accompanied by the music of the bees and the song of the birds. It was the fact that the man sitting beside her seemed also to have a strange enchantment.

'Do you know, Sir Justin,' Sylvina said after they had been talking of the countryside and the Marquis made her laugh when he told her of the escapades in which he had been involved as a young boy, 'that this is the first time, with the exception of my brother, I have ever had luncheon ... or any meal alone with a man?'

'Then I am indeed honoured,' the Marquis replied.

'It is so much more pleasant, is it not,' Sylvina enquired, 'than being with a party of people? I do not know why, but it seems so much easier to talk to a person when one is alone with him. I never realised that until now.'

'You sound as though you are always carefully chaperoned,' the Marquis said, 'except for walking alone in the woods.'

'Does that seem to you very immodest?' Sylvina asked.

'It is, shall we say, a trifle unconventional for a young lady,' the Marquis replied.

'I suppose it is,' Sylvina admitted, 'but there was no one who could come with me. I wanted so much to take Columbus for a run.'

'Where are you staying?' the Marquis asked.

He realised, even as he spoke the words, that he had made a mistake.

Sylvina's self-consciousness returned immediately. He saw her become stiff and her reserve envelop her as though it were a cloud.

'No, no,' he said quickly before she could reply, 'I should not have asked that, I was breaking the rules, forgive me. Tell me instead why the country means so much to you.'

'Does it not mean a lot to you too?' Sylvina asked. 'I feel it must or you would not have been walking in the woods without a hat and cane. Indeed you would not have been walking at all but riding. Gentlemen who live in London seldom take any exercise save on horseback.'

'Is that so?' the Marquis remarked in an indifferent manner.

'Yes, I assure you,' Sylvina said. 'They drive their High Perch Phaetons, their curricles or their four-in-hands and they ride in Rotten Row. Fine horseflesh, it is true, but I always think how those horses would love to be galloping over the countryside, feeling free and untroubled as we are feeling now.'

'What else happens in London?' the Marquis asked.

'Sometimes it is cold, dark and very damp when the mist comes up from the river,' Sylvina answered. 'The streets are dirty, the children that play in them are ragged and hungry and nobody seems to care. The nobility drive by in their grand carriages, and ordinary people like me feel lonely because they do not belong.'

He watched the way her little mouth drooped at the words, and then suddenly the dimples were there again and she said:

'That is why I came into the woods today alone, even though it was trespassing.'

'You are no longer trespassing,' he answered. 'In future the freedom of these woods is yours.'

'Do you mean that?' she asked excitedly, and then the light faded from her eyes. 'I shall remember, Sir Justin, the present you have made me of that freedom. I shall remember it even though I shall never come here again.'

'Why do you say that?' he asked. 'The woods will be waiting for you.'

'And I shall think of them always,' she answered in a soft voice. 'I shall remember the deer coming down to drink, the wood-pigeons cooing in the trees and the feeling that I was safe ... safe from what was waiting for me outside.'

Her voice died away and the Marquis was wise enough not to ask another direct question. Instead he said:

'You seem to predict a very dark future for yourself. Are you in fact a soothsayer?'

She smiled at that.

'I am not a gypsy asking you to cross my palm with silver,' she answered. 'I have in fact known gypsies who could tell fortunes, though many of them are charlatans. But I am at times a little fey, as they say. My mother was Scottish and the seventh child of a seventh child, and I think that she transmitted to me some of her powers.'

'What do you mean?' the Marquis asked, trying to encourage her to go on talking.

'Sometimes when I meet people I can feel intuitively what they are like,' Sylvina said. 'Of course I cannot do it with everyone, but occasionally it – happens.'

She was silent for a moment, and then she said in a voice so low that he could hardly hear her:

'It happened a short while ago. I knew as soon as I had met ... him what ... he was ... like.'

'And what was he like?' the Marquis enquired.

'Bad, wicked, evil!' Sylvina exclaimed. 'It was not anything he said, that was pleasant enough! It was just something that seemed to come out of him, reaching out towards me and I ... could not ... escape.'

Her voice broke on the words and the Marquis saw again a terror in her eyes that he had thought never to see in any woman's face.

'This man,' he asked, 'can you not avoid him?'

Sylvina shook her head.

'No,' she said, 'I cannot avoid ... him.'

The Marquis longed to ask more, but

51

some intuition told him not to press her.

Gradually, like fitting a puzzle together, he was attempting to form a picture; but he knew that, like the deer which had been startled by their proximity, one incautious word could drive Sylvina back into the defences of her reserve where he could not reach her.

'Tell me how you sense these things?' he asked.

She closed her eyes for a moment as if to shut out her thoughts. Then she turned her face towards him.

'Shall I tell you about yourself?' she asked.

'It is a subject that everyone finds fascinating, I believe,' the Marquis answered.

'Then I will tell you,' Sylvina said. 'I knew as soon as you picked up Columbus that you were good and kind. But more than that, there was something in you which everyone could trust, men, women and animals.'

'Is that why you trust me?' the Marquis asked.

'You were a Knight come to help me,' she said simply. 'I knew without anyone having to tell me, without any reassurance from you, that you were my friend, you would do me no harm. I cannot explain why I knew it, it was just there, a conviction so strong, so unshakable that I would have gone anywhere with you and known that I need not be afraid.'

'Thank you,' the Marquis said, 'I think

that is the nicest and the most flattering thing anyone has ever said to me.'

'It is not flattering,' Sylvina corrected, 'because it is the truth. But, if you like, I will tell you something else about yourself, if you will not consider it an impertinence.'

The Marquis smiled.

'Nothing you could ever say to me would be anything but acceptable,' he said. 'Have you not already told me that we are friends?'

Sylvina's eyes were on his face, but he felt as though she did not actually see him.

'I think,' she said in a low voice, 'that someone once hurt you very deeply, someone whom you trusted, someone perhaps whom you loved. And because you would not let anyone know of your hurt, you have put on armour against the world.'

She paused then went on very slowly.

'I cannot explain quite what I mean, but I feel that you stand away from people, you do not give them your warmth – the same warmth and understanding that you have given to me and to Columbus. Sometimes you are hard and bitter: but that is not the real you, not the Knightly Sir Justin who lies inside your heart.'

The Marquis stared at her.

'How do you know these things?' he asked.

She made a little gesture with her hands and looked away from him towards the sunshine outside the temple.

'Is that not the truth?'

'Yes, it is the truth,' the Marquis answered. 'Yet I cannot conceive how you know those things about me.'

For one wild moment he thought perhaps it was a trap. Could Sylvina be a play-actress worming her way into his confidence and ensnaring him for political reasons?

Then he realised such a thing was impossible.

No one could have such untouched innocence of youth in her face and not be honest, no one could have eyes which seemed to reflect at times the sunshine and at others the darkness of the mist rising before nightfall and not be pure.

'Tell me some more,' he begged.

Her eyes came back to him and now her face was troubled.

'No,' she answered, 'I do not want to look further.'

'Look,' he commanded, 'look and tell me what you see.'

He could not have explained why he was so insistent; it was just that he felt that Sylvina could tell him something which he did not even know himself.

'There is something there,' she said, 'but I would rather not look. I have no wish to tell you.'

'Please tell me,' he insisted – it was more of a command than a plea.

'I do not often do this,' she said, 'and Papa did not approve. But once I helped someone who was in trouble and they were very grateful. Give me something you always wear.'

The Marquis drew his watch from his vest pocket. At the end of it dangled his fob. The watch was warm from the proximity of his body, but as he put it into Sylvina's hand he touched her fingers and realised they were icy cold.

Her hands closed over the watch and she shut her eyes.

The Marquis sat looking at her. Her little face had an elfin quality about it, and he could in fact credit quite easily that she could see things that were hidden from more ordinary people.

'You are worried ... worried and I think a little ... angry,' she said after a moment's silence. 'There is a woman ... near you. She does not love you, but ... she wants ... something from you. She is not good and she ... might hurt you. She will reopen those wounds that you thought were healed and forgotten ... you must have nothing ... nothing to do with her.'

As she spoke the last words Sylvina's voice strengthened. Then she said:

'She will try and ... trap you, she will set a snare for ... you. She is beautiful ... very beautiful, but you must be careful because she could have the ... power to hurt ... you.'

There was silence, and after a moment the Marquis prompted her:

'What else do you see?'

'I see you seeking for something ... or it may be a person,' Sylvina said. 'I cannot see what he or she is like ... but you are looking for them. You are worried and anxious ... you cannot find this person and there is emptiness ... and darkness ... around you... And then ... there is ... bloodshed ... blood, and you are ... in danger!'

Sylvina gave a little cry on the words and opened her eyes.

'I cannot look any more,' she said. 'I hate blood, and when I see it I know there is something evil about it. It means violence, hatred and all things that are hurtful. I am sorry, I am sure that what I have told you is not right, but that is ... all I could ... see.'

She looked very pale and her voice was shaken. The Marquis poured her out another glass of wine.

'Drink this, Sylvina,' he said. 'Do as I say.'

She drank a little as he had commanded and the colour came back into her face.

'Forget what I have said, please forget it,' she said. 'I should not have tried, it was ... wrong of me. I am sure none of it is ... true.'

'Now you are trying to reassure me,' he answered. 'You know as well as I do that when you see things like that they are the truth.'

56

'They are muddled,' Sylvina said. 'I could not see the person you sought.'

'Was there anything else?' the Marquis asked. 'Something you did not tell me.'

'No,' she said quickly – too quickly, so that he said accusingly:

'There was, something you are keeping back. Why? What are you afraid to tell me?'

'I saw nothing ... nothing ... more,' Sylvina answered.

'That is not true,' the Marquis insisted. 'Tell me the truth! I promise you,' and his lips twisted in a smile, 'I am courageous enough to hear it.'

'It is not that,' Sylvina said, unhappily.

'Then why are you afraid? It cannot be worse than you have already told me.'

'Please ... do not ... make me,' she pleaded.

She clasped her hands together, her eyes turned to his, begging him not to force her.

There was something hard and determined in the Marquis that made him resist the appeal in her eyes and the sudden quiver of her lips.

'Tell me what it is, Sylvina? Can you not understand that now I cannot bear to go on guessing what it is you were hiding from me. It would haunt me by day and by night. You have gone too far, you must tell me now what you saw.'

Sylvina's head dropped forward so that

her face was hidden from him. In a very low voice she said hardly above a whisper:

'I saw you seeking ... to capture ... a man... You were bringing ... him ... to justice ... you were determined to ... destroy him and you were ... like ... like an avenging angel.'

'And what was the man's appearance?' the Marquis said.

'I could not see ... that I swear ... to you,' Sylvina answered. 'I tried but I could not ... see. He was trying to ... evade you but he could not ... escape.'

The last words were hardly audible, and then Sylvina covered her face with her hands and the Marquis knew she was weeping.

For a moment he stared at her in perplexity, and then he said:

'Why are you so upset? What does this matter to you? What you have told me makes sense, to me at any rate, but it could not possibly affect you in any manner.'

'No, no, of course not,' Sylvina said quickly. 'I cannot think why it perturbs me. The man you are seeking may be just a poacher or indeed a trespasser like myself. You live here in the country, you have no connection with the things that are happening in London. Why I should be so non-sensical about it I do not know.'

She spoke as though she was reassuring herself. The Marquis said lightly:

'Indeed I am sure you are right. We are vastly troubled with poachers in this part of the world, or I might be searching for a highwayman. There is one, I am told, who hides in the woods on another part of this estate. I have been trying to apprehend him for some years.'

As he spoke he watched the colour come back into Sylvina's face.

'There is nothing to make you cry,' he said reassuringly.

'No, of course not,' she answered. 'I am so foolish. I must have confused your life with someone else's. In fact, I shall be very much surprised if everything I have told you is not just moonshine from beginning to end.'

'It should be a lesson to you not to go telling fortunes to strange gentlemen who are curious about themselves,' the Marquis said.

She laughed at that, but he saw that tears lay on her cheeks and glittered on the end of her eyelashes.

He took his handkerchief from his pocket and held it out to her. She took it from him, noting it was of soft linen and smelt of lavender. She wiped her eyes.

'I am ashamed,' she said. 'Papa always said there is nothing gentlemen dislike more than scenes, and here after all your kindness I have been making one for you.'

'There have been no scenes,' the Marquis answered, 'only a little shower of rain which makes the sun shine, now it has come out again, all the brighter.'

She smiled.

'You are getting very poetical, Sir Justin. If you are not careful you will have to go to London and make court to the ladies of quality who like odes written to their eyebrows and who expect to be flattered from the moment they get up in the morning to the moment they go to bed.'

'Do you think I would not enjoy that?' the Marquis said.

'I am persuaded you would not,' Sylvina declared. 'What I expected to see when I most imprudently tried to look into your life was horses and dogs. I know you must have them or Columbus would not have trusted you as he did.'

'Indeed I have quite a number of dogs,' the Marquis answered, 'and as for horses, one day perhaps I will race you; for I too have a feeling that you ride exceeding well.'

'I have always been told I do,' Sylvina smiled, 'but then my father was very particular about the way I was taught. I have, in fact, ridden since the age of four, and even then I was not allowed a child's pony, fat and lazy, but a spirited animal more suited to a boy of fifteen or older.'

'We will race each other,' the Marquis promised. 'There shall be a prize for the winner. What shall it be? Another enchanted day in our magical wood?'

'That would be the most wonderful prize anyone could give me,' Sylvina answered. 'But now fairy stories have to come to an end. You know I must go back. I have played truant for too long, but I shall remember this! Oh, Sir Justin, I shall remember every passing second of it!'

She rose from the table as she spoke and walked down the white marble steps of the temple to stand for a moment silhouetted against the crimson rhododendrons, her bare arms reaching up to touch the blossoms.

She made so beautiful a picture that the Marquis felt it would be etched for ever on his memory.

Then she smiled at him and said beguilingly:

'Come, tell me what you do every day here in this wonderful wood. When I am gone I want to think of you walking bareheaded in the sunshine, riding across the fields, seeing your crops grow, being welcomed home by your dogs.'

'That is the life I like above all others,' the Marquis said and surprised even himself by the ring of truth in the words.

'I knew it,' Sylvina said triumphantly, 'I knew that was what you would like.'

They retraced their steps through the rhododendrons, but now the Marquis led her a quicker way than by the path by which they had come. In a very short time they had reached the edge of the wood.

There was a ride between rows of young fir trees, and at the end of it waiting on the roadway Sylvina could see a carriage.

She stopped instinctively and the Marquis stopped beside her.

'Columbus is waiting for you there,' he said. 'He will be well wrapped and bandaged so try not to disturb him. Carry him gently into your house and tomorrow I will come and see how he fares and if he needs further treatment.'

'Thank you, thank you!' she cried. 'If it were not for you his leg might have been damaged for life. I cannot bear to think what might have happened had you not been there.'

'But I was there,' the Marquis smiled, 'and Columbus will be all right. Let us hope that his mistress will be as lucky.'

Sylvina looked up at him and saw the kindness in his eyes.

'Will you too ... remember ... today?' she asked in a low voice.

'You know I shall,' he answered. 'Do you not think it has been a time of magic for me as well as for you?'

'I hope ... so,' she answered a little breathlessly.

Once again something strange seemed to pass between them until, while he did not move, it was almost as if Sylvina physically dragged herself away from him.

'I must ... g ... go,' she said incoherently.

'I thought you would rather I did not escort you to the carriage,' the Marquis said. 'That would be wisest in case someone sees us together and starts local tongues gossiping.'

'Yes, of course,' Sylvina agreed, 'and it is kind of you to think of my ... my reputation.'

'I shall be thinking of you until tomorrow,' the Marquis said firmly.

Sylvina put her hand into his.

'Good-bye, Sir Justin,' she said softly, 'and thank you again from the very bottom of my heart.'

'It is for me to thank you, a forest maid who has brought so much delight to me so unexpectedly,' the Marquis said.

'Holding her hand close in his, he bent his head and kissed it.

For a moment she was very still, then she snatched her hand from him and was running down the ride, her bonnet dangling from her arm by its ribbons, her hair dancing like liquid gold in the wind which came from between the trees.

He watched her go, watched her reach the carriage, saw the footman jump down from the box and open the door. She stepped in, the door was shut.

He expected her to bend forward and look out of the window, but she did not do so. The coachman whipped up the horses and the carriage moved away out of sight.

Long after it had gone the Marquis stood staring at the empty ride. He felt bewildered, confused and not a little intrigued.

Who was she? Who was frightening her? Why above all things had the thought of him capturing a man distressed her so greatly?

Methodically the Marquis shook himself back into what he hoped was good sense. It was almost as if he had spent three hours in a dream, and yet never had a dream been more compelling.

He walked slowly back through the gardens to his house, and as he walked he knew he was no longer angry, but curious with a curiosity that sooner or later would have to be assuaged.

# 3

'If you pull my hair again, you turnip-handed wench, I will slap you,' Lady Leone said in a furious voice.

Her maid, new from the country and unused to the tantrums of the quality, trembled with fright.

There was a knock at the door and simultaneously it opened and the Viscount Thatford came into the room.

'Oh, it is you, Peregrine!' Lady Leone said disagreeably. 'I cannot think what you want at this early hour. It is enough that I have to put up with nitwitted girls because Papa cannot, or will not, afford to pay a decent Abigail. Look at the manner in which this imbecile is arranging my hair.'

As she spoke Lady Leone put up her hands and in a rage deliberately disarranged the coiffure which her lady's-maid had been painstakingly pinning into place for the past half-hour.

'Leave it!' she screamed. 'Get out, leave me alone! I can stand no more of your fat-fisted muddles.'

The maid, she was little more than a child, burst into tears and ran from the room.

The Viscount settled himself in an arm-chair and crossed his legs, noting with an expression of satisfaction how the high sheen of his boots, achieved by his valet after laborious hours of polishing with champagne, reflected the elegant hangings and shining furniture.

'What do you want to talk to me about?' his sister asked in an unpleasant tone of voice, putting her face near to the mirror to see if there was the slightest blemish on her fine skin.

'Bad temper will give you lines,' her brother announced.

'It is not bad temper that will give me wrinkles – rather a fit of despondency,' Lady Leone answered sharply. 'I have a suspicion of what you wish to discuss.'

'I should credit it is a damned sight more than suspicion,' the Viscount replied. 'It is four days now since you informed us that Alton was about to offer for you. There is Papa sitting expectant in the Library hardly daring to leave the house in case he should miss the noble Marquis; there is Mama reading and rereading her dressmaker's bill in a fit of hysterics; and there are the servants standing with open hands waiting for their wages which are long overdue. As for me, it is a case of imprisonment in the Fleet if you do not bring him up to scratch.'

'Do you suppose I do not know all this?' Lady Leone flashed. 'And it is entirely your fault that we are not by this time official betrothed.'

'My fault!' the Viscount ejaculated in astonishment.

'Yes, indeed,' Lady Leone retorted. 'If you had not come stamping noisily into the Hall that evening when His Lordship was with me, making noises like a frustrated stallion, he would have asked me to be his wife. The question was trembling on his lips, I knew it; but you interrupted us, and then there was nothing I could do but tell him to speak to Papa on the morrow.'

'Then what is preventing his doing that?' the Viscount asked.

'He was not in London the following day,' his sister answered. 'I sent one of the servants to enquire for him at Alton House, only to learn he had posted to the country.'

The Viscount rose from the chair in which he had been sitting and walked across the room.

'If you have frightened him off, Leone, we are indeed under the hatches, every damned one of us.'

'Peregrine, what am I to do?' Lady Leone asked now in a voice of despair.

'Surely you are woman enough to bring him to the point,' her brother replied. 'God knows your attractions have been proclaimed long and loud enough in St James's.'

'Perhaps that is what is wrong,' Lady Leone said in a low voice, 'one never knows with Justin. His own love-affairs have been the talk and gossip of London for years. There is practically no beauty with whom his name has not been associated.'

'That is true,' the Viscount admitted, 'at the same time they have all been married. I have never heard Alton's name being coupled with a girl such as yourself, Leone.'

'To be honest,' Lady Leone said, 'he has not exactly pressed his suit upon me. He has flattered me, made a show of his affection in public, but, I have always felt, only so that he could be in competition with his friends. It is fashionable for me to be acclaimed, yet Justin has always been a fashion unto himself.'

'All the more reason why he should marry you,' the Viscount said sharply. 'You know as well as I do that is something which has been more or less anticipated since you were children together.'

'The other night I was almost sure,' Lady Leone said in a low voice. 'He kissed me and I knew that I excited him. It was the first time I have been almost sure of capturing him.'

'He kissed you, did he?' the Viscount questioned. 'That could compromise him sufficiently for me to call him out if he does not make you a proposal of marriage.'

Lady Leone laughed – it was not a pleasant sound.

'You must be to let in the attic if you can contemplate calling Justin out,' she sneered. 'He is a dead shot, my dear brother, and that is something you have never been with all your roistering. If your hand were steady enough even to point in his direction it would be a miracle.'

'All right, have it your own way,' the Viscount said sulkily. 'I am not moonstruck enough to think I could vanquish the

Corinthian of the Corinthians; at the same time someone should protect your honour.'

Lady Leone got up from the dressing-table and walked to the mantelpiece.

'I have made a muff of the whole thing, have I not?' she said. 'I should have married two or three years ago. Do you realise I shall be twenty-five next birthday? What other woman of my looks has lingered so long?'

'Why did you not accept one of those other lovelorn swains who drink to the beauty of your eyes until they are too foxed to get up from under the table?' the Viscount asked rudely.

'Because, my cork-brained gamester,' Lady Leone replied, 'none of them has been rich enough or in a position to give me what I ask of life. Justin is different, as you well know. He is immensely wealthy, he could lift us all out of the poor-house and not notice that he had even put his hand in his pocket. Besides, he attracts me.'

'I suspicion that is merely because you are finding him hard to get,' the Viscount said shrewdly. 'You always have wanted the moon, Leone, because it was out of reach.'

'Justin is within my reach,' she said harshly. 'I shall marry him, I must. Peregrine! I have an idea!'

'What is that?' the Viscount asked without much enthusiasm.

'It has just come to me,' Lady Leone said.

69

'You remember you said just now that the mere fact that he was kissing me should prove compromising.'

'You laughed at me for the suggestion, if I remember rightly,' the Viscount retorted.

'Yes indeed,' Lady Leone said. 'It could hardly be very compromising for him to be in the house when both Papa and Mama were here. They were asleep upstairs, but when I asked Justin in for a nightcap I am convinced that he thought they would not have yet retired.'

'Then if you were not compromised,' the Viscount said, 'where is this tale leading us?'

'Only to the fact that if I were compromised,' Lady Leone said slowly, 'if you did find me in an unfortunate position, Peregrine, how right you would be to defend my honour, to insist on the Marquis of Alton making your sister a very proper offer of marriage.'

The Viscount's eyes lit up with a sudden understanding.

'This sounds interesting,' he said. 'What is your suggestion?'

Lady Leone sat down in a chair opposite him, and a crafty smile twisted her beautiful mouth as she started to talk.

Later in the day Lady Leone, dressed in the very height of fashion, drove in an open carriage from Grosvenor Square, where the

Earl of Dansby lived, towards Bond Street.

She was accompanied by her mother's Abigail, a hatchet-faced, middle-aged woman of impeccable respectability, who sat subserviently on the seat facing Her Ladyship with her back to the horses.

The carriage turned into Bond Street and Lady Leone leant out to wave to many friends perambulating in the warm sunshine.

She was in very good looks, her dark hair framed by a high-crowned bonnet trimmed with blood-red ostrich feathers and tied with ribbons to match under her pointed chin. 'I am going to call on Madame Zazette,' she told the Abigail, who snorted disapprovingly.

'You went to that charlatan twice last week, M'Lady. I should have thought you'd something better on which to spend your guineas.'

'I will not have you questioning my movements, Martha,' Lady Leone said sharply. 'And what is more, if you tell anyone in the house where I have gone, I swear I will have you dismissed, even though you have been with the family for nigh on forty years.'

'I'm not afraid of your threats, M'Lady,' Martha replied. 'I sees what I sees and I hears what I hears, and luckily for Your Ladyship I keeps my thoughts to myself.'

'That is all I ask you to do,' Lady Leone admonished her, a second later bending forward with a radiant smile to bow to the occupants of a passing carriage.

'Is it true,' Martha continued with the familiarity of an ancient retainer, 'that you are to marry M'Lord Alton?'

Lady Leone was silent for a moment, and then she answered:

'Yes, Martha, I intend to marry him.'

'Then you had best be a trifle more circumspect, M'Lady. Even walls have ears where a lady of quality is concerned, and there are always servants and menials of some sort to carry tales. Not that I'd trust that crafty fortune-teller further than I could see her.'

'Madame Zazette is safe enough,' Lady Leone replied. 'If there were the slightest whisper to the effect that she talked, she would have few visitors and her business would soon be finished.'

'Nevertheless, the woman is dangerous,' Martha said in a low voice.

Lady Leone gave a little laugh and she smiled at the Abigail.

'Dear Martha, you have always been worried about me, have you not? I remember when I was a child you were always in a flutter for fear I should fall down and hurt myself. When I went out hunting you would always be in a tremble lest I would come home with broken bones. Well, sometimes there have been reason in your fears.'

Lady Leone paused, then she said:

'From the moment His Lordship puts the ring on my finger, I will behave like a saint, that I promise you.'

'That you will and no mistake from all I know of His Lordship,' Martha snapped. 'I have seen him agrowing up, same as I have Your Ladyship. I know he is not a man to stand any nonsense, or any of your foolishness.'

'I hope you say the same to him,' Lady Leone said.

Martha snorted again.

'His Lordship is a man, and you know as well as I do, M'Lady, gentlemen can indulge themselves wherever their fancy may take them. But 'tis not expected of a woman, and certainly not one in Your Ladyship's position.'

'You are croaking at me like a black crow!' Lady Leone exclaimed petulantly. 'You take all the pleasure out of life, Martha. If I listened to you I would be sitting dismally at home with nothing to amuse me save the platitudes of a few half-witted beaux, who have no intention of committing themselves to matrimony.'

''Tis time you were married, M'Lady,' Martha said grimly, 'and this is not the right way to set about it.'

Lady Leone shrugged her shoulders.

'You are trying to make my blood run cold, Martha. It has always been your method of trying to control me by fear. Well, I am not easily frightened, and I have already promised you if His Lordship comes up to scratch then all my escapades will be a thing of the past.'

'I can only pray that will be the truth, M'Lady.'

Lady Leone laughed lightly.

'Do you pray for me, Martha? Why indeed, I believe you do, and that in itself should be an inducement for me to turn over a new leaf.'

'I wish I could believe that, Your Lady-ship,' Martha said.

'Well, if anyone could put a damper on my amusing myself, you do,' Lady Leone retorted. 'Take the carriage to the Pantheon Bazaar and do not dare to return for at least an hour. I do not want the carriage to be recognised outside Madame Zazette's.'

'I've a few trifling purchases to make, M'Lady,' Martha said sourly.

'Well, give your instructions to the coach-man,' Lady Leone said, 'and make them sound feasible. You know he is a chatterbox if ever there was one.'

The carriage drew to a standstill outside a small shop in Maddox Street.

There was a small diamond-paned window in which were displayed some lotions for the face, salves for the lips, violet-scented powder and other cosmetics used by Ladies of Quality.

The products all had a tired, rather dusty look as if the window-display had not recently been renewed and the goods on show had been on sale for a long time.

Lady Leone glanced around, but the fashionable Ladies and Dandies strolling in Bond Street were apparently not interested in this side alley.

There were only two ragged urchins to be seen scavenging in the gutter and a few respectable middle-class shoppers going about their business.

Lady Leone seemed to float gracefully up the three steps which led into the shop and disappeared inside.

As the door closed behind her a non-descript middle-aged shop-attendant started to her feet. Lady Leone passed her by without a word, and parting the curtains at the far end of the room she entered the semi-darkness of a small back room, decorated to look like a tent.

Covering the walls there were dark red drapes which fell from the centre of the ceiling, and seated on a low couch with a table in front of her was Madame Zazette.

Of gypsy blood, she had the dark hair, high cheek-bones and almost black eyes of a Romany. She was dressed in a fantastic manner which might have been described as Turkish with touch of Spanish combined with the influence of Egypt.

She was festooned in cheap jewellery and wore huge gold earrings hanging beneath the red-tasselled scarf which swathed her black hair.

She threw out her dark-skinned arms in an exaggerated gesture of welcome as Lady Leone appeared. Her hands, none too clean, were adorned with rings of every type and description, while bracelets jangled round her thin wrists.

'You're late, M'Lady,' she said in a voice with a foreign accent.

'He is here?' Lady Leone asked.

'And waiting impatiently,' Madame Zazette chuckled. 'You put them in a fever, don't you, my pretty. For over half an hour he has been in a sweat and drooling at the mouth in case you should turn him down.'

'That is enough,' Lady Leone said sharply. 'Here is your money.'

She put two guineas down in front of the gypsy. Madame Zazette looked up at her insolently.

'I told you last time, M'Lady, that my fee was increased. Three guineas, if you please.'

'Three!' Lady Leone ejaculated. 'That is too much, as you well know.'

'You're welcome to go elsewhere, M'Lady,' the gypsy said with a shrug of the shoulders.

Lady Leone gave a cry of exasperation, but she pulled another guinea from her

76

reticule and threw it down on the table.

'I may not be coming again.'

Madame Zazette chuckled.

'That's what they all says, but they come back. There's no one as can accommodate them so comfortably or so secretly as Zazette. You'll be back, M'Lady, if not for him for someone else.'

'Do not talk to me like that,' Lady Leone commanded.

She turned towards the door at the far end. It would have been difficult to find if she had not been familiar with the small room. Then as she reached it she turned back.

'As you charge so much,' she said, 'you might as well do a little real fortune-telling for a change. Just tell me one thing, do I get my wish?'

The gypsy threw back her head and laughed.

'You grand ladies are all the same, always wanting a little extra for your money,' she jeered. 'Well, because you're a good customer I'll give it to you. As I've told you before, you'll get what you want out of life – money, that is what you crave, is it not? – and a great position. What more can someone like Your Ladyship be wanting?'

'You are sure that I will have both those things?' Lady Leone asked insistently.

'With a face like yours, it should not be difficult,' the gypsy replied. 'Can it be that your body keeps asking for something different?'

There was again that jeering laugh, but this time Lady Leone turned with an expression of anger and going through the partially hidden door slammed it behind her.

She was now at the bottom of a narrow twisting staircase which led to the first floor. Picking up the front of her dress she climbed swiftly and opened the door on the first landing.

As she entered a man rose from a chair in front of the fireplace.

'You are late,' he said uncompromisingly.

'I am sorry, I could not help it,' Lady Leone replied.

She stood just inside the over-ornamented, pink-curtained room to look at him.

He was a magnificent specimen of manhood. Over 6ft 2in., broad-shouldered, his muscular body was displayed at its very best in the uniform he wore of His Majesty's Dragoon Guards.

He was handsome in a slightly coarse, masculine manner, and there was a kind of animal virility about him which seemed somehow to offer a challenge to any female who looked his way.

'Come here,' he said commandingly as Lady Leone did not move.

'Are you asking me or ordering me?' she enquired, a little smile on her lips.

'You know the answer to that,' he said roughly. 'You have kept me waiting.'

'You came early,' she flushed.

'That old witch downstairs told you, did she?' he said. 'All right, I wanted to see you, and I am convinced you were as anxious to get here as I was.'

'You are intolerably conceited, Gervase,' Lady Leone complained.

'I am not, but I have only to raise my finger and high-steppers like yourself run to my side.'

'God, I hate you when you talk like that,' Lady Leone said. 'I have a good mind not to stay.'

He did not answer but looked at her speculatively, and the expression in his eyes made her go running towards him.

'Gervase, Gervase, we are wasting time!' she cried. 'Kiss me. You know that I have been longing to be with you.'

He reached out and as she looked up at him he gripped her shoulders so hard that she winced a little at the strength of his fingers.

'Is that the truth?' he asked in a deep voice.

'You know it is,' she answered, her lips parted.

He drew her closer and then his lips were on hers. He kissed her roughly, brutally, but after a moment he released her, saying harshly:

79

'Take off the cursed bonnet and let me look at you. You excite me, Leone, but I have no trust in you. You meet me here clandestinely, hidden away from prying eyes, but you will not let me come to your home.'

'What would be the use?' Lady Leone asked, taking off her bonnet as he had commanded her.

She threw it on a chair and reached out her arms towards him.

'Do not let us talk,' she whispered, 'kiss me, love me – set me on fire! That is what I want of you.'

'That is all you want of me,' he said in a hard voice. 'You bewitch me, Leone, and when I am with you I cannot think coherently. And when you are no longer there I know you are but making use of me. You want me as your lover, but you do not want me as a husband. That is the truth, is it not?'

'Do not talk fustian, Gervase,' Lady Leone said wearily. 'You know that we do not lead the same sort of life. I have never concealed from you that I have to marry money. We are poor. Oh, you can smile! My father may not seem a pauper to you, but you have a pitiful income which would not keep an alley rat in comfort – let alone me. I could not live in obscure penury, as you well know.'

'So you have often told me,' the soldier said in a bitter voice.

'I have to be rich,' Lady Leone declared,

'really rich. I have to own jewels and have servants to wait on me, to belong to the Carlton House set, to be admired and fêted, to be someone of consequence.'

'Can any of that give you what I can give you?' the man beside her asked.

She looked up at him and her face softened.

'Oh, Gervase, you know there has never been anyone who can awaken me as you do to the wild excitement of love, to the thrill of knowing we are together, close, close.'

'That is not love,' Gervase answered. 'You may think it is, Leone, because you are spoilt, ruined by the social world in which it is not a person who matters but what he possesses.'

'Do I matter to you?' Lady Leone asked.

'You know, damn you, how much you matter,' he answered hoarsely. 'But even as I hold you in my arms I know that however much I give you of myself, however much I can excite and delight you, it is not enough. You are greedy, Leone, greedy, and those claw-like little hands of yours can squeeze a man's heart dry and give him little in return.'

In reply Lady Leone put her arms round his neck and brought his face down to hers.

'Is this nothing?' she asked, and her lips were on his, hungry, possessive, passionate and irresistible.

He crushed her to him, giving her again those hard, brutal kisses which made her draw him closer and ever closer, until finally with a little cry she threw back her head.

'Love me, oh, Gervase, love me!' she moaned. 'I want you, you are driving me mad – I want you.'

And then, as if he could resist her no longer, the soldier picked her up in his arms and carried her towards an alcove in the room in which was set a soft low divan.

At that very moment the Marquis of Alton was pacing up and down the Library at Alton House, holding in his hand a note from his Agent at Alton Park which had just been delivered by a groom on horseback.

His Lordship had already read the note twice, now he read it again.

'To the most Noble, the Marquis of Alton', it was headed, and the writing-paper was inscribed 'The Estate Office, Alton Park, Hertfordshire'.

'My Lord, I deeply regret being unable to convey to Your Lordship any further information with regard to the Visitors to Furse Cottage, the residence of Miss Rose Trant, who died last month aged seventy-one.

'The Woman in question had been a Tenant of Your Lordship for over twenty years. I have ascertained that her Sister, called Bessie, had never visited her until her last illness overtook her.

'It is believed locally that Bessie Trant was in Domestic Service. Unfortunately, Miss Rose Trant was noted, if Your Lordship will excuse the expression, for "keeping Herself to Herself", and no one seems to know by whom her Sister was Employed.

'Several people say a young Lady was seen at Furse Cottage last Wednesday, but as far as I can ascertain She did not stay for more than twenty-four hours, and left on the Stage-Coach early on Thursday morning with Bessie Trant, their destination presumably being London.

'I deeply regret that I cannot be of further Service to Your Lordship in this matter, but should anything subsequently transpire regarding the Misses Trants or their Visitor, I will communicate with your Lordship immediately.

'I remain Your Lordship's most humble and obedient Servant.

J. Roberts.'

'It is incredible,' the Marquis thought, 'that anyone could disappear so completely and so swiftly.'

He had gone to Furse Cottage the morning following his meeting with Sylvina, having learnt from his coachman where he had deposited the young lady and the injured dog.

To his astonishment he found the cottage with the shutters closed and the door locked.

As it stood by itself a little apart from the village, there was no one from whom he could enquire where the occupants had gone.

He was forced into the somewhat ignominious position of explaining to his Agent that he required information not only about the owner of the cottage but also of the young lady who had visited there.

Sylvina had told him they would not meet again, but not for one moment had he credited that she spoke the truth.

The Marquis was not in the habit of showing an interest in a female without her making it very clear that she welcomed his attentions, much less vanishing.

Sylvina had indeed said very much the opposite, but he had not believed that she meant what she said.

Perhaps for the first time in his life as a reputed breaker of hearts, whose fascinations were so renowned that he had almost come to believe in them himself, the Marquis had discovered someone who was actually eluding him.

His cynicism, which had grown upon him ever since a certain episode in his life in which he had been almost brutally disillusioned, had become so habitual that he was used to questioning if it were possible for innocence and unsophistication to exist.

He had watched Sylvina that afternoon in

the woods and when they had sat in the little Grecian temple.

He had been intrigued by her beauty, but at the same time some critical part of his brain had questioned whether she was, in fact, completely and absolutely genuine.

'Could any woman,' he asked himself, 'be so ingenuous, so utterly unspoilt, so un-touched by the world as she appeared to be?'

The Marquis was used to women who declared their whole-hearted love and devotion for him, but who nevertheless had at the same time their feet set firmly on the social ground.

They were always on the alert lest they should be seen to overstep the bounds of propriety, making sure that, however abandoned they might be in private, they were exceedingly circumspect where public opinion was concerned.

'I love you! I love you!'

How often had he heard these words from a woman, and known at the same time that her passion would swiftly be extinguished by a creak of a stair.

However much she protested her love, she was also determined that her reputation should remain unsullied and that their liaison, however ardent it might appear in his arms, should never be disclosed outside a locked room.

The Marquis was not a man to refuse the

favours that were offered him, but often he had wondered to himself whether he was not the hunted more often than the hunter.

There was never a chase when he did not anticipate what would be the conclusion; he never sought but he knew that he would find.

'You are too damned successful with the fair sex, Justin,' one of his friends said to him once. 'They look on you as a Casanova, and make up their minds from the moment they see you that you will seduce them. The rest of us have to fight for what falls into your arms like an overripe peach.'

At the time the Marquis had laughed at the envious note in his friend's voice, but afterwards he thought to himself that that was exactly what was wrong with his whole relationship with the lovely, desirable women who adorned the world in which he moved.

They were like overripe peaches. He did not even have to reach out for them; they were there, waiting to be consumed, almost anticipating his desire before it was even aroused.

And now for the first time he had met someone different – or had he? He asked himself the question and knew that at all costs he had to find Sylvina again and discover the truth.

She had told him that he was considered to be tenacious. Well, in that she was undoubtedly right!

If he wanted something – and it was seldom he did want something that was not easily obtainable – no difficulties or obstacles were going to prevent him from gaining what he desired.

And yet on this count he seemed up against a brick wall.

How on earth could any man start to find in the teeming labyrinth of London a girl who was called Sylvina, accompanied by a servant named Bessie Trant?

How could he have been so foolish, he asked himself, as not to compel her to tell him her name?

But even as he berated himself, he had the feeling that however hard he had pressed her she would not have yielded to his insistence.

Of what was she so frightened? Who was it who made her face overshadowed and could bring into her eyes a fear he had never seen before in a woman's face.

It must be some man, but what man? Where could he find him? Where indeed could he enquire?

The Marquis still restlessly walked back and forth, his eyes blind to the magnificent Library, the colourful leather books stretching from floor to ceiling, the sunlight glinting on the carved gilt furniture and the ancient mirrors which had been brought into his family during the reign of Queen Anne.

Instead he felt the soft music of the wind blowing through the trees, he saw a little elfin-shaped face turned up to his and he heard a soft almost breathless voice calling him 'Sir Justin'.

He knew it was going to be impossible for him to rest until he discovered where Sylvina was and if she was indeed as entrancing as she had seemed those hours when they had talked together.

'I shall undoubtedly,' he told himself cynically, 'be disillusioned when I do find her. She will inevitably be the daughter of some fat tradesman, or perhaps the by-blow of a nobleman who had not had the inclination to marry her mother!'

Then he hated himself for his own cynicism.

Breeding had been evident in every inch of her body, in the proud carriage of her head, in the high arches of her little feet, in her thin white fingers and the soft musical tones of her voice.

She was educated too, there were not many women who had studied Greek. There were also few women who could talk as she did with a poetry of phrase which could only have come from learning.

Surely during the time they were together she must have given him some clue, if not to her identity at least to where he could find her.

'What is the point,' the Marquis asked himself, 'of my attempting to apprehend Napoleon's spies and to ferret out enemy agents from the length and breadth of England, if I cannot find one girl in whom I am personally interested?'

He threw the Agent's letter with a sudden anger down on his desk.

'The man is a fool!' he said aloud, but he knew even as he spoke that he was being unfair.

The Agent would have done his best, but those old women who keep 'themselves to themselves' would have left few clues, and besides, Rose Trant was dead.

It was Bessie he was seeking, and she had only been staying at Alton Green for three weeks. Where had Sylvina been before she came to the village?

'She had travelled,' he remarked, 'she spoke of the Vienna woods. Had her father been in the Army? That was, of course, a possibility.'

The Marquis walked over to the window and looked out onto the sunshine and the small walled garden which lay at the back of the house.

There were two small rhododendron bushes in flower. Their blossoms were pink and they reminded him of the crimson splendour of the rhododendrons round the Grecian temple.

He could see Sylvina standing against them, her eyes soft and luminous as she reached out her arms to the beauty of them.

'Curse it,' the Marquis ejaculated, 'I will find her if it is the last thing I ever do!'

# 4

The Marquis looked at the pile of letters his Secretary set down in front of him.

The huge desk was already covered with papers of every sort and description, and the Marquis reflected irritably that if this was the amount of work that could accumulate when he had been at the Foreign Office only for a month, there was no knowing what would be waiting for him by the end of the year.

'More letters, Mr Lawson?' he asked in ominous tones.

'I am afraid so, My Lord,' Mr Lawson replied.

He was a quiet, efficient, middle-aged man who had been a Civil Servant all his working life.

The Marquis had detected a faint air of disapproval about Mr Lawson when he had first been appointed as his Secretary.

It was quite understandable that a perm-anent official would resent, if not despise, a newcomer who from what he had heard was more at home in a lady's boudoir than in the austerity of the Foreign Office corridors.

But if these indeed had been Mr Lawson's first thoughts, they quickly underwent a change.

He was to find that the Marquis had an agile brain, a manner in making quick decisions which captured his admiration, and a way of his own in dealing with the most intricate problems, which ensured that soon after he had given his attention to them they usually ceased to present insoluble difficulties.

Mr Lawson's tone was respectful as he placed the heap of correspondence in front of the Marquis and said:

'I have taken the liberty, My Lord, of sorting out those letters which I consider not to be worthy of Your Lordship's attention. Many of them are, I am convinced, nothing but attempts to pay off old grievances by bringing a charge of spying, which in most cases appears to be completely unfounded.'

'I am quite certain you can deal with these as well,' the Marquis said.

He sifted swiftly through the mass of paper noting the illiterate, often illegible handwriting and seeing that in most cases the signature was that of a woman.

'If you will trust me to do that, My Lord, I will be pleased to bring to your attention only those I consider beyond my capabilities.'

The Marquis's eyes twinkled.

'Do you really admit that any such problem exists?'

Mr Lawson smiled faintly. He was never quite certain where he stood when the Marquis joked with him.

The Marquis pushed aside the letters and said:

'If you ask my opinion, we are wasting a great deal of our valuable time in troubling ourselves with these ridiculous complaints. If Napoleon has, in fact, any important spies in England, they would not be so easily detected, they would not have made such obvious mistakes in dealing with the ordinary people as are attributed to these suspects.'

'No, I agree with Your Lordship there,' Mr Lawson said. 'In fact, it appears that the nation is suffering from an epidemic of spymania. It is worse than the mediaeval witch-hunts.'

'Well, sort through those letters and consign the majority, if not all, to the waste-paper-basket. If you think any seem to offer any credibility then send someone to investigate – discreetly, of course. Any real spy would disappear very quickly at the merest suspicion of an enquiry.'

'Of course, My Lord,' Mr Lawson agreed. 'But I should like Your Lordship's approval for taking on two more clerks to carry out these investigations. Your Lordship will agree that we must have men of education and of some presence; otherwise it is unlikely that anyone will give them their confidence.'

The Marquis rose from his seat at the desk and walked across the big oak-panelled room.

'You know, Mr Lawson,' he said reflectively, 'this is not exactly what was envisaged when I consented to work here.'

'No, My Lord?' Mr Lawson asked enquiringly.

The Marquis paused a moment and chose his words carefully; for he did not want to reveal all that Mr Pitt had said to him.

At the same time he thought it only fair that his Secretary should have some idea where he wished to concentrate his attention.

'The fact is,' the Marquis went on, 'I am looking for somewhat bigger fish than some pettifogging little enemy agent who may or may not earn a few louis for any dubious information he can send across the Channel.'

'I think I understand that, My Lord,' Mr Lawson said quietly.

'It is traitors whom I am concerned with, not spies,' the Marquis said. 'And if, as would be most regrettable, there prove to be traitors in our midst, they are not likely to go round the City swearing inadvertently in French, or getting themselves involved with the type of rabble who write to us.'

'No indeed, My Lord,' Mr Lawson replied. 'I think without Your Lordship taking me into your confidence, I knew that this was what lay at the back of your appointment.'

He spoke with satisfaction and went on:

'Nevertheless I am sure Your Lordship will agree that in regard to the people who work here and in other Government departments and, of course, the social world in which Your Lordship moves, it is important to keep up a front, as it were, by dealing publicly with petty informers and unimportant French sympathisers.'

'Yes, of course, Mr Lawson,' the Marquis said, pleased that his Secretary had grasped the point so quickly. 'That is exactly why I persuaded Lord Hawkesbury to give me this most imposing office, to appoint you as my Secretary and to have a number of minor officials acting under you.

'I could have gone to the War Office or the Admiralty, but I preferred to be here. Nevertheless, I am half convinced that it is all a tremendous waste of time.'

'I cannot credit that, My Lord,' Mr Lawson said quietly, 'so long as there is a leakage from the very highest conference tables.'

The Marquis looked startled.

'Good God!' he ejaculated. 'Who told you that? I swear I never breathed a word of it.'

'It is common knowledge, My Lord, amongst the senior officials,' Mr Lawson said.

The Marquis looked irritated for a moment, then he laughed.

'Can anything ever be kept secret from confidential secretaries, or indeed from a gentleman's gentleman?' he asked. 'Well, Mr Lawson, since you know so much I can tell you that it is Mr Pitt who is convinced that revelations of the most secret Cabinet conferences are somehow conveyed to Bonaparte.'

'Mr Pitt is seldom mistaken, My Lord,' Mr Lawson added with a sigh. 'If only he would consent to take office again! It is said that the Prime Minister offered him any post he liked, and even offered to serve under him. But Mr Pitt refused.'

'I know, I know,' the Marquis said testily. 'We all regret his decision because there is no one in time of war we would rather have to lead us than the man who was at the helm for nine years.'

'They say it is only a question of time, My Lord, before Mr Pitt will relent and return to Downing Street.'

'Then let us hope it will not be too long,' the Marquis said. 'Things are sadly chaotic at the moment, as you well know.'

'Indeed, My Lord, that is all too true,' Mr Lawson agreed, 'and I am sure Your Lordship must know...'

Mr Lawson abruptly ceased speaking and looked somewhat apprehensively over his shoulder as the door opened.

The tall, lanky figure of Lord Hawkesbury, Secretary of State for Foreign Affairs, came into the room.

'Good morning, Alton,' he said to the Marquis.

'Good morning, Secretary of State,' the Marquis replied formally. 'Is there anything I can do for you?'

Lord Hawkesbury hesitated and it was obvious that he suddenly changed his mind about what he was going to say.

'I was about to remind you, Alton, not to forget our reception here tonight.'

'Good Lord, is it tonight?' the Marquis ejaculated. 'But surely my presence is not necessary?'

'It is most necessary,' Lord Hawkesbury corrected, 'and remember you are to dine first with His Royal Highness at Carlton House.'

'Not another bonanza,' the Marquis groaned. 'No wonder Prinny's pockets are to let. He spends far too much on entertainment. Besides, if he wines and dines us as he did the other night, most of his guests will not be in a fit state to attend your party.'

'I have already spoken to Mrs Fitzherbert,' Lord Hawkesbury said with a smile, 'and she has promised that the dinner will not be long drawn out. As you know, it was the Prince's idea that this party should be given and it has been planned for a long time.'

'One might have been forgiven for thinking that the outbreak of war would have been a good excuse for cancelling it,' the Marquis said in a disagreeable tone.

'There are still a few diplomats left to entertain,' Lord Hawkesbury said, 'though I admit that with Napoleon rampaging over the map of Europe Ambassadors from other countries are scarce on the ground. That is why my wife has decided to introduce dancing later in the evening. You must not forget, Alton, that I have two marriageable daughters.'

'I had not forgotten,' the Marquis said. 'They are delightful young creatures and I am sure they will find plenty of partners amongst the Corps Diplomatique.'

'My wife will see to that,' the Secretary of State said vaguely. 'Anyway, Alton, we can be sure of your company, and that, if nothing else, will keep the Prince in a good temper. You know he hates this type of party unless he has his special friends around him.'

'I will do my best to ensure that His Royal Highness has a pleasant evening,' the Marquis said in a bored voice.

'That is all I came to ask of you,' Lord Hawkesbury said, and moved languidly from the room.

The door shut behind him and the Marquis ejaculated:

'God damn it! I had no idea there was another of these cursed formal Assemblies to demand my presence.'

'I had written it in your engagement book, My Lord,' Mr Lawson said, 'and I was going to take the liberty of reminding you before you left today that His Lordship was expecting you to be present.'

'I assure you, Mr Lawson,' the Marquis said, 'that had I any idea that the office I now hold was going to oblige me to attend many such functions, I should have refused Mr Pitt's offer, even though it entailed branding myself as a traitor.'

'I am sure the reception will not be as tiring as all that, My Lord,' Mr Lawson ventured, 'and indeed the Ballroom will be a very pretty sight. It is being decorated at this very moment with flowers and ferns, and there are to be fairy lights in the garden.'

'How extremely original!' the Marquis observed sarcastically.

Mr Lawson, taking the pile of letters from the desk, bowed himself from the room.

He had found it wise in his dealings with the Marquis to disappear as soon as that particular note sounded in His Lordship's voice.

When he had gone the Marquis walked to the window. Looking over the immediate roof tops he could see the trees of St James's Park.

They were blowing in the wind, and he thought that so long as the wind continued to blow as it was now, there was little chance of Napoleon crossing the Channel in the flat-bottomed boats which he had been accumulating month by month along the coast of France.

And then inevitably the movement of the trees reminded him of Sylvina.

Again he swore, but this time softly without the irritation in his voice which he had not disguised from Mr Lawson.

It seemed incredible that after a week she should still be present so vividly in his mind that he found it difficult not to find himself wondering at almost any moment of the day where she might be.

'Damme!' he said beneath his breath. 'The whole thing is nonsensical!'

He had met the girl for a few hours, a female of no consequence in the social world in which he moved, someone who, if he had met her in different circumstances, he was certain would not have held his attention for ten minutes.

And yet he would find himself continually thinking of her, of the dimples in her cheeks, of the note of amusement in her voice, of the fear in her eyes and the confiding gesture with which with no trace

99

of self-consciousness she would slip her hand into his.

'I am becoming deranged or senile,' the Marquis told himself sternly.

He remembered with embarrassment how the night before he had planned to visit again one of his latest flirts, a Lady of Quality whom he had pursued whole-heartedly three weeks before.

She had a figure that must, he had been convinced, drive any man to madness unless he were blind.

She had then yielded to his entreaties without too much protestation, and as they had but recently made one another's acquaintance it was not surprising that he had felt a vast urgency to sample again the delights she was all too willing to offer him.

Yet when he had reached the door of her house, having previously ascertained that her husband was away from home, he quite suddenly felt a curious dislike of walking up the stone steps which led into the tall, imposing mansion situated in a fashionable Mayfair street.

He sat back in his carriage, though his footman had flung open the door. He noted that a piece of red carpet was already being rolled across the pavement by powdered flunkeys.

The light from the open door of the house streamed out over the pavement. He could see the butler waiting, and behind him two other footmen ablaze with gold braid, their polished buttons bearing the crest of their distinguished employer.

Quite suddenly the Marquis had known that the affair was over.

He knew that in the Salon she would be waiting for him, her exquisite figure barely concealed beneath a transparent négligée.

Her eyes would be afire with passion, her arms ready to encircle his neck when they were alone.

His wooing had been ardent, since she had not been quite such an easy conquest as others had been. But now, when he had swept away her scruples and became her lover, he no longer desired her.

He had bent forward in the coach.

'Convey my compliments to Her Ladyship,' he said, 'and inform her I deeply regret I am prevented from calling on her this evening.'

The impassive flunkey carried the message to an equally expressionless butler, the red carpet was rolled back, the footman sprang up on the box beside the coachman and the Marquis had been carried home.

'Why?' he now asked of the trees in St James's Park. 'Why? Why?'

He was not prepared to find an answer, he only left the Foreign Office in an exceeding bad temper which made him ignore the greetings of several friends as he passed down the broad steps and into his waiting carriage.

'Why is Alton in one of his sullens?' a young Buck asked as he drove away.

His companion shrugged his shoulders.

'It is obviously a case of *cherchez la femme*.'

His friend held up his hand in mock protest.

'In the name of the devil do not speak French when Alton is about,' he warned him. 'He will clap you in irons and that will be the end of you.'

'I am not afraid,' the young man answered. 'I do not believe that for all his ferocity Alton will catch anything unless it is some pretty little bit o' muslin from Paris who has been smuggled across the Channel for the special delectation of noblemen who are bored with the English variety.'

The sally brought a burst of laughter from his friends.

It was fortunate that the Marquis did not hear them; for it would only have confirmed his own conviction that he was wasting his time.

He thought it even more a waste of time when dinner was finished at Carlton House and the Prince reluctantly told his male cronies that they could linger no longer over their port.

'Mrs Fitzherbert has given me the strictest

instructions that we must not delay in join-
ing the ladies,' H.R.H. said, with a
complacency of a man who rather enjoys
being bullied by the woman he loves.
'Therefore, gentlemen, drink up, for we
must now repair to the party given by our
Secretary of State for Foreign Affairs.'

'I should have thought the plural was
unnecessary,' one of the guests remarked.
'We have only one foreign affair at the
moment which, as far as I am concerned, is
to beat Boney.'

'That is right,' the Prince agreed. 'On your
feet, gentlemen, I will give you a toast. To
the destruction of Bonaparte, may the end
come quickly.'

They raised their glasses, emptied them,
then following their Prince's lead threw
them over their shoulders to smash into a
thousand pieces on the floor behind them.

'What a waste of expensive crystal,' the
Marquis thought to himself.

But he knew how much the Prince enjoyed these theatrical gestures, and indeed
tonight in anticipation of the Reception His
Royal Highness was looking more than
usually dramatic in a coat of strawberry-
pink velvet covered with decorations like a
Christmas tree.

The Marquis had already incurred his
host's displeasure by wearing only one
diamond star on his plain blue evening coat.

The coat had been cut by a master-hand and fitted him without a wrinkle, and it was perhaps the fact that he looked extremely handsome in it rather than the fact that he was under-decorated which had caused the Prince to censure him.

'Really, Alton,' he said, 'you might pay me the compliment of being better dressed when you come to Carlton House.'

'I thought actually that I made a discreet foil to your glittering magnificence, Sire,' the Marquis replied.

The Prince was fond of him and often permitted the Marquis more familiarity than he would stand from anyone else.

For a moment he looked annoyed, then his brow cleared and he laughed.

'Alton, you dog,' he said, 'you are only saying that to flatter me. Yet on occasions like tonight I feel we should show the foreigners that despite the war Englishmen can still outdo a Corsican upstart when it comes to splendour.'

'As the first Gentleman in Europe, and perhaps at the moment the only Gentleman in Europe,' the Marquis replied, 'you have always been able to do that, Sire.'

The Prince was delighted.

'Well said, Alton!' he exclaimed. 'Well said indeed! The only Gentleman in Europe, that is very good. I must remember that.'

'He is not likely to forget it,' the Marquis

thought as he heard the Prince repeating the remark over and over again amongst his guests assembled in the Chinese Room.

Then at last, after a great deal of chatter, the company piled into a long row of waiting carriages to drive the short distance between Carlton House and the Foreign Office.

Mr Lawson had been right when he said it was a pretty sight.

The rather sombre interior had been transformed with garlands of flowers, with forests, as it seemed, of ferns and palm trees, with paper lanterns, and most decorative of all, the guests themselves.

There were men and women from all over the world – Rajahs from India, their turbans glittering with rubies and emeralds the size of pigeons' eggs; Arabs and Chinese from the East; Chileans and Argentinians from the West.

The French refugee-aristocrats with whom London was inundated turned up in force, eager to prove their dislike of the new dictator of France and to vow over and over again their allegiance to Britain.

There was indeed a shortage of Ambassadors, since there were few countries left in Europe where Napoleon was not the master.

Nevertheless there was a sprinkling of them, past and present, and their lack of numbers was made up, as Lord Hawkesbury had prophesied, by a flutter of débutantes accompanied by their bejewelled and tiaraed Mamas.

Obediently, because he had been commanded to do so, the Marquis made himself pleasant, singling out the overseas guests and leaving each one delighted with his charm, his flattery and his wit.

But after two hours of punctiliously doing his duty, he felt suddenly fatigued, and boredom sweeping over him like a tidal wave made him feel he could stand no more.

He went from the Ballroom, down the passage and let himself out by a French window onto a small balcony at the back of the building which overlooked the garden.

There was a flight of steps leading down into the garden, but the Marquis had no desire to join the throng of guests moving amongst the fairy lights or, as he could see from his vantage point, embracing amorously and, as they thought, unperceived behind the shelter of skillfully arranged flowers and ferns.

The Marquis stood there wondering if he could leave the party without being detected, when he heard someone come onto the balcony behind him and a man's voice said:

'Now stay here and do not wander away. I will fetch you a glass of lemonade since you ask for it, but you will wait until I return.'

There was something aggressively authoritative in the voice.

The Marquis, without really consciously thinking about it, felt it must be singularly annoying to whoever was being addressed.

Then he heard a soft breathless voice say: 'I will stay ... here.'

Thinking for a moment that he could not have heard right, he turned and saw her standing alone, her back to the French windows. She was looking up into the sky almost as if she appealed for help.

The Marquis stared at her incredulously; then his boredom and lassitude suddenly vanishing he moved swiftly towards her from the end of the balcony where he had been standing in the shadows.

'Sylvina,' he said in a low voice.

She turned her head and there was no mistaking the almost incredible joy in her eyes.

He put out his hand and took hers.

'Come,' he said, and without protesting she obeyed him.

He drew her down the steps into the garden, and avoiding the crowds they took a small path which led them almost immediately to a door in the wall.

The Marquis opened the door and, as he expected, there was a sentry outside to prevent people who had not been invited to the party from entering.

The man knew the Marquis by sight and

saluted smartly.

Still without speaking the Marquis, leading Sylvina by the hand, drew her across the narrow dusty roadway which led to the Horseguards and entered St James's Park.

He heard her draw in her breath as he led her along a narrow path and over a small bridge to where the silver water flowed beneath the drooping willow trees.

It was very quiet.

Only when he came to a place where the moonlight illuminated the beauty of the trees and glinting on the water lit Sylvina's little face as though by a thousand candles did the Marquis stop.

'Why have you brought me here?' she asked, her eyes raised to his.

As he did not answer she went on:

'Of course I know the answer – because it is so beautiful! Not as beautiful as our magic wood, but still lovely! Do you think the ducks are asleep under the overhanging boughs? My brother brought me here once to see them in the daytime.'

She was talking, the Marquis felt, because she was shy, but now at last he spoke, his voice very deep.

'Where have you been? How could you have vanished like that?'

'Did you look for me?' she questioned.

'You knew I would call the following day to enquire – after Columbus.'

'Oh, he is better,' she answered, her face lighting up, 'in fact, his leg is nearly well. You must have thought me very ... ungrateful.'

'I could not have believed it possible that you would vanish back to Olympus or wherever you had come from so swiftly and so completely.'

She laughed a little at that.

'Not Olympus,' she replied, 'merely London, which you could not describe as being the home of the gods, except perhaps when we stand here.'

She had no idea how lovely she looked, her eyes dark pools of mystery in the moonlight, her hair soft and pale as a summer's cloud.

The Marquis noted that she was fashionably gowned. Her dress was of gauze threaded through with silver, and there were silver ribbons over her shoulders which crossed over her small swelling breasts and hung down in a many-ended sash behind her.

Her hair was fashionably arranged, and yet it seemed to him that she was unchanged, the forest maid with whom he had laughed and talked for some enchanted unforgettable hours.

'Sylvina, I have been searching for you.'

'You should not have done that,' she answered. 'I told you we would never meet again.'

'And yet we have met.'

'Why are you here?' she asked wonderingly. 'I thought of you as living in the country, farming your land, unable to afford to come to London.'

She looked at him and her eyes caught the moonlight gleaming in his diamond star.

'But you ... you are of ... consequence,' she said accusingly, 'you wear a decoration.'

'What I wear tonight,' the Marquis replied, 'I won in battle. I have been a soldier, Sylvina.'

He saw the sudden anxiety on her face clear.

'A soldier!' she breathed. 'I might have guessed. No wonder you were my Knight-Errant, Sir Justin. There are many soldiers here tonight, and you would wish to be with your comrades.'

She was offering herself an explanation for his presence, and the Marquis did not contradict her.

'Fancy dress is not important, Sylvina,' he said, 'what is important is that I have found you again.'

'You wanted to see me?'

It was a child's question, and the Marquis's voice was deep as he replied:

'I wanted to find you – more than anything in the world.'

She turned away from him and he knew that she blushed.

'There is nothing more we can say to each other,' she said quickly. 'I have told you, it is impossible for us to meet. Oh, Sir Justin, do not spoil the memory of those wonderful, wonderful hours – or was it a whole lifetime? – that we spent together. I have thought of it ... it has helped me ... it has made it possible for me to bear...'

She stopped suddenly.

'To bear what?' he asked.

'I cannot tell you,' she said quickly.

'Then let us talk of something else,' he suggested.

'No, I must go back... I should not have come ... you know I should not have come.'

'But you came,' the Marquis said gently.

'I was so surprised at seeing you that I could not think, I did not have time to protest.'

'Was that not fate?' the Marquis asked. 'Look round you, Sylvina is this not also an enchanted place?'

He watched her look round as he had told her to do, noting the deep mysterious shadows beneath the trees, the radiance of the moonbeams seeping through the leaves which fluttered in the wind, the rippled surface of the water, the stars twinkling above in the dark purple of the sky.

'It is very ... lovely,' Sylvina breathed.

'Very lovely,' the Marquis agreed.

But he was watching her face, knowing

with the instinct of a man who is conversant with women that she was tinglingly aware of him standing beside her.

'Look at me, Sylvina,' he said commandingly.

She obeyed him, the moonlight on her face; and with that expression he knew so well of trust and fear mingled together which made her seem half child and half woman.

'I have to see you again,' the Marquis said firmly. 'You said our meeting was like a story-book; then what has happened between us cannot end so pointlessly.'

'There can be no other ... ending,' Sylvina said in a low voice.

'Why not?' the Marquis insisted.

'Because of the things... I cannot tell you,' she answered, 'because there are ... obstacles and ... difficulties, problems and ... fears which I cannot ... relate.'

'Do you realise what it is like,' the Marquis asked, 'to search for one elusive forest nymph called Sylvina amongst the teeming crowds who dwell in London?'

'You have been searching for me?'

'But of course,' he answered.

'But why?' she enquired innocently.

'Do you really want the answer to that?' the Marquis asked in a deep voice.

She looked up into his face and he knew that she was trembling, but not from fear.

'I must ... go,' she whispered, but there

was an excited breathlessness in her voice.

She would have turned away from him, but he reached out and taking her by the shoulders prevented her from moving.

At his touch she was suddenly very still.

Her eyes widened as they met his and it seemed to the Marquis as though he too was unable to move. A spell such as he had never known before in his whole life held him bound to her.

There was no need for their lips to speak because something magical and strange passed between them and they knew each other's need without words.

For a moment it seemed as though Sylvina hardly breathed, but he felt her whole body quiver beneath his hands.

Very, very slowly, as if he was compelled by something stronger than himself, by something completely irresistible, the Marquis bent towards her.

His mouth sought hers and he found that her lips were as soft and sweet as the petals of a flower.

Just for one moment they were joined together, until with a little exclamation which was almost a sob Sylvina twisted herself from his grasp and was gone.

She moved so swiftly that he was unable to stop her, unable to do anything but stare helplessly after her as he watched her disappearing along the path they had come back towards the Foreign Office.

Her dress was white against the darkness of the trees, until finally she vanished and he could see her no more.

It was then that the Marquis realised almost despairingly that he still had no knowledge of her name or where she lived.

# 5

The Marquis walked slowly back to the Ballroom.

He knew instinctively that Sylvina would not be there, and yet he could not help looking amongst the dancers to see if he could catch a glimpse of her.

There were many people standing round the dance floor conversing with each other or just watching those who were more energetic.

The Marquis scanned their faces, but there was no small graceful figure in a white dress sparkling with silver ribbons.

'Could you by any chance be looking for me?' a voice said at his elbow.

He turned round and saw Leone looking exceedingly beautiful in a dress daringly cut to reveal her white shoulders. Her neck was encircled with rubies.

'Leone! I did not expect to see you here tonight!' the Marquis exclaimed. 'I should have thought this would be too staid a company for someone as gay as yourself – unless you have a special reason for invading the Foreign Office.'

'You are trying to be disagreeable, Justin,' she replied. 'But my presence is accounted for without any ulterior motive. Papa insisted that it was his duty to be present, and so I accompanied him.'

'Very filial,' the Marquis remarked sarcastically.

'I suppose it is useless to ask you to stand up with me in the country-dance?' Leone enquired softly.

She drew a little nearer to him as she spoke and he could smell the exotic eastern scent which she habitually used.

It was, he thought, characteristic of her: there was something oriental about Leone, it showed in the way she moved and the almost serpent-like manner in which she insinuated herself close to a man and made him feel that she was enticing him into wild indiscretions merely because she glanced at him through her dark eyelashes.

'I regret if I appear discourteous,' the Marquis said formally, 'but I am in fact, on the point of departure.'

'The lure of some gambling hell? Or can it be that I have a rival?' Leone asked.

'Neither,' the Marquis replied. 'It may sound very banal, but I am retiring to bed.'

'At so early an hour!' she exclaimed.

'You forget,' the Marquis answered, 'that I am now a working man.'

'How could I forget?' Leone smiled. 'All London is talking of your untiring search for Napoleon's spies. Indeed every time I swear in French I expect to have you drag me to the Tower.'

'I can promise you that is not my intention,' the Marquis replied.

'Then if not to the Tower – where?' Leone asked.

He looked away from the invitation in her eyes.

'Your servant, Leone,' he said bowing, 'but you must excuse me. I am sure my place as your partner on the dance floor will be eagerly sought by one of your ever increasing number of admirers.'

The Marquis would have turned away, but he felt Leone's hand on his arm.

'Is that the truth, Justin?' she asked insistently. 'You are indeed refusing me not for some fair charmer but because you are fatigued?'

'If you are really interested I can assure you,' the Marquis replied, 'that the only encircling arms I seek at this particular moment are those of Morpheus.'

'Then let me bid you a very pleasant

night, My Lord,' Leone replied, 'and I hope that you will dream of me.'

'It would, of course, be impossible not to do so,' the Marquis replied with that cynical note in his voice which invariably incited women to pursue him with heightened ardour.

He walked away through the Ballroom. Leone watched him go.

There was something in the breadth of his shoulders, in the proud carriage of his head and the elegance of his whole appearance which made her draw in her breath sharply.

He would not escape her, she vowed to herself.

The Marquis proceeded from the Ballroom down the flower-decorated corridors until he reached the front door. There was the usual crowds of linkmen calling up the carriages, and the moment he appeared a resplendent flunkey on the doorstep bawled out his name.

'The carriage of The Most Noble the Marquis of Alton,' he shouted.

Almost immediately the Marquis's elegant black and yellow cabriolet appeared drawn by two perfectly matched roans.

He was just about to walk down the steps towards it when a thought struck him.

'Tell me,' he said to the flunkey who had called his carriage, 'did a lady leave here alone about twenty minutes ago – a young lady, very young?'

The man thought for a moment, then he said:

'Yes, you are right, M'Lord. There was a young lady. I remember now I was surprised she was not accompanied. She asked for a hackney carriage.'

'What was her destination,' the Marquis enquired.

The man left his post at the door and went to speak to one of the linkmen. When he returned he said:

'The address, M'Lord, was Number 9, Queen's Walk, Chelsea,' and transferred a guinea unobtrusively into his coat pocket.

But as the Marquis started to descend the steps towards his cabriolet he was hailed by a voice he knew well.

'Wait a minute, Alton,' Lord Hawkesbury said coming down the steps behind him.

'Anything wrong, Secretary of State?' the Marquis enquired.

Lord Hawkesbury shook his head.

'Nothing, except that I am as fatigued with the proceedings as I expect you are. I am playing truant, Alton. Will you give me a lift in your carriage? It is not far out of your way.'

'Yes of course,' the Marquis said. 'I shall be delighted to do so.'

Lord Hawkesbury stepped into the Marquis's well-padded cabriolet which was built for speed and the Marquis gave instructions to drive to His Lordship's house in Hanover Square.

Inside the carriage the Secretary of State leant back with a sigh of relief and put his feet up on the seat opposite.

'Damned exhausting, these affairs!' he grumbled. 'We are fortunate that His Royal Highness left as early as he did.'

The Marquis thought a trifle shame-facedly that he had forgotten his dinner-host and had indeed been absent when His Royal Highness had retired.

He only hoped that Lord Hawkesbury had not noticed his absence amongst the courtiers saying farewell to the Prince.

'No one of importance left now,' Lord Hawkesbury was saying, 'or rather no one with whom my wife cannot deal competently. She enjoys functions of this sort. If you ask my opinion, Alton, they are a dead bore.'

'I agree with you, M'Lord,' the Marquis remarked drily, 'and if you remember, it was you who insisted that I should be present.'

'Yes, I remember,' Lord Hawkesbury said, 'but there was something else I was going to say to you when I came to your room this morning and found you had Lawson with you.'

'He is a reliable fellow,' the Marquis replied. 'All the same, one cannot be too careful these days.'

'Yes, indeed,' Lord Hawkesbury said. 'We sometimes forget that all those who wait on us – our domestic staff, for instance – have ears.'

'What was it you wished to tell me, My Lord?'

'We had a secret dispatch this morning from one of our agents on the other side of the Channel,' Lord Hawkesbury answered. 'He tells us that Bonaparte's invasion fleet is enormous. He did not know the exact number of barges, of course, or the amount of men that the enemy intends to carry, but apparently Bonaparte is said to have remarked that "it would matter little if ten or even twenty thousand troops were sunk on the way over".'

'Good God!' the Marquis ejaculated. 'The invasion must indeed be on a grand scale.'

'It is what we anticipated,' Lord Hawkesbury said, 'but this is the first verifiable confirmation of our fears. But I have not finished my story.'

'What else?' the Marquis asked.

'Apparently Bonaparte continued: "One expects to lose that number in battle, and what battle ever promised such results as a landing in England?"'

'Can we repel them?' the Marquis asked.

'I believe we can,' Lord Hawkesbury said. 'We had a secret Cabinet meeting this afternoon, and though we shall have to rely a great deal on the Volunteers, we can muster a formidable army of men. However it would help greatly if we knew from what ports the barges were to commence their journey.'

'Are the Dutch involved?' the Marquis enquired.

Lord Hawkesbury spread out his hands.

'Reports are very confused,' he said, 'and even though we have a number of informants, as you well know, they tell conflicting tales. There is only one thing of which we can be completely certain – that Napoleon will invade us if he can. The time, the day, the month depends undoubtedly on what the weather is like in the Channel.'

'Let us hope that this wind continues,' the Marquis muttered. 'Mr Pitt assured me only yesterday that the Channel was far too rough for a flat-bottomed boat.'

'If only we had more time,' Lord Hawkesbury sighed.

'We need a great deal of time if we are to arm our army as it should be armed,' the Marquis said sharply. 'I cannot believe it gives an Englishman much confidence to have to face Napoleon's victorious veterans with nothing better than a pike in his hand.'

The Marquis spoke angrily, and Lord Hawkesbury from his corner of the carriage said drily:

'What can you expect when we have a Prime Minister like Addington, prone to appeasement and conciliation.'

'The most important thing now,' the Marquis said as though he saw the futility of abusing the Administration, 'is to ensure that Bonaparte does not put a large number of troops ashore where we least expect it. If a body of well-trained men could get behind our lines of defence, then we should indeed be in serious trouble.'

'You may be certain,' Lord Hawkesbury said, 'I am trying to discover everything I can. I have sent two of our best agents to France this week.'

'By the usual method?' the Marquis asked with a smile.

'With the best gang of smugglers on the whole of the South-East coast. They will land them undetected, and they have also promised to bring back every scrap of information about the size of the invasion fleet.'

'What have you promised in return?' the Marquis enquired.

'Just that the coastguards on the Romney Marshes will not be too assiduous in their duties in the next month or so.'

The Marquis laughed.

'I congratulate you, My Lord! I can see you have a real aptitude for intrigue.'

'It would be amusing,' Lord Hawkesbury said, 'if it were not so curst serious, Alton. I do not think that ever before in my life I have been afraid. But I am afraid now –

afraid for my country and the future of our people.'

The Secretary of State spoke with an unusual depth of passion in his voice. Then as if he felt embarrassed by his own protestations he said quickly:

'I must not bore you.'

'You would never do that, My Lord,' the Marquis assured him. 'In this matter we are both unashamedly patriotic. However I am convinced in my heart that, whatever happens, we will beat Bonaparte. It is not going to be easy, it may take many years and may involve a great loss of British lives.'

As he spoke the carriage came to a standstill. Lord Hawkesbury looked out.

'Thank you, Alton, for bringing me home,' he said. 'Keep what I have told you to yourself, although I told the members of the Cabinet that I intended to inform you of what was happening.

'Like Mr Pitt, they are absolutely convinced there is a vital leak somewhere, and they are relying on you to discover who this damned rat may be. For until he is exposed all our defence plans are in jeopardy.'

'I am well aware of that, My Lord,' the Marquis said solemnly, 'and I assure you I am doing everything within my power to unmask this traitor.'

The Secretary of State put his hand on the Marquis's shoulder.

'Good man,' he said, 'I knew we could put our trust in you.'

He tapped on the window of the carriage and the footman, who was already standing outside waiting for the signal, opened the door.

'Good night, Alton, and thank you again for bringing me back. No, do not get out,' he added hastily, 'I have a feeling you are as much in need of sleep as I am.'

Lord Hawkesbury waved his hand and hurried up the steps of his house to where in the lighted doorway his servants stood waiting for him.

The footman at the door of the carriage asked respectfully:

'Home, M'Lord?'

'Home,' the Marquis replied.

He yawned, while at the same time his brain was busy thinking over what Lord Hawkesbury had told him.

If Napoleon was prepared to risk 20,000 troops being sunk in the Channel, that could only mean that he intended to launch an army of at least 80,000, if not 100,000, against England.

They would be trained men, the majority of them seasoned veterans of many battles and many victories.

Would the English troops and inexperienced Volunteers be in any way their match?

It seemed incredible, the Marquis

thought, that during the two years of Armistice while Bonaparte had continued to maintain vast armaments and had used the raising of the blockade to replenish his empty dockyards, England had disbanded the Volunteers and halved her army.

Yet what was the use now of moaning and regretting the stupidity of a policy already put into effect?

What mattered now was that they should be waiting and ready when Bonaparte attempted to land.

The Marquis was sunk in his thoughts as the carriage journeyed the short distance from Hanover Square to Alton House.

The coachman drew up the horses with a flourish, the Marquis stepped across the carpeted pavement and in through the doorway.

The Major-domo was waiting for him in the Hall.

'There is a lady to see Your Lordship,' he said in a low voice.

'A lady?' the Marquis ejaculated. 'At this hour!'

Just for a moment his mind went to Sylvina, but he knew it was impossible.

Then he wondered who amongst his flirts would be likely to behave so outrageously as to call at a bachelor establishment even though her husband might be away from home.

'Who is it?' he asked the Major-domo.

The man hesitated.

'The lady is veiled, M'Lord.'

The Marquis smiled cynically. He was well aware that no veil, however thick or disguising, would prevent a servant from knowing the truth.

'Who do you think it is, Newman?' he enquired.

The Major-domo replied in a tone quiet enough not to be overheard by the attending flunkeys:

'If you will pardon my presumption, M'Lord,' he said, 'I suspicion it is the Lady Leone Harlington.'

'Lady Leone!' the Marquis ejaculated. 'Surely she would not be so indiscreet...?'

Then he stopped.

Somewhere in the back of his mind he remembered Sylvina's little voice saying to him:

'She will set a trap for you.'

With a swiftness born of his army training, the Marquis turned on his heels.

'Inform the Lady,' he said, 'that my carriage has returned empty, and that I sent a message to say I will not be sleeping at home tonight.'

The expression on the Major-domo's face was wholly impassive as he replied:

'Very good, M'Lord.'

The Marquis stepped through the front

door and onto the pavement.

'Your carriage, M'Lord? Shall I send for one?' a flunkey asked.

The Marquis shook his head.

'I will walk,' he replied to the man's astonishment, and set out at a brisk rate.

As soon as he reached the corner of the Square he turned, and out of sight of the house stepped into the flower-filled garden which stood in the centre of the Square itself.

Here he moved slowly and quietly between the great bushes of lilac which stood in the shadows beneath the high trees.

There was the fragrance of night stock which reminded him of Alton Park, and he had only to think of Alton to remember the woods and Sylvina's warning of a woman who would try to trap him.

He was certain, almost completely certain, that this was the trap which she had foreseen when she had told him of his past and future in so strange and uncanny a manner.

Threading his way through the garden the Marquis was soon opposite to his own front door.

He was hidden by a huge bush of syringa, and as he brushed against it the white blossoms fell to the ground and the yellow pollen centres brushed off against his coat. He stood still amongst the sweet-scented branches waiting.

The door of Alton House was flung open

and the light from the great crystal chandeliers in the Hall flowed out warm and golden onto the pavement.

A flunkey emerged and ran hurriedly down the street. The Marquis guessed that he had gone in search of a hackney carriage.

In a few minutes he returned with one, and then from the door of the house a veiled figure hurried across the pavement and stepped into the carriage.

There was no mistaking the blood-red dress with its low *décolleté* that Leone had worn at the Foreign Office reception, and the light wrap with which she had covered her shoulders fell back to reveal the necklace of rubies which encircled the white column of her neck.

The hackney carriage drove away, but still the Marquis did not move.

He stood behind the syringa bush for perhaps ten minutes, until driven at an almost reckless speed round the Square there arrived a sporting curricle conveying four young men.

They were all obviously in a cheerful mood and what Mr James Fox would have called 'a trifle bosky'.

The driver was particularly well wined, with his top-hat balanced at a jaunty angle on the side of his head.

He rose unsteadily to his feet, threw the reins to a groom and climbing down from the box of the curricle marched across the pavement to lift the knocker of Alton House.

The other gentlemen followed him, some taking longer than others to disengage themselves from the comfort of the cushioned seats.

'The witnesses!' the Marquis told himself with a tightening of his lips.

The door of Alton House opened and he heard the Viscount Thatford say loudly:

'I desire to speak with the Marquis of Alton. Take me to His Lordship.'

'His Lordship is not at home, Sir.'

'I beg leave to doubt that statement,' the Viscount replied aggressively.

He pushed his way into the Hall, followed by his companions.

The Marquis could hear sounds of altercation between the gentlemen and the flunkeys, and then he knew that the Viscount, accompanied by his friends, was opening the door of the small Salon on the ground floor, the Library and the Dining Room.

From where he stood he could see down the long passage and could perceive his servants trying to expostulate, but being thrust on one side by first the Viscount and then his companions.

Finally the Viscount went up the stairway, and the Marquis knew that he intended to search the bedrooms.

The sheer outrageousness of the young

Bucks' behaviour enraged him, but he was wise enough to know that nothing could be gained by his appearance at this particular moment.

He only vowed to himself that he would seek out each one of the young men who had dared to intrude on the privacy of his house and he would make them pay dearly for their impertinence.

Finally, discomfited and somewhat deflated, the gentlemen reappeared on the pavement.

The Marquis could not see the expression on the Viscount's face, but he felt certain it portrayed not only disappointment but also apprehension.

They all climbed into the curricle and drove off, almost silent and in a mood very different from the joviality of their arrival.

When they were out of sight the Marquis stepped from the shadows of the syringa bush and walked across the pavement to his own house.

His hand on the knocker brought a footman quickly to the door. When he saw who stood there he looked astonished.

'M'Lord!' he exclaimed. 'I understood...'

'I have changed my mind,' the Marquis interrupted.

'There were some gentlemen here, M'Lord, who...'

'I know all about it,' the Marquis said in

his most abrupt manner. 'They shall be dealt with, make no mistake, I shall deal with them.'

He walked into his Library and sat down in an armchair. The footman brought a decanter of brandy and set it down beside him.

The man hesitated for a moment in case his master should ask for something, but as the Marquis did not speak he went from the room, closing the door quietly behind him.

The Marquis sat very still. He felt like a man who had piloted a frail craft down the rapids of an unnavigable river and by a miracle survived.

He saw now why Leone had been so insistent in finding out whether he intended to go home. She had planned this, he thought, planned it for some night, any night when she was sure that he would be at home.

She intended to come to him and tempt him to make love to her, and then they were to be discovered by her brother.

There would have been no possibility of extrication. The Marquis would have been expected to behave honourably and make requital for Leone's smeared reputation.

The only recompense possible would have been an offer of marriage.

He had been saved, the Marquis thought, saved because Sylvina had warned him that someone would set a trap for him.

Had she not done so, he might unsuspectingly have gone into the Salon where Leone was waiting, expecting to find not her but some other lady not so vulnerable because she was already married.

The Marquis reached out his hand and poured himself a glass of brandy.

He felt that he needed it, for he was well aware that his freedom had been saved by a hair's breadth.

If indeed he had married Leone, which at one time he had felt was inevitable, would she not indeed have hurt him as Sylvina had predicted?

Would she not have reopened those wounds which he had hoped were healed and forgotten?

And yet he knew that what had happened to him in the past was something which he never could forget.

Lying back in his armchair, a glass of brandy in his hand, the Marquis remembered all too vividly the wild elation of his first love affair.

He had been very young, very impressionable, and having joined the Army straight from Oxford he had thought that Heloise was not a woman but a goddess.

He realised now that he had been absurdly idealistic in setting her upon a pedestal.

She had, in fact, been very attractive, with a wide-eyed virginal loveliness which, if she had been born amongst the *Beau Ton,* would have ensured her being acclaimed a beauty.

As it was, she was the wife of an obscure British officer, and undoubtedly her attractions were enhanced because she suffered little or no competition from the other wives and sweethearts congregated in a camp where the soldiers of several different Regiments were being trained.

Heloise was small and fragile in appearance, and when she confided to the Marquis, who was then the Viscount Bourne, how badly her husband treated her, he declared he would challenge his brother officer to a duel.

But Heloise had restrained him from doing anything so foolish.

There was no doubt she enjoyed the ardour of his love-making and was flattered by the social rank of her young admirer, but at the same time she was afraid of a scandal.

The Marquis thought with a little twist of his lips how deeply he had respected this lovely woman who had given him her affection.

At first he could not believe that she not only loved him in return, but was indeed willing to surrender herself to him.

He did not dare even to dream of such a benefaction, let alone ask her to make such a sacrifice; but when she did so, he believed that the heavens had opened and he was indeed blessed.

While he approached her in reverence and thanked God on his knees for her love, her husband was killed on manœuvres.

It was then that the Marquis realised that he was the most fortunate man in the whole world.

This perfect woman, this creature from another planet who had stooped to accept him as her lover, was now free to become his wife.

When the formalities of the military funeral and the first weeks of deep mourning were over, the Marquis went to Heloise and told her that he was asking for special leave to visit his father.

'I know we shall have to wait for a long time yet,' he told her. 'You will be in mourning for the conventional twelve months, but I intend to speak to my father about you, I want to tell him what you mean to me, and I know that when he hears how deeply I love you he will understand and will accept you into the family.'

The Marquis had spoken more confidently than he really felt.

He was well aware that his father was exceedingly proud of the family name and the great position at Court and in politics that the Altons had held for many centuries.

Besotted as he might be, the Marquis knew that the interview in which he had to explain why he had lost his heart to someone outside the usual sphere of his parents' acquaintances was not going to be easy.

He was not so foolish as to credit that the daughter of an obscure country solicitor and the widow of an officer in a not particularly distinguished Regiment of Foot was the type of female his father and mother would welcome as the future Marchioness of Alton.

But he believed his love would conquer everything, and he set off to Alton Park in a jubilant mood, determined as he had never been determined about anything in his life before that he would make his father understand how perfect Heloise was in every way.

He had gone for perhaps ten miles and his high spirits were sinking a little when he had an idea.

Surely it would be better not to explain what Heloise was like but to let his parents see for themselves?

If he took her with him to Alton Park would they not be completely captivated, as he had been, by her beauty, her gentleness, her sympathy and above all her compliance?

'They will see that she is indeed the type of person who would adopt herself successfully to our way of life,' he told himself. 'They will realise there is no barrier of class or breeding which cannot be bridged by someone who is by nature a great lady, even if she has no family tree to proclaim it.'

He turned his horses round and drove back

to the camp. He drew up at Heloise's house and walked in without being announced.

They had long dispensed with any formality. Finding the Sitting Room empty he bounded up the stairs to the bedroom.

He opened the door and found Heloise as he expected in bed – but she was not alone.

Even to think of it now, the Marquis ruminated, was to bring back that sudden numb feeling in the chest as though he had been struck by a cannon-ball.

He could still recall his stupefaction as he saw Heloise lying there, the dark head of a brother officer on the pillow beside her.

His whole world had seemed to turn upside down, and he had known as he tooled his horses away from the camp that while he could never bear to see her again, he would never forget what she had done to him.

He had arranged a transfer to another battalion of his regiment which was leaving immediately for the continent, and with the desperation of youth he had done his best to get himself killed.

He had fought so wildly and with so little consideration for his own safety that he had been decorated on the field for gallantry.

If he could have done so he would have refused the medal. He received other distinctions during his Army career, but the first was one he never wore.

But time, as always, softened the violence

of his feelings. Some of his misery left him, his unhappiness gradually faded.

Never while he lived, he thought, would he again be so besotted as to believe there was any woman so pure and innocent that she could not be seduced by a man who desired her.

He had never spoken to anyone of what had occurred, and because Heloise was unimportant and not a member of Society, no one who knew the Marquis had any idea why he had become so cynical.

Yet for every married woman he seduced the Marquis felt that he avenged himself on Heloise. She had left him disconsolate, she had left him empty of all emotion save that of revenge.

When lovely women wept and vowed he had broken their hearts, the Marquis felt each one had the face and voice of Heloise.

The Marquis rose from his chair. He had grown stiff sitting and thinking over the past, remembering Heloise, thinking that Leone in her own way was not unlike her.

How many there were of them – greedy, avaricious, self-seeking women sucking a man dry of everything that appertained to manhood.

He walked across the room and flung back the curtains from the window.

Outside the pale dawn was creeping over the roof-tops, the first faint yellow of the sun was dispelling the purple darkness of night.

There was still one small star twinkling directly overhead.

'Damn all women!' the Marquis said aloud. 'I shall never marry.'

And as he said it, it seemed to him that he heard the sound of laughter in his ears.

Then he felt soft against his mouth, softer than the petals of a flower, gentle as the touch of a butterfly's wing, Sylvina's lips.

And he knew – fool that he was, he would swear on everything he held sacred – that he was the first man who had ever touched her.

# 6

Sylvina came slowly into the Dining Room, an anxious look on her face which was justified when her brother, looking up from his breakfast, asked:

'What maggot in the brain made you behave in such a reprehensible manner last night?'

Sylvina sat down at the end of the table and was silent for a few seconds before she answered.

'I left a message for you,' she said. 'One of the flunkeys said he knew you by sight and

I told him to inform you that I had gone home.'

'I received it,' her brother replied, 'but only after Mr Cuddington, mad as fire, had been raging about the place demanding where you could have gone after he left you on the balcony.'

'I did not ... wish to stay any ... longer,' Sylvina said in a low voice.

'You did not wish to stay!' her brother repeated angrily. 'And how do you think I felt with Cuddington shouting at me as though I were a lackey and roaring round the garden like a wild animal in search of you? I must say, Sylvina, it was a poor way to repay his hospitality. After all, he had given us dinner and paid for your...'

The sentence trailed away awkwardly as Sylvina, suddenly alert, looked at her brother enquiringly.

'He paid for what?' she asked sharply.

'Forget it,' her brother answered.

'Paid for what?' Sylvina insisted.

Her eyes were very large in a face that had suddenly been drained of colour.

Her brother did not answer, and after a moment she said in a low voice:

'You were going to say that he paid for my gown, were you not? You told me, when I thanked you, that you had bought it yourself.'

'Well, I did not have the blunt, and that is the truth,' her brother replied. 'Besides,

Cuddington was making such a flapdoodle about your looking smart and impressing his friends. He is proud of you, you know that.'

'Proud of me!' Sylvina exclaimed bitterly. 'He wants to own me! That you should have let him spend money on my gown is a humiliation such as I have never endured ... never.'

Her voice broke on a little sob. Her brother, pushing back his plate and looking embarrassed, said:

'I could not see any harm in it. After all, you are going to marry him.'

'A man I loathe and detest with every fibre of my being,' Sylvina said passionately.

'I cannot think what you are making such a dust-up about. We have been through all this before, and you know as well as I do that if you do not marry him I shall be put in front of a firing squad.'

'Yes, I know,' Sylvina said, and her voice softened. 'I am doing it for you, Clyde ... because ... I love you, because it is a case of saving ... the family honour. But you know what sort ... of man ... he is.'

'I know nothing of the sort!' her brother retorted angrily. 'You have made this ridiculous fuss about Cuddington since the very first moment you met him. After all, he is behaving quite decently over the whole thing. And you might do worse.

'They say he is the most brilliant man

there has ever been at the Foreign Office. He is not yet forty and he is Under-Secretary of State for Foreign Affairs. There is every chance, if Hawkesbury retires, that he will step into his shoes.'

Her brother paused, but as Sylvina said nothing he went on as if encouraged:

'Oh, I know that Mama would think him a Cit! After all, his father was only a wool merchant, but that has made him extremely wealthy. And he is ambitious, everyone knows that.'

'Can you not see that that is one of the reasons why he wants me?' Sylvina said. 'He wants a blue-blooded wife, he said so! He wants to cut a dash in fashionable circles. That is why he wants to doll me up like a Lady of Fashion, that is why he is prepared to spend money paying for my gown – although had I known about it I would have died rather than wear it.'

'Oh, fustian!' her brother said sharply. 'You always talk in such an exaggerated fashion. What does a gown matter one way or the other? He will be paying for all of them as soon as you are married.'

'If I ... marry him,' Sylvina said in a low voice.

Her brother rose from the table, and walking round to where she was sitting put his arm round her shoulder.

'I know I am asking a lot of you,' he said,

'but Sylvina, what else can I do? You know that Alton is sitting there ready to pounce on anyone about whom there is the least suspicion. Cuddington has only to murmur my name to him and I am absolutely convinced I would be in irons without a defence of any sort.'

The young man's voice was so bitter that Sylvina turned and laid her cheek against her arm.

'It is all right, dearest,' she said, 'I will do it, you know I will do it. But there is something about him that repels me, and last night ... well I could not face ... him again.'

'He will get over it,' her brother said cheerfully. 'And by the way, that reminds me. He is coming here about noon to see you.'

'Coming here?'

Sylvina repeated the words with horror in her voice.

'But I told you that I will not be ... alone with him, and you ... promised me!'

'All right, all right,' her brother said soothingly. 'He is bringing someone with him to see you, someone you used to know when you were in Spain.'

'When I was in Spain?' Sylvina repeated wonderingly.

'Yes. Comte Armand de Vallien. Does that name mean anything to you?'

'Of course,' Sylvina exclaimed. 'His father was the French Ambassador in Madrid; and then I saw him again the year before last when Papa and I first went to Paris.'

'Well, apparently he wants something from you,' her brother said.

'From me?' Sylvina questioned. 'But what can I give him?'

'Cuddington will tell you all about it. They are coming together, so do not get in a flippety-flap.'

'At least I have Bessie here with me now,' Sylvina said almost beneath her breath.

Her brother looked at her down-turned eyes, opened his lips as if to say something and then turned towards the door.

'I shall be late at the office,' he said. 'Cheer up, Syl, things will not be as bad as you think, and Cuddington will have recovered by now. He was in a state fit for Bedlam at your behaviour. I should not do it again.'

Sylvina merely sighed, and when her brother had left she sat for a long time at the breakfast table, staring with unseeing eyes across the small room and making no effort to help herself from the dishes which Bessie had laid on the table.

Finally she rose and went to the window, looking out onto the small garden which lay just across the roadway and which separated the two rows of small, elegant houses, each one ornamented with a wrought-iron balcony.

It was the garden with its high trees that

had persuaded Sylvina to choose this house.

At least here there was some green in what had seemed to her at first sight the pervading gloom and darkness of London.

Now she had come to find beauty in unexpected places; in the blue mist which lay over the river at night, in the pale sunshine which glinted on the roofs and chimney-pots when they were wet and turned them to liquid gold, and in the flowers and ornamental water of the parks.

The thought of the Park made her remember last night, and instinctively she put her fingers to her lips.

She could still feel Sir Justin's mouth as it had touched hers, she could still hear the deep note in his voice, still feel that sudden inexplicable ecstasy within her breasts because he was close, so close that his arms encircled her.

He had kissed her!

She felt a little thrill go through her at the thought, and then resolutely she went from the room, calling for Bessie, telling her she was ready to help her with the myriad household tasks they regularly performed together after Clyde had left for the office.

Clyde's clothes must be tidied and pressed, his boots polished until they shone like mirrors. There must never be a button awry or a stitch out of place.

It was Clyde who must look smart however poverty-stricken they might be, Clyde who was now head of the family, Clyde whom their mother had adored and whose name she had whispered as she died.

Sylvina had never been jealous, even though her mother had meant everything in her life. It had seemed right that Clyde should have everything, and she what little could be spared.

'He is a man,' she told Bessie, 'he must keep up appearances among his friends.'

She and Bessie were prepared to do without almost everything so that Clyde could go to the Balls and Assemblies, the Routs and Masques to which he was invited night after night; and indeed even if she had been asked, Sylvina had no wish to accompany him.

She was content to stay at home, content to read and to study, sometimes until the early hours of the morning.

'What are you awearing out your eyes with now?' Bessie would ask her.

'It is my Spanish,' Sylvina would answer. 'It is becoming lamentably rusty. Let me see, it was in 1796, seven years ago, that Spain declared war on England and we had to leave the Embassy at Madrid. I remember how angry Papa was, too angry to give any orders.'

She smiled. 'It was Mama who saw to everything being packed up, and I helped her because I could speak Spanish better

145

than she could.'

'There's not much likelihood of your wanting Spanish again, Miss Sylvina,' Bessie said, 'not with Napoleon ruling the country.'

'Napoleon will not rule for ever,' Sylvina had answered with something like a touch of prophecy in her voice.

She had laughed as Bessie had snorted and answered:

'The world be full of upstarts, there's no place for decent bodies amongst them.'

'Speaking for yourself, Bessie, of course,' Sylvina had remarked with a little glint of amusement in her eyes.

'Well, if I'm not decent,' Bessie retorted, 'I would like to know who is?'

It was Bessie who now tried to cheer Sylvina out of her apprehension at the thought of Mr Cuddington visiting her at noon. But she was not to be persuaded.

'I hate his even coming to this house,' she declared. 'I hate to see him amongst the things which belonged to Mama. Even when he has gone the atmosphere he has created seems to linger in the Drawing Room.'

'What cannot be cured must be endured, Miss Sylvina,' Bessie said severely. 'You have told me that you have to endure him for Master Clyde's sake. So there's no use in aworking yourself up into a ferment before he even arrives. Take Columbus out into the garden. His leg has nearly healed, as you

146

well know.'

'Yes, I will do that, Bessie,' Sylvina answered, her eyes lighting up. 'It will be wonderful when he is well enough for us to walk in the Park again.'

She picked Columbus up in her arms, cuddling her cheek against the little dog's soft head.

'Come along, my poor wounded soldier,' she said. 'Let us go walkies in the sunshine and pretend we are far away in the woods.'

Sylvina's voice softened suddenly at the words, and old Bessie watching her drew in her breath at the sudden beauty which illuminated the little pointed face.

Then Sylvina was gone, running down the stairs, out through the front door and into the small flower-filled garden which belonged to all the inhabitants of Queen's Walk.

Among the flowers, the shrubs and the trees Sylvina lost all count of time.

She was remembering what she had felt in the Grecian temple. She could see Sir Justin's eyes looking at her, eyes which she knew she could trust, grey and steady, and yet they sometimes held an expression which made her feel as though her heart throbbed in her breast and it was difficult to breathe.

She could almost see him in the shining armour and plumed helmet of a Knight-Errant.

'Sir Justin.'

She whispered the words to herself and realised time was passing and her guests would be arriving.

'Come along, Columbus,' she said to the little dog sitting on the grass at her feet, 'it must be nearly time for your dinner.'

She picked him up in her arms and whispering endearments carried him across the narrow street towards the house.

It was thus the Marquis saw her, the sunlight on her fair hair, her muslin skirt blowing in the wind, her head bent protectively towards the small animal in her arms.

He reined in the team, threw the reins to his groom and jumped down from his Phaeton.

'Walk the horses, John,' he said, and hurried down the pavement.

Sylvina was actually on the steps when he reached her side.

Hearing someone approach she looked up casually, only to feel as if her heart turned over in her breast.

'Y ... you!'

The word came stammeringly from between her lips.

'Did you really think you could escape me?' the Marquis asked.

'I do not ... know what...' Sylvina began incoherently.

'Shall we talk inside?' he asked quietly.

Almost before she had realised what was

happening she had entered the house and the Marquis had closed the door behind him.

Somehow bereft of words she preceded him up the narrow staircase into the Drawing Room on the first floor.

Again he turned to close the door behind him, and he saw that she had retreated to the very far end of the room, a room which he vaguely realised was furnished in perfect taste.

Sylvina put down Columbus on his cushion, and the Marquis watching her thought he had never seen anyone move with such grace.

'H ... how did you ... f ... find me?' she asked at length.

'Why did you run away?'

'I meant ... never to see ... you again.'

He moved towards her, a smile on his lips.

'Did you really believe that was possible?' he asked. 'Surely you know that fate has decreed that we should come together – and one should never try to elude fate.'

'I do not understand ... how you found me,' Sylvina said, not looking at him. 'But please, you must go away ... now ... at once.'

He did not answer, and she said:

'Forget me ... forget we have ever ... met.'

'Do you really think that is possible after last night?' he enquired. 'Have you forgotten, Sylvina, that I kissed you?'

The colour rushed into her face like a crimson tide. For a fleeting moment she looked at him, and then her eyelashes touched her cheeks.

'It was w ... wrong and ... im ... immodest,' she stammered.

'It was wonderful,' he corrected, 'a wonder beyond words, a moment of beauty such as I have never known.'

She trembled but she did not raise her eyes.

'I had the conceit,' the Marquis said quietly, 'of thinking that I was the first man who had ever touched your lips. Is that true?'

'Of course ... it is ... true,' she answered almost fiercely.

'Then, my darling, why are you trying to send me away?' the Marquis asked.

She turned towards the mantelpiece, gripping it with both hands so that he saw her knuckles go white.

'I am ... to be ... married,' she said, so inaudibly that he could hardly hear her.

Just for a moment the sentence made him pause, then he came nearer still and said:

'You are to be married – and yet you are in love.'

'No ... no it is not ... true,' she said quickly.

'Then why are you trembling because I am near you?' he asked. 'If it is not fear, Sylvina, why is your heart beating so fast?'

150

One little hand went to her breast as if to quell the tumult there.

'Why,' he went on, 'is the breath coming quickly between your parted lips? And why are your eyes shining like stars – if it is not with love?'

'It is not! It is not!' she protested. 'Oh please … I beg of you … do not make me … feel like … this.'

It was the cry of a child. Then the Marquis said:

'Look at me, Sylvina.'

She shook her head, turning further away from him.

'Look at me,' he commanded her.

As she did not move he put his fingers under her chin and turned her little face up to his.

'Look at me, look into my eyes and tell me that you do not love me. Then I swear to you I will go away.'

He felt her whole body quiver at his touch, as bravely, with an effort, she looked up at him; and while she trembled she had the strangest feeling that he was trembling too.

There was something they saw in each other's eyes, something so magical, so beautiful that they were both spellbound.

How long they looked at one another it was impossible to know, but suddenly they broke beneath the strain and with a little inarticulate murmur Sylvina melted into the

Marquis's arms and he held her against him.

He bent his head and found her mouth, and this time his kiss was not the gentle touch that their lips had known the night before.

It was a kiss demanding, possessive, a kiss which drew her soul between her lips and made her irrevocably his.

They were indivisible, they were one person, man and woman complete in each other, everything else in the world forgotten.

As he held her closer and still closer the clock on the mantelpiece chimed the hour.

For a moment the sound hardly penetrated Sylvina's consciousness, until with a cry of sheer horror she struggled free of him.

'You must go! You must go at once!' she said with something like terror in her voice. 'Please, I beg of you, do not dispute, do not argue, but go now!'

The Marquis would have spoken, but she put up her fingers to touch his lips.

'I cannot explain ... there is not time. But if you have the least affection for me, show it by leaving quickly ... quickly.'

He saw the desperation in her eyes, and holding her hand against his lips kissed it.

'I will go because you ask me to, Sylvina,' he said, and his voice was very deep and moved, 'but you know I will come back.'

'Yes ... but go now,' she pleaded. 'It is of

desperate import – or I would not ... beg it of ... you.'

The Marquis released her hand, and picking up his tall hat where he had laid it on a chair on entering the room, he opened the door.

'You are quite certain I must leave you?' he asked.

'Quite ... quite certain,' she replied, 'but hurry ... oh please ... hurry.'

Her obvious terror forced him almost against his better judgment down the stairs and out through the front door.

Sylvina made no move to see him out, she only stood in the centre of the Drawing Room, her hands to her heart, tense and still until she heard the front door shut behind him.

Then she ran from the room and up the next flight of stairs to her bedroom.

She stood for a moment, resisting the impulse to throw herself down on the small white bed and bury her face in the pillow.

With an effort she went to the dressing-table, and sitting down stared at her reflection in the mirror as if she felt her image must have been changed by someone waving a magical wand over her.

She did, in fact, look positively different. Her eyes seemed to have caught and held the sunshine, her mouth was warm and tremulous.

There was a blush on her cheeks and she knew that because the Marquis had kissed her she had never been more lovely.

Yet as she stared at herself there came a knock at the door. She did not reply and the door opened.

'The Gentlemen are here, Miss Sylvina,' Bessie announced.

'Already!' Sylvina ejaculated. 'Oh, I pray they did not meet him leaving the house.'

'The clock in the Drawing Room is fast,' Bessie said. 'It gains nigh on four minutes a day. I meant to have it seen to.'

'Then they will not have seen … him,' Sylvina said in a low voice.

'You must go down, Miss Sylvina.'

'Yes, I know.'

Sylvina took a deep breath, tidied her hair absent-mindedly, and walked slowly step by step down the narrow staircase, forcing herself to calm the quickened beating of her heart, forcing herself to remember the man who awaited her.

He must never guess what she was feeling or indeed what rapture had been awoken within her.

She reached the door to the Drawing Room and realised that she was still far from composed and that her blood seemed to be hammering almost like waves within her head.

She stood there striving to be calm, and

then almost without realising at first that she was listening, she heard two men talking in the room. They were speaking in French.

Some part of herself responded to the elegant tones of the Frenchman's voice, the manner in which he phrased his sentences.

The music of the words themselves, brought back to her memories of the chestnuts in bud in the Bois, the Seine reflecting the blue of the sky, the flower-sellers on the steps of the Madeleine.

Then Mr Cuddington's harsh and ugly speech broke her dream. How she hated the very sound of him!

His French was good, he had obviously studied hard to be proficient, but never in a thousand years would he be able to capture the poetry and the rhythm of the French language!

'*Quand doit commencer l'invasion?*' the Comte asked.

It was some minutes later Sylvina realised she was eavesdropping and turned the handle of the door.

The two men stopped speaking, and as she entered the room Mr Cuddington came towards her with a smile.

'Good morning, my dear. You must forgive us for calling on you so early.'

He took her hand and raised it to his lips. She strove not to shudder.

'Now I have a surprise for you,' he said,

'an old friend – a friend of your childhood, le Comte Armand de Vallien. Do you remember him?'

'But of course I remember you, Monsieur,' Sylvina answered with a smile. 'We met again only two years ago in Paris.'

'Am I likely to forget?' the Comte asked gallantly, bowing over her hand. 'You were with your most distinguished father. May I offer you my deepest condolences? The news of his death was indeed a very great shock both to my family and myself.'

'Thank you,' Sylvina said, inclining her head.

'And now the Comte has a favour to ask of you, Sylvina,' Mr Cuddington said, almost as though he were impatient with the courtesies which were being exchanged between them.

'A favour?' Sylvina enquired. 'Forgive me, gentlemen, will you not be seated?'

She took a chair which had its back to the window, and which obliged both Mr Cuddington and the Comte to sit opposite her on the velvet-covered French sofa with its gilt frame.

She noted how completely in contrast the two men were. Mr Cuddington, thick-set, broad-shouldered, his slightly coarse features betraying his humble origin, was handsome enough, while his high forehead bespoke a quick, intelligent mind.

His eyes, however, were too close together, and his lips were unexpectedly thick, the lips of a sensuous man.

The Comte was thin, elegant and aristocratic.

He was affectedly dressed in the fashionable Dandy style, the high points of his collar reaching over his chin, his snowy cravat meticulously tied, and his yellow knitted pantaloons so tight that it must have been a work of art to get into them.

'How can I help you, Monsieur?' Sylvina asked when the gentlemen were seated.

The Comte glanced at Mr Cuddington as though expecting him to be the spokesman.

The Englishman cleared his throat.

'The Comte has just arrived in England,' he said, 'having managed to escape from France where he is under suspicion for opposing the Bonaparte regime. He has expressed a wish to help us fight the Dictator, and he thinks he would be best employed if he assisted the Marquis of Alton in his effort to ferret out those Frenchmen in our midst, and perhaps even Englishmen, who are prepared to assist Bonaparte to vanquish this country.'

'You want to join the Marquis of Alton?' Sylvina said to the Comte. 'But how can I help you?'

'The Comte feels that someone should vouch for him,' Mr Cuddington replied before the Frenchman could speak, 'some-one should explain to the Marquis that he is indeed a *bona fide* sympathiser with this country in our efforts to defy the might and majesty of the all-victorious Corsican.'

'But I do not know the Marquis,' Sylvina said.

'That is immaterial,' Mr Cuddington replied. 'What the Comte wants is for you to relate your childhood association with him, the manner in which your father knew his father and trusted him, and the fact that when your father was at the Embassy in Paris two years ago the Comte and his family were known to be friends of Great Britain.'

'I cannot ... I cannot possibly say this to the ... Marquis of Alton,' Sylvina said agitatedly.

'You would rather I asked – Clyde to oblige?' Mr Cuddington enquired.

There was a meaning in his voice which she could not misunderstand.

'No ... no, of course ... not,' she answered.

'It will not be difficult,' Mr Cuddington went on. 'I have, in fact, already made an appointment for you to see the Marquis this afternoon. The Comte will go with you, and now you have but to write a letter explaining the reason for your visit. I will help by dictating it to you.'

'But why the Marquis of Alton?' Sylvina

protested. 'Is there no one else with whom the Comte would rather work?'

'I know where my gifts will be of most use,' the Comte replied, speaking for the first time. 'I assure you, Mademoiselle Sylvina – if I may call you that in memory of the old days – I have much valuable information to offer the Marquis. I think, in fact, His Lordship will be extremely grateful for the introduction.'

Sylvina glanced at Mr Cuddington.

There was appeal in her eyes, but she found he was watching her with a speculative smile on his lips which made her feel a sudden loathing of him well up inside her.

All she wanted was to be rid of him, and if it meant the writing of a letter what did it matter?

She went to her bureau which stood at one side of the room and picked up a white quill pen.

'You had best tell me what I am to say,' she said.

'That is a good girl,' Mr Cuddington approved with what she felt was an odious familiarity. 'Now write as I tell you.'

The Marquis of Alton was taking very little interest in the letters that Mr Lawson was placing before him one after the other.

He signed them in an absent-minded fashion which was quite unlike his usual habit of scrutinising everything before affixing his signature.

'Have we not finished yet, Lawson?' he asked irritably. 'I have an engagement this afternoon. Surely everything else can wait until tomorrow?'

'There is something else, My Lord,' Mr Lawson said, 'an appointment made for you to see the Comte Armand de Vallien.'

'Who the devil is he?' the Marquis enquired.

'I have here a letter from Miss Blaine,' Mr Lawson explained. 'You will remember Sir Rendell Blaine, My Lord, a most distinguished member of the Diplomatic Corps with a great future in front of him.

'He would, in fact, have been appointed our Ambassador in Paris in 1802 had he not died the year before in the most unfortunate circumstances, which necessitated Lord Whitworth taking over the post.'

'Yes, yes, I remember,' the Marquis said. 'Sir Rendell was killed in a duel or something like that, was he not?'

'It was, in fact, a duel,' Mr Lawson replied, 'and it proved a very unfortunate end to what had been the distinguished career of one of our senior diplomats. No one knows quite how Sir Rendell became involved with the lady in question. It was one of her French admirers who called him out, and Sir Rendell was shot through the heart.'

160

'I remember hearing about it,' the Marquis said, 'although it was all hushed up.'

'Sir Rendell's son, Mr Clyde Blaine, is working here, My Lord,' Mr Lawson continued. 'We have too many young diplomats, of course, but because of his father's services to Great Britain, Lord Hawkesbury thought it was the least we could do to recompense the family.'

'I am sure Lord Hawkesbury was right,' the Marquis said in a bored voice. 'But why should I see this Frenchman? What does he want?'

'I have here the letter from Miss Blaine,' Mr Lawson said, 'in which she begs that Your Lordship will give the Comte an audience, and is prepared, should Your Lordship consider it necessary, to speak to you herself. I understand that the young lady is here and the Comte is with her.'

'I should have thought it was quite obvious that we do not need any more people, especially in my department,' the Marquis said.

'I think, my Lord, it would be extremely discourteous if you did not at least see the Comte,' Mr Lawson answered apologetically. 'Moreover it has always been Lord Hawkesbury's principle that if anyone sponsors another person, it is wise to see them separately: the sponsor first, the applicant afterwards. In that way it is easier to draw a true picture of the person under consideration.'

'Very well,' the Marquis agreed impatiently. 'Have it your own way, Lawson. Send this lady in, and pray Heaven it does not take long.'

'I am sure Your Lordship will manage to prevent that occurrence,' Mr Lawson said with a touch of humour that the Marquis had not known him possess.

The Marquis fidgeted with his paper-knife. He was anxious to be away from the Foreign Office.

He had already ordered his Phaeton, which would be waiting outside to carry him back to Chelsea. He wondered if Sylvina would try to elude him, but this time he swore that she would not succeed.

He was deep in his thoughts of her when the door opened. 'Miss Sylvina Blaine, My Lord,' Mr Lawson announced.

The Marquis glanced up and froze into immobility.

Sylvina advanced almost to the centre of the room before she realised who was facing her from behind the desk.

For one fleeting second there was a sudden light in her eyes and her lips parted, and then in a voice of utter bewilderment she said:

'They said – I was to see – the Marquis of Alton. Why are – you here?'

There was a pause until she continued

with a note of incredulity in her voice:

'It ... it cannot ... be that ... you, that ... you...'

The Marquis rose to his feet.

'I am the Marquis of Alton,' he said.

She stared at him as though he had taken leave of his senses.

Then with a little strangled sound in her throat she ejaculated:

'How can it be the ... truth ... after all you have ... said to me ... all that has ... happened?... It cannot ... be.'

'I meant to tell you, Sylvina, I swear I meant to tell you this afternoon,' the Marquis said. 'I would have told you this morning but you sent me away.'

'You were deceiving ... me all the ... time,' she said piteously. 'You let me tell you how ... afraid I was of ... the Marquis, you ... pretended to me that I was not on ... his land, in his ... woods, eating his ... food!'

'I told you the truth,' the Marquis interrupted her. 'I told you the woods and the Temple belonged to me, which is true, they do.'

'But you know I did not think that ... you were ... the Marquis of Alton.'

'Was it so very important?' he asked.

'You know it was,' she flashed, 'you know I thought the Marquis was...'

'Old and frightening,' he finished the sentence.

163

'But you never corrected me, you let me go on thinking that you were a farmer ... a poor man, someone who did not want to ... come to London.'

'Be fair, Sylvina,' the Marquis begged. 'You thought those things and they were partly true. I do farm, I have an affection for the country.'

'You were lying ... lying and pretending,' Sylvina cried accusingly. 'How you must have laughed at my ... foolishness, my ... un-sophistication, my childish ... id ... ideas.'

Her voice broke on the words.

'I have never laughed at you,' he said in a deep voice, 'you know that. Those moments in the woods, last night in the Park and this morning were moments of enchantment such as I have never known in my whole life.'

There was a silence so that Sylvina thought he must hear her heart beating.

Then with an almost superhuman effort she drew herself up proudly.

'You cannot expect me to believe you, My Lord,' she answered. 'It must have passed an idle hour for Your Lordship to trifle with someone so ignorant of your social world, but I assure you there is no necessity for you to go on pretending.'

'Damn it, I am not pretending!' the Marquis said violently.

He stepped towards her as though he would have taken her in his arms, and then he remembered where he was and was half afraid that even in his office the walls might have eyes and ears or that Lawson might come in unexpectedly.

'Have I Your Lordship's permission to withdraw?' Sylvina asked, and her voice was icy, her face very pale.

The Marquis glanced at her, and then in his most formal tones he replied: 'I understood that you wished to speak to me on a matter of business.'

'Oh yes, of course,' she said quickly.

'Then will you not sit down?' he enquired, indicating a chair on the further side of his desk.

She sat on the edge of it, her back very straight, her eyes veiled so that the lashes lay dark against the transparency of her cheeks.

The Marquis watched her, an expression in his eyes that was unfathomable.

'You wish to bring to my notice the petition of the Comte Armand de Vallien,' he said, 'who desires employment in this office. Is that correct?'

'It is correct.'

'You have known the Comte for some time?'

'Since I was a child.'

'Your father, I understand, was Sir Rendell Blaine, a very distinguished diplomat.'

She inclined her head.

'Then where did you meet the Comte?'

'In Spain at our Embassy and again in Paris.'

'And when were you in Vienna?' the Marquis enquired.

She flushed a little as if she remembered why he asked, but her voice was still cold and distant as she replied:

'My father was the Counsellor in Vienna until the French invasion. We left when I was aged nine and he was posted to Spain.'

'Thank you, I think that will be all,' the Marquis said. 'Perhaps now I should make the acquaintance of the Comte.'

'I must thank Your Lordship for hearing me,' Sylvina said formally.

She rose to her feet and moved towards the door.

'One moment!' the Marquis said.

He came from behind his desk to stand beside her.

'Do not let us leave each other like this,' he said in a low voice.

'I have no more to say to Your Lordship,' Sylvina replied.

He knew it was her pride and indeed her breeding which made her so controlled.

'Will you not forgive me?' he asked very gently.

She looked up at him then and he was astonished at the anger in her eyes.

'I can never forgive you!' she answered. 'Never! Never! I hate you! Do you not understand? You have killed the only beautiful thing left in my life … you have killed … m … my dreams.'

Just for a moment they stared at each other, and then she repeated almost beneath her breath:

'I h … hate … you!'

'Very well,' the Marquis replied, 'but I swear to you, Sylvina, I will do my utmost to make you change your mind.'

'I shall never do that,' she retorted.

'In which case,' he said, 'perhaps, as we have learnt so much about each other, you would care to tell me who is this most fortunate and enviable gentleman to whom you have promised your hand in marriage.'

Sylvina drew herself up, and for a moment she seemed taller than she actually was.

Then clearly, in a voice which did not falter, she replied:

'His name, My Lord, is Mr Roger Cuddington. He is the Under-Secretary of State for Foreign Affairs and is indeed a colleague of Your Lordship. I know you will respect both Mr Cuddington's and my wishes when I inform you that our betrothal is at present secret, and therefore I must trust you to speak of it to no one.'

She did not wait for the Marquis's reply but went from the room, opening the door herself. The Marquis saw Mr Lawson, who must have been hovering outside, hurry to close it after her.

He stood staring at the closed door, a look of sheer astonishment on his face.

Then he walked backwards and forwards across the room.

A man bedevilled within himself and faced with a problem of such unprecedented and unexpected dimensions that he could not think for the moment how to tackle it.

# 7

'How are you, Alton? A trifle blue around the gills?' the Honourable Percival Lillington jested as the Marquis got down from his High Perch Phaeton to ascend the steps of the Foreign Office.

He spoke with the familiarity of an old friend, but the Marquis withered him with a glance through his quizzing-glass and passed on without speaking.

'What rot has got into Alton's attic?' the Honourable Percival exclaimed in surprise. 'Can it be that the last rumour is true and Bonaparte is arriving in a fleet of balloons? Or has some Incomparable shut her bedroom door against him?'

His friend laughed.

'The first contingency is far more likely

than the second. The only time an Incomparable would shut her door where the Marquis is concerned would be when he is inside.'

Their laugher echoed behind the Marquis and merely accentuated the black mood which had settled over him like a November fog.

He passed into the marble hall and along the corridors without acknowledging the salutes of the flunkeys in attendance, and entering his own office he slammed the door and threw himself down in the armchair behind his desk to stare across the room with unseeing eyes, tapping his fingers mechanically on the silver blotter as he did so.

It seemed so incredible that he could hardly believe it himself!

This was the fifth time Sylvina had refused to see him – a man to whom every door was open in London.

The most sought-after bachelor in the whole of the *Beau Ton,* whose invitations every week reached astronomical figures, could not get through the small, cheap, green painted door of Number 9, Queen's Walk.

He had written to Sylvina, only to have his letters returned unopened. That morning he had swallowed his pride and begged Bessie to assist him.

'I must see Miss Blaine,' he said insistently. 'Will you not help me?'

He knew that no money he could offer Bessie would make the slightest difference to her attitude: and he was intuitive enough not to try to bribe her.

But he could not believe that his far-famed charm would not work on this elderly, grey-haired Abigail who carried all over her the mark of a family servant.

'There be nothing I can do, M'Lord,' Bessie replied.

'Have you told Miss Sylvina of my visits? Did you give her the flowers I brought her yesterday?'

'You'll not soften her with flowers, M'Lord, they're just a waste of good money,' Bessie said sharply.

'Did Miss Sylvina throw them away?'

Bessie shook her head.

'She wouldn't countenance a wicked waste like that. No, she comes downstairs when Your Lordship's Phaeton was out of sight and gives them to the first beggar she meets. She tells him to sell them for what he can obtain for them. And if I am not mistook, the old varmint will be round this door for ever more hoping for another windfall.'

The Marquis laughed, he could not help it. But his expression was serious a moment later as he pleaded:

'I have to talk with her, Bessie. Surely you can make her understand that.'

'There's nothing I can do, M'Lord, and

that's a fact,' Bessie repeated. 'She'll not listen to me any more than she'll listen to Your Lordship. When Miss Sylvina has made up her mind as to what's right and what's wrong, there's nothing as'll change her.'

'Is she unhappy?' the Marquis asked in a low voice.

'Unhappy is not the word for it,' Bessie replied. ''Tis more like the heart has gone out of her. I've not seen Miss Sylvina like this since Her Ladyship died. Took it real hard, she did then, seeing what a devoted family they were. And now there is the same blind look in her eyes as though she has lost something – precious.'

There was silence for a moment and then Bessie went on:

'I can't suspicion what Your Lordship was adoing of, upsetting Miss Sylvina as you must have done. She's enough to bear as it is with that Mr Cuddington bullying her whenever he gets the chance.'

'Bullies her, does he,' the Marquis ejaculated sharply, a frown between his eyebrows. 'By what right?'

He saw by Bessie's face that she was about to tell him politely to mind his own business. Then she changed her mind.

'I don't know, M'Lord, I don't know what it all means and that's the Gospel truth. I only knows if Her Ladyship were alive he's not the sort of suitor that would be welcomed for Miss Sylvina's hand.'

'Then why has she accepted him?' the Marquis enquired.

Bessie shook her head.

'Miss Sylvina's not confided in me since we returned here from Alton Green, M'Lord. Before that she'd talk to me as if I were her closest friend and I could swear there were few secrets between us. But when she comes to the village after m'sister's death she was changed.'

'In what way?' the Marquis asked.

''Tis hard to put my finger on it, M'Lord. She was frightened for one thing, frightened in a manner as I have never known her to be. She was always a sensitive child, and often when I was alooking after her if her nurse had left or we were travelling to another country, I'd think to myself she was like a fairy creature.'

Bessie was smiling at the memory.

'Even as a baby,' she continued, 'she used to hold her hands out to the sun and the flowers, and when she grew up I used to think she was happiest when she could be in a garden or the woods.'

'She told me she loved woods,' the Marquis said softly.

'That's true enough, M'Lord. She used to badger Sir Rendell to take her into the woods when we were in Vienna, and in the Embassy garden in Spain there were trees she used to call her very own. She'd look sort of radiant when she was adreaming under them, same as she looked after you'd called that morning and she hustled you out quick before Mr Cuddington could see you.'

'She looked radiant – and happy?' the Marquis questioned in a quiet voice.

'Happy as a bird in a tree,' Bessie declared. 'Her eyes shining, her lips smiling, and I thinks to myself that Your Lordship, and I didn't know then who you might be, could make everything right for her.'

The Marquis did not speak and the old woman continued:

'After Mr Cuddington leaves, Miss Sylvina says to me: "I have to go out, Bessie, to do something unpleasant which I have no wish to do. But if while I am away the same Gentleman who was here a little while ago calls to see me, please ask him to wait!"

'I knows who she means right enough, M'Lord, and she adds:

'"I want to see him again! Oh, Bessie! I want so very, very much to see him again!"'

The Marquis was still silent, a frown between his eyes.

'But you never came back that day, M'Lord, and Miss Sylvina returns looking as if she'd been struck down by a flash of lightning. Not a word could I get out of her, nor has she shed a tear in front of me. But I hears her, M'Lord, night after night acrying so piteous that it fair breaks my heart to hear her.'

The Marquis's lips tightened as if in pain.

'Curse it! This cannot continue!' he said harshly. 'Did Miss Sylvina tell you why she came to Alton Green to fetch you?'

'She said little, M'Lord,' Bessie replied, 'but I understands without her atelling me that she didn't want to be alone with that Mr Cuddington. You see, when Miss Sylvina and Master Clyde first came to Queen's Walk, Sir Rendell's sister was living with them. A proper chaperon she was for Miss Sylvina. But then she was taken ill and had to go away to Harrogate to take the waters. I've been expecting her to return, but 'tis my belief she'll never be well enough to come back.'

'So Miss Sylvina fetched you from Alton Green as a chaperon,' the Marquis said reflectively.

'You can put it in those words, M'Lord; for Miss Sylvina says to me:

'"You are never to leave me alone if gentlemen call on me, Bessie. Whatever they may say to you, you are to come into the Drawing Room and remain there."'

'Gentlemen?' the Marquis said, raising his eyebrows.

'That was her way of putting it, M'Lord, but I knows as well as if she had said his name who she meant. 'Tis always the same when he comes. She becomes pale and frightened, and sometimes I've seen her shaking almost as if a cold wind was blowing through her after he has been here telling her to do this and not do that.'

Bessie snorted with anger.

'I knows he's Master Clyde's boss,' she went on, 'but even so you would think a young gentleman could stand up to such pretensions, especially if a person is not of the quality.'

If the Marquis had not been so perturbed he would have smiled at the scorn in Bessie's voice.

There was no one more disdainful of social upstarts than a family retainer. All servants, he thought, were snobs, and Bessie was no exception.

'Tell me about Lady Blaine,' he said.

'I shouldn't be standing here talking to Your Lordship like this,' Bessie retorted. 'If Miss Sylvina knew about it she'd be upset.'

'Would she be angry with you?' the Marquis asked.

Bessie shook her head.

'No, 'tis very seldom that Miss Sylvina is ever angry, M'Lord. If things go wrong she is hurt, and somehow that is more of a set down than if she ranted and raged like some I've known. But there, I've always said that she is as sweet-tempered and gentle as an angel. She's too good for this world, and that's the truth, M'Lord.'

'I can well believe it,' the Marquis said drily. 'Unfortunately she has to live in this world, and that is why I must help her. She cannot go on being frightened in this manner.'

'That's just what I've told her often enough,' Bessie said triumphantly. 'But she has always said there be no help for it.'

'Take me up to her, Bessie,' the Marquis said coaxingly.

'No indeed, M'Lord, I couldn't do that; for she's in her bedchamber; and that is something Lady Blaine – God rest her – would never forgive me for doing.'

'I asked you to tell me about Lady Blaine,' the Marquis prompted.

'Yes indeed. A beautiful lady she was. Scottish, as you doubtless know, a niece of His Grace the Duke of Argyll, and loved and respected by all who knew her.'

'The Duke of Argyll,' the Marquis said reflectively, 'that is interesting.'

'You have His Grace's acquaintance, M'Lord?'

'We have met once or twice on the Duke's rare visits to London,' the Marquis replied.

For a moment he seemed deep in thought, and then he said:

'I beg you, Bessie, carry one more plea on my behalf. This is the fifth time you have shut the door on me. Go upstairs now and ask Miss Sylvina to grant me just five minutes of her time. I will not keep her longer, tell her I swear I will leave the house the moment she asks it of me. But I must speak with her.'

'I will ask her, M'Lord,' Bessie said reluctantly, 'and I only pray Miss Sylvina'll agree to your request. But if Your Lordship will excuse me, I would not be doing my duty if I did not shut you outside while I climb the stairs.'

'Then you must do your duty,' the Marquis said quietly.

He stood waiting on the doorstep, a handsome elegant figure who drew the eyes of every passer-by while deep in his thoughts he was completely oblivious of them.

He turned quickly as the door opened again, and he knew by the expression on Bessie's face what the verdict was before she said:

'I'm real sorry, M'Lord.'

'What did she say?' the Marquis asked. 'Tell me her exact words.'

'Miss Sylvina says, M'Lord,' Bessie replied sadly, '"I have nothing to say to the Marquis of Alton now – or ever."'

Driving back to the Foreign Office the Marquis wondered whether in his whole life he had ever been so blue-devilled as he was at this particular moment.

Never had he known himself up against such an unscalable obstacle, especially where a female was concerned.

The only possible hope was to enlist the help of Clyde Blaine – but he shrank from doing this, knowing it would place him in a most invidious position. How could he say to a young man:

'I wish to pay my advances to your sister, even though I know she is already promised to another.'

No, that, of course, was impossible, but now that Bessie had failed him, where, where could he turn?

The Marquis rose from the desk and walked across to the window.

He could see the trees in St James's Park bending in the wind, and he thought how Sylvina had looked up at him in the moonlight, her face breath-takingly beautiful, the expression in her big eyes one of anxiety as she asked him about the decoration he wore on his evening coat.

Why at that moment had he not been honest with her? Why had he not told her who he was? He knew the answer was because he had been afraid of losing her!

He had not forgotten how she had refused to go near Alton Park. It was impossible to forget how she had asked if the food waiting for them in the Grecian temple had belonged to the dreaded Marquis.

'Old and frightening' was how she had described him. He could see the darkness in her green eyes, the manner in which her lips trembled in an unexplained dread at the thought of meeting the Marquis or of going to his house.

Why was she afraid of him? What did it mean? Where could he find a solution to such a tangled coil?

He remembered how he had told Sylvina that he was good at solving problems, but this one seemed insoluble. How could he, who had never failed, be defeated by a small, socially inconsequent young girl.

It seemed absurd, but the Marquis thought it was Sylvina's innocence of the world which made her a more difficult adversary than any worldly-wise sophisticate.

'I have to find a clue,' the Marquis said out loud, and he started as a voice from the door said:

'I apologise, My Lord, for not being in attendance on you. I did not realise you had returned.'

'It is all right, Lawson, come in,' the Marquis replied.

'There is something perturbing you, My Lord?'

'There is indeed,' the Marquis said grimly.

Mr Lawson waited a moment as if expecting the Marquis to confide in him, but as he did not do so he said:

'I have no wish to trouble Your Lordship, but the Comte Armand de Vallien has called again hoping for a favourable acquiescence to his request.'

'Damn the fellow!' the Marquis ejaculated. 'Why can he not leave me alone.'

'Shall I tell him to depart, My Lord?'

'No, wait a minute,' the Marquis said, 'I have an idea!'

Anyone who knew him well would have been aware from the expression on his face that he was at that moment at his most formidable.

There was in the Marquis self-reliance and inner strength which he could fall back on when all seemed lost. Now out of the ashes of desperation a new fire flickered into life.

Sylvina had called him tenacious! He would show her he was that if nothing else.

Then, almost as though it had been conjured up by magic at the thought of her, a plan took shape in his mind.

It was this attribute in the Marquis which made Sylvina also describe him as being 'uncannily perceptive'.

It was something that had made him a brilliant commander of troops during the war. When defeat had seemed inevitable, when there was no chance, it appeared, of gaining their objective, suddenly some quite unexpected and often quite outrageous scheme would present itself to the Marquis.

He could see what his troops must do as clearly as if the instructions lay on a map in front of him. And because he half believed these inspirations came from something outside himself, he was always prepared to act on them.

'Do not send the Comte away yet, Mr Lawson,' he said. 'Let him cool his heels in the anteroom, it will do him no harm. Kindly take a message to the Under-Secretary of State for Foreign Affairs. Ask Mr Cuddington, if he is not otherwise engaged, whether he would be gracious enough to grant me a few moments of his time.'

'I will do that, My Lord,' Mr Lawson said.

The Marquis sat at his desk concentrating on Cuddington. He had made many enquires about him this last week and discovered very little.

The man was extremely wealthy and was considered brilliant. Everyone who spoke of the Under-Secretary of State had said the same.

But there was no one, the Marquis discovered, who was willing to call Mr Cuddington a friend or even to speak warmly of him, save as regards his capacity for work.

He appeared to have few acquaintances except in a social stratum lower than his own.

The Marquis had also learnt that he was a frequenter of bawdy-houses, usually those which catered for the clients with more unusual erotic tastes than the ordinary run of such places.

'He does not have a particularly savoury reputation where women are concerned,' an elderly man whom the Marquis had questioned explained.

In all fairness the Marquis had to admit that this was something which might be said of himself also; at the same time the females to whom he devoted his hours of leisure were not to be found in brothels, nor was he required to purchase their favours.

The Marquis had, in fact, drawn almost a blank where Mr Cuddington was concerned. There was little unusual to be discovered about the man save that he was outstandingly clever.

He spoke several languages fluently, had obtained a first at Oxford, and there was no doubt at all that if Lord Hawkesbury were to retire tomorrow, the Under-Secretary would step into his shoes.

Until now the Marquis had not been interested enough to notice Mr Cuddington's existence.

A week ago outside the Foreign Office he would have been hard put to it to recognise him.

He was still thinking about the Under-Secretary when the door opened and Mr Lawson announced:

'The Under-Secretary of State for Foreign Affairs, My Lord.'

The Marquis sprang to his feet.

'My dear fellow,' he said in tones of great affability. 'I had no intention of asking you to come to my office, but merely sent my Secretary to find out if you would receive me in yours.'

'My office is crowded, and I thought if you wished to talk to me it would be almost impossible for us to exchange a private word,' Mr Cuddington said.

'Well, it is indeed kind of you,' the Marquis said. 'Knowing how busy you must be at this particular moment, I hesitate to encroach upon your time. Nevertheless, I must pray your assistance.'

'My assistance, My Lord?'

There was no doubt that Mr Cuddington was surprised, but pleasantly so. He seated himself beside the Marquis's desk, crossed his legs and lay back. He appeared at ease, and yet the Marquis felt that in some way he was wary.

He glanced at Mr Cuddington's face and thought he had never disliked a man more. Sylvina had felt he was evil.

It might be too strong a word for him, and yet the Marquis thought, though he might personally be prejudiced, there was something about the closeness of his eyes and the thickness of his lips which was strangely repulsive.

Nevertheless the Marquis's voice was

pleasant and his smile engaging as he said:

'You may think I am making a mountain out of a molehill, but as I do not like to bother Lord Hawkesbury I feel I must ask your help.'

'I am only too ready to help you in any way that you desire, My Lord,' Mr Cuddington replied.

'Ah, but before I begin,' the Marquis said, 'I understand I must congratulate you. I am told you are to be married.'

He saw the sudden surprise in Mr Cuddington's eyes as he said:

'I wonder who told you that, My Lord.'

'If it is an unwarranted rumour, I must apologise,' the Marquis said. 'But I was informed you were to be wed. It was someone at the Ball, I think. Perhaps it was Lord Hawkesbury. But whoever it was, they told me you were there with the lady in question.'

'I was,' Mr Cuddington said briefly, 'and my betrothal is a fact, My Lord. But for private reasons I would be grateful if Your Lordship would keep such information to yourself, at any rate for the time being.'

'But naturally,' the Marquis smiled. 'I regret that I mentioned it. At the same time let me felicitate you. I understand your intended is Miss Sylvina Blaine. She called on me a few days ago and I found her most charming.'

'She is the daughter of Sir Rendell Blaine,'

Mr Cuddington explained. 'I dare say Your Lordship remembers him, and Sylvina will make me, I think, a comfortable wife when I have trained her. All women need a master.'

Mr Cuddington spoke the last words almost as though he were speaking to himself. There was a smile on his thick lips which made the Marquis look away from him quickly.

The Under-Secretary of State for Foreign Affairs had no idea how near he was to death at that moment.

'Like yourself, My Lord, I have been a bachelor for a long time,' Mr Cuddington went on, quite unaware that the Marquis who had been toying with an ivory paper-knife had snapped it in two, 'but I feel that those of us who are in politics need a woman at our side to entertain, to grace our dinner tables and, of course, to warm our beds on a cold night.'

Mr Cuddington laughed. The conversation seemed out of keeping with the man's reputation for brilliance, but the Marquis, an acknowledged judge of men, suddenly understood.

Cuddington was trying to speak as an equal.

He knew the Marquis's reputation for being a heartbreaker, a friend of the Prince of Wales, the cream of the *Beau Ton*, a Corinthian; and he imagined in his abysmal ignorance that this was how the Bucks and Dandies of whom he had heard so much talked when they were alone together.

He was putting on an act, he was giving a performance of one gentleman of the world talking to another.

He thought he was being witty and sophisticated, and he had no idea that the Marquis was as nauseated with him as though he had found himself in the same room as a reptile.

'But I must not bore you with my private affairs,' Mr Cuddington said deprecatingly. 'Now, My Lord, tell me why you wished to see me.'

It was with the greatest difficulty that the Marquis forced his voice to betray none of the loathing and disgust he felt for the man sitting opposite him.

'Three days ago, Mr Cuddington,' he said, 'Miss Sylvina Blaine brought me a warmly written introduction on behalf of the Comte Armand de Vallien. I interviewed her and she explained to me that she had known the Comte for many years, in fact, since she had been a child.

'Afterwards I saw the Comte, talked with him and thought him pleasant enough. At the same time I was slightly surprised he was so eager to join me in this particular department. However he explained how greatly he and his family disliked the Bonaparte regime in France, and how because of this dislike he had crossed the Channel to join Great Britain in fighting to restore the balance of power in Europe.'

The Marquis paused, and Mr Cuddington asked:

'You liked the young man?'

'You have met him?' the Marquis enquired.

'Only once, at some function or other,' Mr Cuddington replied casually. 'Miss Blaine informed me, of course, that he had begged her to further his ambition to serve this country in a place in which he felt he would be well suited. I am afraid if you are asking me for a reference for the Comte, I can be of no assistance, I have so little personal knowledge of him.'

'I think the Frenchman might be quite useful,' the Marquis remarked. 'He could doubtless ferret at some of his compatriots among the *émigrés* who are only waiting to betray our weaknesses, despite the fact that we have offered them continuous hospitality since the Revolution.

'At the same time Lord Hawkesbury has asked us to be particularly careful to whom we give our confidence, and I think you know, Mr Cuddington, that I am here at Mr Pitt's special request.'

Mr Cuddington smiled in a superior manner.

'Mr Pitt has always had an obsession that

there are spies under every dining-table,' he said. 'Nevertheless I would agree with Your Lordship that we should take the greatest possible care.'

'Then I feel sure you will accede to what I am about to suggest, Mr Cuddington,' the Marquis said.

Again he thought he saw that flicker of alertness in the older man's eyes.

'I have always thought,' the Marquis continued, 'that it is almost hopeless to assess a man's character or his capabilities merely by talking to him across a desk. Sometimes the applicant is nervous, sometimes he is over-confident, and always he is putting on some sort of act. He is never at his ease, never completely himself. How could he be, when perhaps his whole career is at stake?'

'I agree with you there, My Lord,' Mr Cuddington remarked.

'So what I suggest,' the Marquis said, 'is that I invite the Comte to Alton Park for a short visit, perhaps of two nights; and if you, Mr Cuddington, could spare the time to be my guest on that occasion, then together we could find out whether indeed he is as genuine in his desire to help Great Britain as he professes, and whether, in fact, he would be of any use to us.'

'You wish to invite me to Alton Park, My Lord?'

Mr Cuddington spoke in level tones, but

he could not sufficiently disguise the expression of satisfaction on his face.

The Marquis was well aware that invitations to Alton Park were greatly prized, even among his most intimate companions. He had always been very selective about whom he entertained in his house, and it had been said often enough that the Prince of Wales preferred the comforts of Alton Park to any other house in which he ever stayed.

The Marquis had suspected that Mr Cuddington was a social climber, and now he knew he had not been mistaken.

There was an undisguised eagerness in the man which had not been there before, and there was a smile on his lips as the Marquis replied:

'I should be extremely grateful if you could see your way to accepting my invitation.'

'Indeed I accept with pleasure,' Mr Cuddington said quickly.

'Then what about this coming Friday,' the Marquis suggested. 'I think however it would be a mistake to make it too obvious to the Comte what we are about. Suppose Miss Blaine, as his sponsor, were to be invited also, and, of course, her brother, who I understand works in this very building. That would make it appear quite an ordinary social occasion without any underlying reason for your being my guest.'

'I think it is an excellent idea, My Lord,'

Mr Cuddington said.

'I will ask my grandmother, the Dowager Duchess of Wendover, who acts as hostess when I entertain, to write Miss Blaine a formal invitation,' the Marquis said. 'But as time is short I wonder if you would be kind enough to persuade Miss Blaine and her brother to accept before the formalities are completed.'

'I am sure I can do that, My Lord,' Mr Cuddington said confidently.

'Then I am extremely grateful to you, Under-Secretary,' the Marquis said. 'One, of course, wants to be fair to someone like the Comte, whose father had, I believe, a most distinguished career as French Ambassador to various countries in Europe. At the same time one must be cautious: this is not a time to take any risks.'

'No indeed, My Lord.'

'I believe the Comte is outside waiting my decision whether he can hope for employment here in the Foreign Office or not,' the Marquis went on. 'I will see him and tell him that as I am so busy at the moment it will be best if we can continue our discussion at Alton Park.'

Mr Cuddington rose to his feet.

'In which case you will not want me here, My Lord. As you say, it must not appear a conspiracy between us to approve or disapprove of the Comte.'

'I cannot thank you enough for your kindness,' the Marquis said. 'You have lifted a weight off my shoulders. I felt it was too big a decision to make on my own without assistance from someone like yourself, who has had long experience of foreign affairs.'

'What time would you like us to arrive at Alton Park on Friday?' Mr Cuddington enquired.

'I expect you will be busy here on Friday, as on every other day,' the Marquis said with a smile. 'But Alton Park is but an hour's drive from London, and if you could manage to arrive somewhere about five o'clock that will give us plenty of time before dinner. I will, of course, ask some friends to meet you. I am fortunate in that I have very charming neighbours, and I think you will find there will be plenty to entertain you both on Saturday and Sunday.'

'I am sure of that, My Lord,' Mr Cuddington said.

The Marquis felt he almost purred like a cat sipping cream at the prospect of what lay ahead.

'Although it is a dead bore,' the Marquis continued, 'I fear we must return on Sunday night. There is nothing I should like better than to have you as my guest until Monday, but with the war at this crucial state I cannot believe that the Foreign Office can spare you, at any rate, for longer.'

'Your Lordship is indeed flattering,' Mr Cuddington said, 'and I assure you that at the moment you are more indispensable than I am.'

'I wish that were the truth,' the Marquis remarked.

The two men bowed to each other and the Under-Secretary of State for Foreign Affairs left the room.

The Marquis sat down again at his desk, but now the darkness that had encompassed him when he first entered his office had gone.

He was planning, he was manœvering, he was anticipating the battle which lay ahead.

He felt with an absolute certainty that however much Sylvina might resent or try to refuse the invitation to Alton Park, the ambitious, social-climbing Mr Cuddington would force her to accept it.

The mere thought, however, of Mr Cuddington with his thick lips near to Sylvina made the Marquis feel a rage smoulder within him which was almost murderous.

He looked down at the broken pieces of ivory paper-knife and wondered what would have happened if he had obeyed the urge to seize Mr Cuddington's thick neck between his two hands and throttle him to death.

It was what the man deserved! How dare he speak of Sylvina in such a fashion – Sylvina of all people!

And now at last the Marquis understood why she was afraid, why her exquisite little body shrank from the proximity of a man who by some inexplicable means had persuaded her to accept his offer of marriage.

How could he have done it? What hold had he over her?

The Marquis felt suddenly sick at the thought that Sylvina, with her sensitiveness, should be subjected to the company of a man who could not even speak of the woman he would marry with decency and respect.

'I will save her,' the Marquis vowed, 'by God, I will save her if I have to kill Cuddington to do it!'

# 8

'Stay at Alton Park!' Sylvina ejaculated. 'Are you crazed?'

'No indeed,' her brother replied, 'and quite frankly, Syl, it is an invitation that people of social consequence yearn to receive.'

'But not you!' Sylvina cried in tones of horror. 'Not you, Clyde!'

'You do not suppose Mr Cuddington would have accepted for us both if he had thought there was any danger in it,' Clyde protested. 'He is not so cork-brained as to run me into trouble with the Marquis deliberately; and besides if anyone is swaggering about like a peacock with two tails, it is Cuddington.'

'You mean he wants to go to Alton Park?' Sylvina asked.

'Wants! That's blowing off the froth!' her brother retorted. 'He's excited, elated, puffed up with pride, boasting about the invitation to whoever will listen.'

'But why? Why?' Sylvina asked, a desperate note in her voice.

'Do not be so bird-witted,' Clyde answered. 'Surely you know that invitations from the Marquis of Alton are more prized than diamonds. Everyone in the *Beau Ton* hopes against hope to receive one, and it is said that even the Prince of Wales never refuses an invitation to Alton Park.'

Sylvina was silent for a moment, and then she said in a low voice:

'Well, I for one will not accept His Lordship's hospitality.'

'How can you be so obstinate?' her brother asked in exasperation. 'Why, the Marquis spoke to me himself and he could not have been more gracious. I wish I could afford a tailor who could cut me a coat like his! Perhaps when I am at Alton Park I can learn to tie my cravat in the same intricate folds with never a crease. I just cannot conceive how his valet achieves it.'

'Can you not understand,' Sylvina said, 'that His Lordship must have some reason for asking us.'

'Why should you always look on the black side of everything?' Clyde protested irritably. 'If you ask me, the Marquis wants to entertain your protégé the Comte, and it is only good manners to include us in the invitation. That is what Cuddington thinks, at any rate.'

'Then why has Mr Cuddington been invited?' Sylvina enquired.

'That puzzles me, I admit,' her brother replied, 'but I suppose if the Comte is to join the Foreign Office he has to have either Mr Cuddington's or Lord Hawkesbury's approval.'

'I will not go with you,' Sylvina asserted.

'Very well then, I shall go without you,' Clyde retorted. 'I have no intention of being as hoity-toity as you apparently wish to be, nor am I in a position to refuse an invitation which any man of my age would envy.'

He preened himself for a second.

'If you wish me to rise in the Diplomatic Service,' he went on, 'I obviously must make myself pleasant to my chiefs, apart from the fact that to have spent a few nights at Alton Park will do me a deal of good socially.'

'There is something behind it,' Sylvina insisted. 'Can you not understand, Clyde, that the Marquis has not asked you because he wants to be pleasant or gracious; he has not asked you because he wants your company. Why should he? Perhaps he is suspicious and is trying to catch you off your guard.'

'And what will he find?' Clyde replied. 'Nothing, as you well know.'

'But even a hint of suspicion would ruin your career,' Sylvina insisted.

Her brother shrugged his shoulders.

'You are damned depressing, Syl,' he said. 'Quite frankly, I cannot go through life for ever in the dismals because of what Cuddington holds over me. I am young and I am going to enjoy myself; and that means accepting an invitation to Alton Park.'

'Just the same, I shall refuse it,' Sylvina said firmly.

'That, I am afraid, is something you cannot do, my dear,' a voice said from the doorway.

She turned sharply to see that Mr Cuddington had arrived unnoticed.

He had ascended the stairs unheard and had entered at such a telling moment that she was convinced that he had crept up on them deliberately so he could overhear what was being said.

But this suspicion, naturally, she could not put into words.

'Clyde, you did not tell me Mr Cuddington was coming here,' she said accusingly to her brother.

'You did not give me time,' Clyde expostulated. 'I had every intention of informing you that he was on his way, but you were so busy arguing with me that I had no opportunity to prepare you for his arrival.'

Sylvina swept the newcomer a curtsy, and then as she did not invite him to sit down, her brother, somewhat embarrassed, pulled forward a chair.'

'Will you not be seated, Sir?' he asked.

'I was hoping that your sister would be more welcoming,' he replied, observing Sylvina's downcast eyes.

'You must excuse me,' she said, 'my conversation with Clyde has made me forget my manners. Can I offer you any refreshment?'

'No thank you,' Mr Cuddington said. 'I cannot stay long. We have a great deal to do, all of us, if we are to leave for Alton Park as I have planned about four of the clock on Friday afternoon. It will be necessary for Clyde and me to leave the Foreign Office a trifle early, but I think that may be forgiven in the circumstances.'

'But as you have already overheard, Sir,' Sylvina said, 'I regret that I am unable to accept the Marquis's hospitality.'

Mr Cuddington raised his eyebrows.

'Indeed! And what may be your excuse?'

'I have no wish to visit Alton Park.'

'If I may say so,' Mr Cuddington said, 'that is an extremely childish and rude remark which I would not undertake to convey to the Marquis. He most expressly asked that you should be included in the invitation, and his grandmother, the Dowager Duchess of Wendover, is writing to you personally a letter you will doubtless receive by hand tomorrow morning.'

'I shall thank Her Grace for her kindness,' Sylvina said, 'with regret that I cannot accompany you. You will, I am convinced, fare better without me.'

'That, of course, is problematical,' Mr Cuddington retorted, 'but nevertheless I insist that we do as the Marquis suggests and spend Friday and Saturday under his roof.'

'I cannot see any reason why the Marquis should wish for my company,' Sylvina argued. 'I understand from Clyde that the party is being given for the Comte Armand de Vallien. You will be present with Clyde to support him, and my absence will for sure pass quite unnoticed.'

'Nevertheless, you sponsored the Comte,' Mr Cuddington said in the over-calm voice of one who was deliberately controlling his temper.

'On your insistence, Sir, if you recall,' Sylvina replied, 'and although I was pleased to do so, remembering my parents' friendship with the Comte's father, I cannot see that there is any reason for me to assist him further.'

'There is no time for further argument,' Mr Cuddington said briskly. 'We are all going to Alton Park, and my carriage will collect you here at four o'clock precisely on Friday afternoon.'

'I will not accept the invitation,' Sylvina said firmly.

For the first time her eyes met those of the man watching her.

His eyes were hard and determined, and there was an unpleasant smile on his lips, almost, she thought, as though he watched a bird fluttering in a trap and knew there was no escape.

'You will travel with us to Alton Park,' he said, and his voice was dangerously quiet, 'for one reason because I have already accepted the Marquis's invitation on your behalf, and for another because I wish it.'

'And if I persist in my determination,' Sylvina asked breathlessly, 'if I refuse to be ready at four o'clock on Friday afternoon, will you drag me there forcibly?'

'No, my dear,' he replied, 'I would not lower myself to drag you anywhere. All I shall do is take to Alton Park a certain black book that I have locked up in my desk. I think the Marquis might be quite interested to peruse it at his leisure.'

'Syl, for God's sake!' Clyde ejaculated.

She turned away to stand at the window, and both men realised she was fighting desperately for self-control.

'I never had … any choice … did I?' she asked at length in a voice hardly above a whisper.

'None,' Mr Cuddington replied. 'And that is why I advise you, my dear, in future to leave such decisions to me. As I have told you before, your social sense is lamentably lacking for an Ambassador's daughter. You are unsophisticated to the point of absurdity. You will, unfortunately, need a lot of training before you make the type of wife a man in my position needs.'

'If I have all these deficiencies,' Sylvina said with a sob in her voice, 'why, why do you wish to marry me?'

'I think it is hardly the moment for me to answer that question,' Mr Cuddington said with a sudden thickness in his voice which made her shudder. 'But it is a question I can answer very competently, I assure you, and at the right time and place I will certainly do so.'

Sylvina laced her fingers together and felt herself shiver as though a cold wind had blown suddenly through the room.

'And now to business,' Mr Cuddington said with a change of tone. 'I have decided, Clyde, that we will travel in style. I am going to purchase a new curricle. I have already seen one which has been ordered by a nobleman who cannot meet his debts.'

There was an obvious smear in the last three words.

'It is a very dashing and elegant vehicle,' he continued, 'built for speed, and I think the pair of bays I already own will not disgrace His Lordship's stable. The Comte will travel with me, and you will escort your sister in my carriage. It is fortunate that I had it painted but a short time ago. There will, of course, be two men on the box and one behind.'

Clyde did not speak, and after a moment Mr Cuddington continued, looking at Sylvina:

'Now you, my dear, have a great deal to do in a very short time. Your attire must be worthy of the occasion. You have, it is true, the gown I gave you for the reception at the Foreign Office, but nothing else.'

'Do you really think I would allow you to pay for my clothes?' Sylvina asked angrily. 'There are some matters, Sir, in which I still am determined to behave with propriety. You may threaten me into accepting the Marquis's invitation, but you cannot force me to wear gowns that you have paid for as though I were ... your fancy ... woman!'

'That is a quite nonsensical argument considering we are affianced,' Mr Cuddington said, 'and no one knows better than you do that you have not the money to provide yourself with any type of trousseau required by a Lady of Quality.'

'Clyde and I will manage somehow,' Sylvina said defiantly.

Mr Cuddington laughed unpleasantly.

'Well, Clyde, and what do you say to that? How much blunt have you to spend on your sister, considering, as I well know, you yourself are in debt?'

Clyde Blaine's lips tightened, and with an effort he forced himself to say:

'It is no use, Syl, I have no ready, which apparently Mr Cuddington knows better than I do myself.'

'Then I will come as I am,' Sylvina said. 'Do you suppose my Mother, if she were alive, or my Father would allow any man other than my husband to provide me with clothing? They would be humiliated at the suggestion, as indeed I am myself.'

'When we arrive at Alton Park,' Mr Cuddington said, 'in style, in my new curricle; with the Comte and Clyde looking like gentlemen of fashion, as indeed they are; with my coachmen, footmen, valet and doubtless your maid – Bessie; do you intend to appear as the beggar maid in rags and tatters and be the laughing-stock not only of the Marquis himself but of the important friends he will invite to meet us?'

He paused for Sylvina's reply but she did not speak. 'We are to be his guests of honour, girl!' he continued. 'Do you really propose to appear as you are now, draped in muslin which could not have cost more than a few pence, and if not made up by yourself then by some incompetent seamstress?'

'It is not clothes that ... matter,' Sylvina said unsteadily.

'The world in which the Marquis lives takes a person at his face value,' Mr Cuddington snapped. 'They judge a man by his cloth and a woman by her gown. What do you think the Marquis will think of your appearance after he has so warmly congratulated me on my betrothal?'

Sylvina was very still, and then in a voice that was hardly audible she said:

'The Marquis ... congratulated you?'

'Yes indeed. And there was no doubt in my mind that His Lordship thought it a most suitable match.'

It seemed to Sylvina as if the whole room had gone dark.

If the Marquis had congratulated Mr Cuddington, it could mean only one thing – that he had given up his quest of her.

She had sent him away from the front door for long enough, she had refused to open his letters, she had given away his flowers.

He must see her now for what she was, a tiresome, inconsequent girl who had engaged his attention for a short time, but who no longer aroused the affection which she thought once to have awakened within him.

She felt her whole being cry out in protest.

Then she remembered that the Marquis had destroyed her trust, broken her dreams and deceived her when she had believed in him as she had never believed in any man before.

She had thought as she went from the Foreign Office that there was nothing left for her to live for, and now she knew that the only thing she wanted was to die.

She wondered how long it would take before this agony within her heart no longer tortured her. But pride, the pride which even while she suffered had kept her dry-eyed in public made her say:

'I will … do as you … wish.'

She looked up as she spoke and saw the light of triumph in Mr Cuddington's eyes, and realised he had been playing with her from the very beginning.

He had known the inevitable outcome of every argument, he was the conqueror and he was enjoying every moment of it.

'You will go to Madame Bertin in Bond Street,' he said. 'I have already sent a message to say that she should expect you. I have informed her that I am aware that there is little time to provide the various dresses, driving coats and other female fal-de-lals that are necessary, but I am certain she will contrive if the price is right. The account will be sent to me, and I think you will find the woman not unobliging.'

Sylvina shut her eyes momentarily and wondered if it were possible to sink lower than go to a shop knowing that they must suppose that she was nothing but a doxy under the protection of a wealthy man.

Then she heard Mr Cuddington say:

'You will apologise. I have been very patient with you, Sylvina, but I assure you I shall not put up with such obstinacy once we are married.'

'I ... apologise,' Sylvina said meekly.

What did it matter what she said or what she did?

The Marquis had congratulated him – she was alone, utterly and completely alone, with nothing left, not even her dreams.

'That is hardly the manner in which an apology should be made,' Mr Cuddington complained.

Some last vestige of spirit made her turn round angrily.

'Then what do you require?' she asked. 'That I should fall on my knees before you, rend my garments and tear my hair as I beseech your forgiveness?'

'I can think of a better way,' Mr Cuddington replied. 'Come to me, Sylvina.'

He put out his hand, and as he did so Sylvina, with a frightened leap of her heart, realised that Clyde, perhaps because he could no longer bear to see his sister being bullied, had left the room.

'I apologise also for my ... rudeness,' Sylvina said quickly. 'Sometimes my temper gets the better of me. It is something that I am well aware I must learn to curb.'

Mr Cuddington was smiling.

'I will show you how to do that too,' he said. 'Start by obeying me.'

His hand was still outstretched, and in a panic of fear because of the sudden fire in his eyes and the cruel smile on this thick lips, Sylvina moved, but only to pick up Columbus from his cushion by the fireplace.

'It is ... time for Columbus ... to go for a ... walk,' she said. Even to herself her voice sounded weak and frightened.

'Columbus can wait,' Mr Cuddington said decisively. 'I have given you an order, Sylvina. If you are ever to be a commendable wife you must first learn to obey me.'

'What do you ... want?' Sylvina asked fearfully.

'Shall we say a kiss of peace?' Mr Cuddington suggested. 'Put down that dog and come here.'

'No ... no!' Sylvina cried, and the fear in her trembling body transmitted itself to Columbus, who, realising something was wrong, growled.

'Damn the animal!' Mr Cuddington said

furiously. 'You know I dislike dogs. Put him down and do as I command you.'

Just for a moment she stood facing him, Columbus growling fiercely in his throat as she held him to her breast.

Then, before Mr Cuddington could prevent her, with a little frightened sob she was gone from the room, running upstairs in a panic which was to leave her white and shaking long after he had left the house.

As she went she heard him laugh.

It was the sound of a man amused, yet not annoyed because he was confident that ultimately he would get what he wanted.

Mr Cuddington's coach, drawn by four well-matched horses, raised a cloud of dry dust in its wake.

It travelled at speed, yet it was easily passed by a shining yellow curricle tooled by Mr Cuddington, wearing his high conical hat at what he thought was a fashionable angle, and accompanied by the Comte elegantly garbed as a Tulip of fashion.

'Curse it!' Clyde ejaculated, leaning forward to watch them pass. 'It is enough that I must be driven sedately with you like a spinster maiden when I might be tooling a Phaeton or riding a decent piece of horseflesh.'

'Somebody had to accompany me,' Sylvina said in an apologetic voice. 'And Mr Cuddington insisted on Bessie going in the baggage coach.'

'He is trying to show the Marquis what money will do,' Clyde Blaine said bitterly. 'But he will always be an outsider, and well he knows it.'

'That is not much consolation where I am concerned,' Sylvina answered.

Her brother had the grace to look shame-faced.

'I am sorry, Syl, I am really, that I should have got you into this. God knows it was none of my contriving, but as things are what can I do? At least Cuddington has money and is prepared to spend it.'

'Only as it suits him,' Sylvina said. 'I doubt if you will find him over-generous as a brother-in-law.'

'Oh God, was there ever such a toil?' her brother complained. 'You may think I am unfeeling, Syl, but I love you. However, if I were in the Tower you would starve to death, as you well know; and, as it is, at least you will be rich and important.'

Sylvina did not answer, and he went on:

'They say that Cuddington is certain to be in the next Honours List. He will end up with a peerage, you can be certain of that. If Hawkesbury resigns, or even if Pitt returns, he is almost certain to be given a Ministry. There is no one who does not talk of his brilliance and his meteoric ascent in the Government.'

'There is something about him which frightens me,' Sylvina said in a very small voice. 'He is bad and evil, I know he is. I knew it from the first moment I saw him.'

Her brother looked uncomfortable.

'Some women would be glad to make such an advantageous marriage,' he said. 'What chance have you of meeting anyone, living as we do in a back street? I have made a few good friends since I came to London and there are still some acquaintances of Papa's who invite me to their houses. They would ask you too if you did not refuse every invitation you receive.'

'How could I go anywhere dressed as Mr Cuddington says ... in rags?'

'That was unnecessarily brutal,' Clyde said quickly. 'You have never been in rags, Syl, and to me you have always looked very pretty. However I must say your new garments are exceedingly becoming. They really are right up to scratch.'

'Ordering them made me feel lower than the dust,' Sylvina replied. 'I wondered what Mama would have thought, and Madam Bertin kept saying:

'"Mr Cuddington tells me that no expense is to be spared – Miss."

'There was something insulting in the way she did not call me Madam. I thought that I could not have been humiliated much further if he had bid for me in a slave-market.'

'I cannot think why he does not insist on your marrying him at once and get on with it,' Clyde ejaculated.

Sylvina gave a little cry.

'Oh pray, do not put such ideas into his head! He says he is waiting for some special occasion, but I am not certain what it is. I keep feeling it is coming nearer and nearer, and then I only want to die.'

'Oh, for Heaven's sake, Syl, you always exaggerate,' Clyde said crossly. 'Cuddington is infatuated with you – that is obvious. What is more, he will take you into the fashionable world in which we lived when Papa was alive.'

'You may enjoy that world,' Sylvina said, 'I do not.'

'And why not?' Clyde asked. 'It is unnatural for a female to think as you do. What have you got against the fashionable world that you should be so censorious of it?'

'It does sound presumptuous of me, does it not?' Sylvina said with a brief smile. 'But if you really desire to know the answer, I will tell you why. It was when we were in Spain – Papa was First Secretary under Lord Bath at our Embassy in Madrid – that Mama first told me she felt ill. She was in pain, Clyde, terrible pain.'

Sylvina's voice deepened at the memory.

'She never let Papa know,' she went on, 'and sometimes I saw her white and shaking and almost unable to walk because of the agony she was suffering.'

Sylvina paused and there were tears in her eyes before she continued:

'I would beg Mama to send for a physician, but she told me she had seen one and there was nothing he could do to help her. She would take some medicine he gave her to control the pain, and with an incredibly courageous effort she would go down to the party laughing and being gay so long as she was with Papa.'

Sylvina closed her eyes as if to shut out the memory.

'You know,' she continued after a second, 'that everyone always said she was the most valuable asset that Great Britain had on the Continent, but no one realised it was achieved at the cost of her health.'

'I had no idea,' Clyde admitted.

'You were away most of the time, either at school or at Oxford,' Sylvina explained. 'I was only a child, so I was kept in the background. But I would be with Mama whenever I could, and with me she never pretended.'

She sighed. 'The pain became much worse when we returned to England.' She went on, 'Papa was anxious that he should keep well in the forefront of society so that if there was a diplomatic post vacant he might be offered it. You remember how much Mama entertained at our house in Curzon Street? But her attacks of pain got worse and worse. Once or twice even Papa was suspicious and begged her not to overtax her strength.'

Sylvina's voice broke for a moment, and then she went on bravely:

'I think Mama knew she was going to die, but she was determined to help Papa. I often think it was only after she was dead that he knew how much she had meant to him.'

'Then he was posted to Paris,' Clyde said. 'I only wish I could have been with Papa, perhaps I could have prevented him...'

'No one could have prevented him,' Sylvina interrupted. 'You must not blame yourself. He was lonely and miserable without Mama, and that Frenchwoman fell in love with him. She never left him alone. She was very beautiful, Clyde, one of the most beautiful women I have ever seen, and I think in her own way she made Papa happier.

'But she was too famous and too beautiful, she was bound to have other admirers. Poor dear Papa, he may have been a good diplomat, but he was always a very bad shot.'

'You should see his personal reports at the Foreign Office,' Clyde said. 'Every one reiterates over and over again how brilliant he was. It was a tragedy he should die.'

'You must take his place,' Sylvina said softly.

'If nothing happens to prevent it,' Clyde answered.

She put her hand on his arm and laid her cheek against his shoulder.

'I will help you,' she said, 'I swear I will, because I know Papa would have been so proud of you and Mama loved you so much. I will try to be nice to Mr Cuddington, I will try my ... hardest, Clyde.'

'Then everything will be fine and dandy,' he said. 'If you do that, Syl, there will be no more problems, I am sure of it. Be the fashionable lady he wants you to be! He is terribly proud that Mama was the daughter of a Duke: I have heard him boasting about it to his friends. He wants to show you off, he wants people to envy him. Perhaps being married to him may not be so bad as you suspicion it is going to be.'

Sylvina swallowed.

'I will ... try,' she whispered, 'I promise you ... I will ... try.'

She told herself that the most important thing was to behave as both Mr Cuddington and Clyde would expect of her when they arrived at Alton Park.

She would be charming to everyone except the Marquis. But if she were cold and distant to him that would not create any particular comment.

Neither her brother nor the man to whom she was betrothed had any idea that she had ever met His Lordship except on the one occasion when she had gone to the Foreign Office to introduce the Comte.

'I hate him,' she whispered in her heart as the horses turned in through the high arched gateway of Alton Park.

It was flanked by stone lions holding heraldic shields on either side of the wrought-iron gates tipped with gold.

Then they were passing down a long avenue of oak trees until suddenly the house lay before them, exquisite in the summer sunshine.

Black and white swans, arching their necks, floated on the silver lakes which were linked with bridges like a necklace in front of the house.

A flag was fluttering on the flagpole above the grey gabled roofs, and a flight of white pigeons swooped against the blue of the sky to circle in front of the glittering diamond-paned windows, and vanished in a flutter of wings towards the verdant green of the woods which protected the house to the north.

Sylvina drew in her breath. It was beautiful, even more beautiful than the last time she had seen it; and then her thoughts shied away from the memory like a horse not completely under control.

'I hate him,' she whispered to herself, as if the words were a kind of talisman to prevent her heart throbbing with a strange excitement within her.

'I hate him,' she murmured again as she climbed from the coach up the broad marble steps and entered the big square Hall with its Grecian statues poised in niches and furnished with exquisitely carved and gilded tables specially designed for Alton Park by the brothers Adam.

The Major-domo bowed as they entered and one of the six footmen took Clyde's hat and cane.

Then they proceeded slowly towards a door at the far end of the Hall which Sylvina knew must be the entrance to the Salon.

She had a quick glimpse of the carved oak staircase rising towards the first floor, and then suddenly from behind her when she least expected it a voice she knew only too well said:

'May I welcome you to Alton Park?'

She wondered why the sound made her heart turn over in her breast.

With downcast eyes she curtsied as Clyde replied:

'Good evening, My Lord, my sister and I are delighted to be here.'

Sylvina felt the Marquis's hand take hers. He raised it perfunctorily to his lips, and though his touch was firm and strong there was nothing in his conventional greeting that he would not have accorded to any female, whoever she might be.

'It is finished, it is all over,' Sylvina told herself.

She wondered why the thought made her feel so unaccountably depressed, despite the fact that her heart was still beating so loudly that she was afraid he must hear it.

'Will you not come into the Salon?' the Marquis asked.

She had not yet raised her eyes to his face, but she could see the high polish on his boots as he walked a little ahead of them showing the way to where Sylvina knew the others would be waiting.

'Mr Cuddington and the Comte arrived some half an hour ago,' the Marquis was saying. 'We were afraid that something untoward might have delayed you.'

'Our horses were unfortunately not so fast,' Clyde said. 'I assure you, My Lord, I would much rather have been riding, except, of course, I had to accompany my sister.'

'We must see if we can find you a spirited bit of horseflesh for tomorrow,' the Marquis said genially. 'I have several in my stable which I feel would meet with your approval.'

'That would indeed be kind,' Clyde said excitedly.

His very eagerness made Sylvina feel he was still only a schoolboy enjoying every moment of an unexpected treat.

'I will not let him down,' she told herself.

Instinctively her chin went up and she made herself walk a littler taller as they entered the Salon.

It was a magnificent room, with six French windows opening out onto the Terrace. Its furnishings were worthy of a museum rather than a private house, and the pictures of the Marquis's ancestors by Van Dyck and Holbein would have been the envy of any connoisseur.

But Sylvina had eyes only for the woman standing at the far end of the room talking to Mr Cuddington and the Comte.

She was small and yet she gave the impression of height simply because of her dignity. She must once have been very beautiful; now her hair was white, her skin wrinkled.

Nevertheless she still had that indefinable aura of beauty which a woman, having once possessed, never loses, however old she has become.

The Dowager Duchess, now dressed all in white and wearing fabulous emeralds, had been a great personality in the middle of the previous century. She was still, though few people realised it, a force to be reckoned with.

Politicians consulted her; it was said that Mr Pitt wrote continually to her; and more than one member of the House of Lords had laid his heart at her feet.

Nevertheless she preferred the country,

staying in London for only a few months of the year, and making her garden at the Dower House, a few miles west of Alton Park, one of the most famous in England.

Her shrewd eyes, quite undimmed by age, watched Sylvina's progress across the room, and what she saw obviously pleased her.

For when the girl curtsied she held out her hand with a warmth she accorded to few of her contemporaries and said in a deep musical voice:

'I am delighted to meet you, Miss Blaine. Your mother was a very dear friend of mine, and I was, of course, a great admirer of your father.'

Sylvina raised her eyes and there was a light in them for the first time since she left London.

'You knew my Mama, Ma'am?'

'Yes indeed, child, and we must talk about her. But let me first say how delighted I am to meet you. I have been very remiss in not discovering before what after your father's death had happened to you and your brother.'

She turned as she spoke to Clyde, and as he bent over her hand there was no doubt there was approval in her expression as she saw how handsome he was and how elegant his manners.

'This may be your first visit,' the Duchess said, 'but I assure you it is not to be your last. My conscience pricks me that it has been delayed so long, and I am most grateful to my grandson for bringing you here today.'

For the first time Sylvina ventured to look at the Marquis. He looked kind and relaxed, she thought, and not hard and intimidating as he had been at the Foreign Office.

Perhaps here at Alton Park he was more like the man she had met in the woods, the man she had so foolishly believed to be a poor and undistinguished farmer.

She felt herself blush at how incredibly naïve she had been, and then she remembered that it did not matter.

She hated the Marquis – he was nothing in her life. The episode in the woods was finished, they would neither of them refer to it again.

'May I offer you a glass of wine, Miss Blaine?' the Marquis asked.

She wondered why the very sound of his voice could throw her into a confusion.

'No ... no thank you, My Lord,' she said quickly.

'I think you would be wise to have something after such a long journey,' he insisted.

Because she did not wish to appear rude she took from him the crystal glass which she guessed would contain Madeira.

'Have you any partiality for wine?' the Dowager enquired. 'Or would you prefer a cup of chocolate. That is what I always desire after jolting over the bumpy roads. Our local authorities are always promising to do something about the disgraceful state of the King's Highways, but I am sure it will be long delayed and I will still be jolted at my funeral.'

Sylvina felt the Marquis take the glass from her hand.

'It was stupid of me,' he said, 'I should have thought of chocolate, or indeed tea if you would prefer it.'

'I am sure Sylvina would prefer tea to anything else,' Mr Cuddington said in a proprietory tone. 'It is, I am informed, her one extravagance, and I have already made a note to provide her in the future with a plenteous supply, whatever the expense.'

'Then it shall be tea,' the Dowager said quietly.

A footman put down the tray which carried a decanter of wine and hurried from the room.

'I would not wish to put you to any inconvenience, Ma'am,' Sylvia said shyly, speaking to the Duchess.

But it was the Marquis who answered her.

'Our guests' wishes, whatever they may be, are never an inconvenience,' he said firmly. 'We have, I assure you, quite a magical way of providing anything that is required.'

She knew exactly what he was trying to say

to her.

She wondered how he dared, after all he had done, remind her of that magical meal they had eaten together in the little Greek Temple.

Just for a moment she glanced at him with what she hoped was a look of contempt in her eyes, but which instead only made her look very young and very defenceless.

She had no idea that the Marquis as he saw her standing in the Hall had overcome an almost irresistible impulse to take her in his arms and tell her that she need not be frightened, that no one would hurt her and that he himself would keep her safe.

She looked so small and pathetic in her pale blue driving-coat and her high-crowned fashionable bonnet trimmed with tiny blue ostrich feathers and ribbons to match tied under her little chin.

She was elegant, she was chic; but the Marquis thought she had been even lovelier in her unfashionable green gauze gown.

He was, however, well aware now that Mr Cuddington was watching him, and he did not underrate for a moment the shrewdness of the man's brain, however much he might dislike him.

He turned from Sylvina with an effort.

'Another glass of wine?' he enquired of Clyde. 'I wonder if there is time for me to show you some of the gardens before dinner.

We have a party tonight, especially arranged for you, Mr Cuddington. We shall be about thirty, I think, all people who are anxious to make your acquaintance, though some may already be known to you.

'We are fortunate that we live in a county where there are many congenial neighbours. The Prince is staying with the Duke of Bilston, and there is a chance that he may be coming over to see us tomorrow.'

The delight on Mr Cuddington's face was very obvious. The Marquis, as he went on talking, wondered if he could get under the Under-Secretary's guard through his snobbery.

Somehow during these next two days he had to find the secret of Sylvina's fear and of Mr Cuddington's ascendency over her. He told himself it was not going to be easy.

Cuddington was an astute, brilliant adversary whom he must not under-estimate. At the same time he had never yet known failure, and he had no intention of experiencing it now.

'If you gentlemen are going out into the garden,' the Dowager said, 'then I shall take Miss Blaine – and I hope, my dear, I may call you Sylvina – upstairs. She will wish to rest before the festivities this evening, and besides it will be an opportunity for us to have a little talk.'

'That is a good idea, Your Grace,' Mr Cuddington interposed before Sylvina could speak. 'I have told Sylvina what an extremely fortunate girl she is to visit such a famous house as Alton Park. I am waiting now for her to express her appreciation of your kind hospitality and to tell me that I was right in my anticipation of both the pleasures and treasures we should find here.'

He paused, and Sylvina, obedient as a puppet on a string, replied dully:

'You were ... right, Sir, it is all ... very ... fine.'

Just for one fleeting second as she finished speaking her eyes met those of the Marquis.

He saw, though he was convinced she did not mean him to see it, a despair so poignant that it was with difficulty that he prevented himself from telling her that however hard it might prove to be he would save her.

# 9

'I have failed,' the Marquis told himself as he walked wearily up the Grand Staircase.

Behind him he could hear the drunken laughter and the slurred voices of his dinner guests.

He had been making a last effort to try to

break down what seemed the impenetrable defences of Mr Cuddington.

The more he saw of the Under-Secretary of State for Foreign Affairs, the more the Marquis realised that he loathed the man with an intensity of feeling which made him wish to commit murder.

Never in his whole life had he hated anyone so violently.

Even to be in close proximity with him was almost unbearable: it was not only because of his relationship with Sylvina, there was something odious about the man's own personality.

The Marquis acknowledged that Mr Cuddington had a brilliant brain. As a conversationalist he could be extremely interesting when he did not try to dominate the whole party.

He was well-read and well-educated, and yet there was something about him which made the flesh creep.

The Marquis would have supposed that he was over-imaginative where Mr Cuddington was concerned because his own feelings were so deeply involved, had not each one of his friends during the day taken him on one side to enquire what 'that outsider' was doing at Alton Park.

The expression they used was not always so polite, and indeed the usual description was one used only by men about men.

The Marquis had flattered the Under-Secretary of State, he had tried conversing confidentially with him, he had used every wile to trap him into some admission or even some faint indication as to why Sylvina, though so frightened of him, had at the same time promised him her hand in marriage.

But he had to admit that he had drawn blank after blank. Mr Cuddington had remained bland, good-tempered and impervious to every assault.

Using as his excuse his investigation of the Comte, the Marquis had talked to Mr Cuddington alone for some time about affairs at the Foreign Office, Addington's incompetence as Prime Minister, and then had gradually worked the conversation round to Sylvina.

'Have you known the Blaines a long time?' he enquired tentatively.

'Not so very long,' Mr Cuddington replied.

'And what do you think of young Blaine? I understood Lord Hawkesbury accepted him because of his father's very distinguished career.'

Mr Cuddington shrugged his shoulders.

'A likeable young man,' he said, 'but I doubt if he will go far. Like most would-be Bucks, his ambition does not rise much further than to be seen frequenting the best Salons.'

'And you yourself are ambitious?' the

Marquis asked quietly.

He thought he saw a flicker in Mr Cuddington's eyes, a smile on his lips as if he looked into the future and found it good.

Then he replied in a cleverly deprecating voice:

'I have had to work hard, My Lord, to reach the position I am now in.'

'A very creditable one, if I may say so,' the Marquis replied drily. 'And now tell me about the charming Miss Blaine.'

He had meant to lead Mr Cuddington on to discuss her, but even as he said the words he knew he could not bear it, could not sit still and listen to this man, who he sensed rather than knew was yellow-livered, discussing Sylvina.

Before Mr Cuddington could reply to his question he glanced at the clock and said with a start:

'I am afraid I am neglecting my other guests. We must talk together another time, perhaps next week in the office.'

'Yes, of course,' Mr Cuddington said, 'my time is always at your disposal, My Lord.'

'I am indeed grateful for your assistance,' the Marquis answered.

He went from the room feeling as though he was free to breathe the fresh air again.

And yet there was nothing that he could really say was wrong with Mr Cuddington.

He behaved impeccably, he paid the Duchess fulsome compliments, he was ready to take part in any activity that was suggested.

He admired the house, praised the grounds; in fact, the Marquis thought, his interest was almost embarrassing.

He asked innumerable questions about the running of the Estate, the cost of the upkeep, the disposition of the farms, and once surprisingly the Marquis found him questioning the Major-domo about the economical details of the household.

The thought that the reason for so many questions might be that Mr Cuddington was interested in buying a country house for Sylvina sent the Marquis away with a frown between his eyebrows, which those who knew him well regarded ominously.

Finally in a last despairing throw the Marquis decided he must get Mr Cuddington drunk.

'In vino veritas.' How often had he quoted the old adage to his friends when someone in their cups had been all too self-revealing.

While his dinner party on Friday night had been designed to bedazzle Mr Cuddington and play up to his worst instincts as a social climber, the Marquis decided that the party on Saturday should be of a very different calibre.

He sent over an urgent note to an old friend, Lord Hornblotton, a man renowned as a *raconteur*, a *bon vivant* and a great connoisseur of wines.

Lord Hornblotton was an elderly man, but there were few people who did not value him as a guest at their table.

Another crony was Sir Lucas Powell, Deputy Lieutenant of the County, a hard rider to hounds and well known to be addicted to the bottle.

The Marquis limited the number, feeling that conversation was likely to be more intimate and that he could, in fact, watch Mr Cuddington more closely.

But after the ladies had left the room and as bottle after bottle of the most delectable wines were served to the gentlemen and cheeks became flushed, foreheads moist and speech a little indistinct, the Marquis noted that Mr Cuddington had himself admirably under control.

He drank a great deal, it was true, indeed as much as anyone present, but while his legs might be unsteady his head apparently was unaffected.

Only his stories grew more obscene.

It was not that they were coarse and vulgar, it was rather that they were revoltingly licentious; and there was something about the way he told them which made the Marquis long to strangle him.

The drinking continued even after the gentlemen had repaired to the Salon.

The Marquis had warned the Duchess to

take Sylvina to bed early, and the men could sprawl in the brocade chairs with their legs stuck out in front of them, a glass in their hand which was filled and refilled by the ever attentive flunkeys.

Finally, as Mr Cuddington embarked on a story so disgustingly indelicate that the Marquis felt physically sick, he rose to his feet.

He did not bid his guest good night, he just slipped away and went upstairs in a darkness of despair such as he had never known in his whole life.

His valet took one look at his face when he entered the room and hurried about his duties in silence.

He had served with the Marquis in the Army and he thought it was not since his master's two best friends had fallen beside him in battle that he had seen him look so stricken.

He collected the Marquis's clothes and went noiselessly from the room.

The Marquis sat for a long time in a high-winged armchair looking into the fire.

It had been a warm day in the sunshine, but the wind that was keeping Napoleon's ships in harbour on the other side of the Channel had freshened as evening fell and there was a chill which seemed to penetrate down the chimneys and even through the closed windows into every corner and cranny of the house.

The housekeeper, well versed in seeing to the comfort of the guests at Alton Park, had hastily lit fires in every bedroom.

But even so the wind was persistent, and as the flames sank lower and lower the Marquis realised he was cold.

He took off his robe and climbed into the huge four-poster bed which had been used by the owners of Alton Park for centuries.

There were curtains hanging on either side to keep out draughts and make the occupant feel safe from prying eyes.

Propped against his pillows the Marquis could see in the dying light of the flames the exquisitely carved pillars which supported the canopy. Some master of his craft centuries ago had carved what he knew best, the leaves and trees which were so familiar to him.

There were oak leaves with their acorns, beech and ash leaves, elm and willow, all faithfully reproduced by a man who must have taken pride in his craftsmanship.

Now inevitably, since every thought he had, it seemed to the Marquis, led in the same direction, the carved leaves with which his very bed was decorated made him think of Sylvina.

He started to think over what had happened since she had arrived at Alton Park.

He had never thought it possible that any woman on whom he had set his affection should treat him as Sylvina had done.

It was not only the coldness of her voice when she spoke to him; it was that she had seemed to wrap herself in an impenetrable reserve and it was almost impossible to draw any response from her.

He thought of how he had held her in his arms, how her lips had responded to his and how they had both known an ecstasy which had carried them into a world beyond the world, where there was no one but themselves and only the all-consuming wonder of their love.

How was it possible that after that had happened she now could hate him as she obviously did?

He clenched his fists together in the darkness and longed to smash something, to destroy anything, as an expression of his inability to cope with a situation that was completely out of his control.

And yet he felt in his heart that Sylvina's hatred was fundamentally a pretence.

She was trying to hurt him simply because she herself was so hurt and unhappy. And yet he could not even be sure of that.

When she had come down to dinner the first night before the guests arrived he had said to her:

'I hope you are comfortable in your bed-chamber, Miss Blaine. I deliberately put you in the old part of the house because I thought you would find it more romantic.'

She looked at him without speaking, and the expression in her eyes he could not fathom.

'Bonnie Prince Charlie is said to have used the room in which you will be sleeping,' he said. 'I hope the idea does not make you afraid. Your brother is only one bedroom from you, but there has never been a report of any haunting at Alton Park.'

'I am not afraid of ghosts,' Sylvina said quietly. 'Their power to hurt and betray is finished.'

She turned away from him as she spoke and he found it impossible to approach her again the whole evening.

The following day he suggested that everyone should ride in the morning, but at the last moment Sylvina had excused herself, even though he knew that she eyed longingly the thoroughbred horse with Arab blood in him he had chosen specially for her.

He knew then that she was deliberately refusing a ride she would have enjoyed because they had talked of racing each other when they had been together in the Grecian Temple.

Instead of Sylvina he found himself saddled with Mr Cuddington, the Comte and young Clyde, and he had returned them to the house as soon as was possible without causing comment.

Although Sylvina might refuse the Marquis's horse, she could not refuse his dogs.

As soon as she had arrived at Alton Park she had seen his two gun-dogs, brown and white springer spaniels, who jumped to their feet with excitement every time he entered a room and followed him wherever they could.

Once when the Marquis entered the Salon unexpectedly he found Sylvina down on the hearth-rug, her arms round the two animals, her face tender with affection.

But on his entrance the spaniels had sprung to their feet and rushed towards him, forgetting their new-found friend.

For a moment he thought she looked at him reproachfully as though he would take even the comfort of a dumb animal away from her.

'I am glad you like Romulus and Remus,' he said. 'I purchased them as puppies after I had been to Rome.'

He had known that as a classical scholar she would have read the story of the two orphan children who were suckled by a she-wolf and grew up to found the city of Rome.

'I think the names are singularly appropriate for your dogs, My Lord,' Sylvina said demurely.

There was a twinkle in the Marquis's eyes.

'Sylvina, you little wretch!' he exclaimed.

'How dare you imply that I am a female wolf!'

Just for a moment two dimples appeared in her cheeks and she looked up at him with an expression of mischief.

Then from the Terrace where he had been looking at the view, Mr Cuddington entered the Salon.

There was a frown on his face as he saw Sylvina seated on the floor.

'Are you indisposed?' he asked sharply.

Aware of his disapproval and the rebuke in his voice she flushed as she rose to her feet and moved away to the end of the room where the Duchess was explaining an intricate game of patience to Clyde.

The Prince of Wales, Mrs Fitzherbert, with a number of other guests of the Duke and Duchess of Bilston arrived for lunch.

Their presence had undoubtedly delighted Mr Cuddington, but the Marquis noted that although Sylvina was quiet and unassuming, she made herself charming to anyone with whom she was conversing.

In fact, both men and women seemed to gravitate towards her, as if she drew them by an invisible magnet. The Marquis could not help remembering with clenched teeth that it was Mr Cuddington who had sensed she would make a commendable hostess.

When the Prince was leaving and Sylvina curtsied low, he said:

'I remember your father well, Miss Blaine, a most gifted man. And when I was a boy every man in London was in love with your mother. She was very beautiful.'

For a moment Sylvina's face had lit up, and she had smiled as the Marquis had longed for her to do ever since she came to Alton Park.

'Thank you, Sire,' she said softly, 'I am so touched that you remember my mother.'

'It would be impossible to forget her,' the Prince said with the genial charm which helped him to win from so many people both their allegiance and their hearts.

He patted Sylvina's hand and said:

'You are very like her, my dear.'

He left behind him an atmosphere of good-humour which even Mr Cuddington could not disperse.

They had all eaten too much in the middle of the day, so the party adjourned into the garden to admire the blossom-filled flower-beds, the rose-covered trellis work, the strange shapes of the topiary and, of course, the maze.

The Duchess stopped to speak to one of the gardeners, and the Marquis showed Mr Cuddington and Clyde the intricacies of the maze which had first been grown in the reign of Henry VIII.

Then as the two men disappeared between the yew hedges he saw that Sylvina was standing alone at the end of a grass walk staring at the woods in the distance.

He came up beside her very quietly so that she did not hear him coming, and she started when he said:

'You look a very forlorn, unhappy little Princess. Would it not be feasible for a Knight-Errant to sweep you up in his arms and carry you away from the Dragon that frightens you and ensure that you need no longer be afraid?'

He watched her face as he spoke, hoping almost against hope to see the lovely child-like look in her eyes which he had never seen before in a woman's face.

Instead in a hard, cold little voice she replied:

'I have been reading recently about Knights-Errant, My Lord, and I find that down the centuries they have been distinctly over-glamorised. Many of them were no better than knaves who used their knightly rank to deceive the foolish maidens who trusted them.'

She meant to hurt him, and because he was hurt he struck back.

'I am sure you are right, Miss Blaine,' he said. 'I hope that Mr Cuddington will not be long in the maze. I want to ask his opinion on how best I can demolish a certain Grecian Temple that stands not far from here.'

He had slipped under her guard!

'Demolish it?' she ejaculated. 'But you cannot do that!'

'Why not?' the Marquis enquired.

'It would be sacrilege,' she asserted almost passionately.

'I have decided I have no further use for it,' the Marquis replied coolly. 'To keep it there is merely to encourage dreams and fantasies that you yourself would be the first to describe as nonsensical. It had better go – I have decided that it must be levelled to the ground.'

'No! Please … please do not do … that,' Sylvina pleaded, and for the first time she turned to look at him.

'Sylvina!' he said, and his voice was deep and moved.

Then at that moment they were interrupted.

'My Lord, we need your help.'

It was Clyde who called, hurrying towards them across the green lawn. It was with difficulty that the Marquis managed to answer him civilly.

'How can I help you?' he asked.

'Mr Cuddington is lost in the maze,' Clyde announced. 'He went ahead of me, and now I cannot reach him, nor can he discover his way out.'

'Dear me, that is extremely unfortunate,' the Marquis said drily. 'I will come and rescue the Under-Secretary of State for Foreign Affairs. What a tragedy it would be if he were incarcerated there until his bones turned white.'

He glanced at Sylvina as he spoke, and just for a moment he saw those irrepressible dimples.

Then as they neared the maze and could hear Mr Cuddington shouting, he knew that her reserve swept over her again and she shivered.

Later the Marquis tried to seize a moment alone with Sylvina by suggesting that he should show her the Library. He knew without being told that she would love the huge walls lined from floor to ceiling with books.

There were volumes collected all down the centuries, and each succeeding holder of the title had made it his business to add to the collection, which had been started in the fifteenth century.

The Marquis himself had recently purchased some very ancient editions of the Greek classics, and one of the oldest books in Latin ever printed was in his possession.

He had hoped Sylvina would accompany him alone but she had insisted, much against his will, that Clyde should be one of the party.

'I am no scholar,' the young man had admitted frankly. 'It is Sylvina who is the bookworm. And she has a fantastic memory!

She can read pages of ancient Greek or Latin and memorise it word for word. My father always said that if she had been a man she would have been a Professor.'

'I imagine you are good enough in modern languages,' the Marquis said.

'That is different,' Clyde replied. 'I picked those up when I was with my parents in foreign countries, and even from my nurse.'

'But you prefer the classics,' the Marquis said, turning to Sylvina.

'I find them interesting,' she admitted primly.

But as he offered various books for her to examine, he knew by the way she handled them and turned the pages that she was thrilled as no other woman of his acquaintance would have been thrilled by the treasures he had thought peculiarly male in their appeal.

For some moments she stood reading a sentence here and another there, with a look of concentration.

Then with a little sigh she shut the book he had last shown to her and handed it back to him.

'Thank you,' she said, 'I am glad to have seen it.'

'It is yours,' the Marquis said. 'Allow me to make you a present of it.'

'No, no, that I cannot accept,' she protested.

'Why not?' the Marquis enquired.

'Go on, Syl,' her brother admonished her. 'Do not be so foolish. You know you would rather have a book any day than a diamond necklace.'

'That is true,' Sylvina answered. 'But, My Lord, just as I could not accept a diamond necklace from you, neither can I accept a book of this value. You must understand it is impossible.'

'I see no analogy,' the Marquis said and appealed to Clyde: 'Can you not persuade your sister?'

'She is difficult to persuade, My Lord,' Clyde laughed, 'and she always makes a fuss about presents. Why, she created blue murder the other morning when she learnt that Mr...'

'Clyde, will you be quiet!' Sylvina said in a voice that shook.

Her brother looked at her face and was instantly apologetic.

'Sorry, Syl,' he said, 'I am gabbing too much, am I not?'

Sylvina dropped the Marquis a small curtsy.

'If you will excuse me, My Lord, I wish to find your Grandmother,' she said, and went from the room.

'Your sister is a very unusual young woman,' the Marquis remarked when the two men were alone. 'Most females today are only too willing to accept presents from anyone who offers them.'

'I know that, of course,' Clyde said with a boyish grin. 'But Sylvina is very proud.'

'You were saying, I think, that she did not wish to accept presents from Mr Cuddington,' the Marquis prompted.

'Yes, indeed,' Clyde replied. 'She says it humiliates her and all that sort of moonshine. After all, we have been living below decks since my father died and there simply has not been enough money for Sylvina's fal-de-rals.'

'But you yourself have managed quite well, I can see,' the Marquis said.

His tone was so affable that Clyde was not alarmed.

'Well, seeing the position I have, and as the man in the family, I have to be decently garbed,' he said. 'But not up to your standard, My Lord.'

'Perhaps it had never struck you that it would be wiser for your sister not to accept gifts from any man until she is actually married to him,' the Marquis said sternly, 'even if that meant some sacrifice where you are concerned.'

Clyde Blaine suddenly looked embarrassed – a schoolboy caught out for being unsportsmanlike.

Without labouring the point the Marquis put his books back on the shelf.

'Shall we join the ladies?' he suggested.

He had no opportunity of being alone with Sylvina again. The guests settled themselves to play piquet until it was time to change for dinner, and very shortly Sylvina withdrew from the room on the excuse that she would like to rest.

She was looking very pale, the Marquis noted, and wondered if the strain he himself was feeling was in any degree as intense for her.

He felt that the encompassing bands of steel were growing tighter and tighter, and there was nothing he could do to prevent their imprisoning him and squeezing his very life-blood from him.

He had never before known what it was to feel that he was being manipulated rather than being the manipulator, that events were stronger than himself, and nowhere could he see any solution to the problem that beset him.

Time was drawing on; they would all return to London tomorrow, and what had he gained by his carefully planned, his meticulously organised house party? Absolutely nothing!

He felt he was drawing further away from Sylvina at every moment; he was almost beginning to believe to himself that she hated him.

He came down to find his Grandmother

already in the Salon.

She looked up as he approached, and he thought as he had done so often before how remarkably beautiful she still was in her old age.

The light from the candles glittered on her jewellery, her white dress was most becoming and she carried herself superbly, the thinness of her arms hidden by a gauze scarf, her wrists weighed down by jewelled bracelets.

'Well, Justin,' she said as her grandson approached her, 'has your party come up to your expectations?'

He felt that she knew the answer before he replied:

'You know full well it has not.'

'I have news for you,' she said. 'I have just received a note from Emily Dansby.'

She paused, but as the Marquis made no comment she went on:

'Leone has become affianced to the Duke of Farringdon.'

'To Farringdon?' the Marquis ejaculated. 'That is impossible. He is eighty if he is a day!'

'Seventy-six to be exact,' the Dowager corrected, 'and a very rich man.'

'I suppose that is what Leone wanted,' the Marquis said, 'but to me it is singularly unpleasant to think of a young woman married to that aged old tortoise.'

'I thought at one time,' the Dowager said, 'that you and Leone would make a match of it, but I suppose she did not engage your heart.'

'I believed in those days that I had no heart,' the Marquis replied.

'And now?' the Dowager asked quietly.

'I find it an unpredictable, irritating and extremely painful part of my anatomy,' the Marquis said bitterly.

'You have never said anything that pleased me more,' the Dowager smiled.

The Marquis was so surprised that he snapped angrily:

'What the devil do you mean by that? I apologise, Grandmama, I was not expecting you of all people to make such a statement.'

'And I mean every word of it,' his Grandmother said with a smile. 'If you are in love, Justin, as I have suspicioned since the first moment that enchanting creature crossed the threshold, then it will be the making of you.'

'And I thought you were fond of me,' the Marquis said with a wry smile.

'I have always loved you,' the Dowager replied simply. 'You are my favourite grandson, and I think I have wanted your happiness more than I wanted that most elusive blessing even for my own children.'

She smiled at him before she continued.

'And because I wanted it so desperately, I

cannot tell you how hard it has been to watch you year after year growing more cynical and more bored, wasting your time, your brain and your energy pursuing those birdwitted females who flew into your arms almost before you asked their name.'

The Marquis threw back his head and laughed.

'Grandmama, you are incorrigible!' he protested. 'And I thought you were so proud of me!'

'I was proud of you when you were in the Army,' she said, 'and I am glad now that Mr Pitt has chosen to place you in a position of responsibility. But the years in between have been a waste-land of thistles about which I would rather not speak.'

'Nor I neither,' the Marquis agreed. 'It is all over now, at least I sincerely hope it is. Tell me about Sylvina's mother.'

'I thought you would ask me that sooner or later,' the Dowager said. 'Jeannie Campbell was a delightful creature, lovely, gay, unspoilt, and when she came to London she captured the hearts of almost everyone who saw her. Both men and women loved Jeannie, she was that type of person. She was kind, she was sympathetic, she was intensely grateful for the love and affection which she seemed to evoke by right, but which she never took for granted.'

'Why did she marry Sir Rendell?' the

Marquis asked.

'He was not Sir Rendell then,' the Dowager said, 'he was an unknown, unimportant young man who had just entered the Foreign Office – rather like his son. Jeannie could have married anyone. Half the Peerage laid their hearts, their coronets and their fortunes at her feet; but she fell in love. That was what you wanted to know, was it not?'

'She fell in love,' the Marquis repeated.

'Hopelessly, irretrievably from the moment she met young Blaine,' his Grandmother said. 'He had nothing much to recommend him save that he was a gentleman; for he came of good stock. It was a bitter blow to the Duke, but he realised that when a woman loved a man as his daughter loved Rendell Blaine, there was nothing he or anyone else could say to stop her. She was the type of person who would love once in her life and once only, and I am persuaded her daughter is like her.'

The Marquis was very still. After a moment in a strangled voice he said:

'Grandmama, what am I to do? I have lost her. I have tried everything, but I think she really does hate me.'

The Dowager looked up at him with a smile on her lips.

'If you are so chicken-hearted as to believe that,' she said, 'I wash my hands of you.'

'Do you think there is hope?' the Marquis asked quickly.

'I do not know what is keeping you apart,' the Dowager replied, 'but I do not think I have ever seen a young person suffer as Sylvina Blaine is suffering at this moment. Whatever else it may be, I would stake my hope of Heaven that she is not indifferent to you.'

'Then I have to find out somehow what is wrong,' the Marquis declared. 'I must win her, Grandmama, if I have to kill to do it.'

'I believe you would,' his Grandmother said, 'and incidentally I have not heard you say anything so intelligent for a long time. Do you mean to say that after all your experience with women – and from all accounts that is very considerable – with your looks and your much-vaunted charm you cannot persuade one young and inexperienced female to love you? Justin, I am ashamed of you.'

There was deep affection in his Grandmother's voice behind the mockery. The Marquis answered her quite seriously.

'You give me courage, Grandmama. I was almost in despair. But now I know that I will win through eventually. I must, I must!'

He hit the mantelpiece with his clenched fist as he spoke, and the Dowager Duchess watched him with approval in her eyes.

'If there is one thing I have always detested,' she said, 'it is a drawling, la-de-da, indifferent way of facing life. You have woken up, boy, and I must say it is a vast improvement.'

The Marquis did not answer her, and after a moment she said in a softer tone:

'Now that I realise you are more serious than I had hitherto believed, I will tell you something that happened this afternoon.'

'What is it?' the Marquis asked quickly.

'I was alone with Sylvina,' the Dowager replied. 'We had been talking of her mother and she had wept a little as only a child can weep when she realises how forlorn and empty life seems when she no longer has a mother to turn to in her troubles and difficulties. Then Sylvina said to me:

'"Tell me, Ma'am, since you are so wise, if you knew that life was utterly intolerable, with no hope of reprieve, nothing but a hell in store so indescribably loathsome that one could not contemplate it, would you think it wrong to die...?"'

The Marquis's eyes were fixed on his Grandmother's face.

'What did you answer?' he asked.

'I said,' the Dowager replied, 'that one is never without hope because when all else fails one can always pray. And Sylvina replied:

'"Do you not imagine I have prayed and prayed? I thought perhaps Mama would help me, but I cannot reach her."'

The Dowager's eyes were misty with tears.

'I think to all of us,' she said to her grandson, 'there comes a moment when we think we really are alone. We feel forsaken, forgotten, and that was what that child was experiencing at that moment.'

'And did you comfort her?' the Marquis asked almost fiercely.

The Dowager looked up to him and said simply:

'I told her I was sure her mother was very near to her, that she was not alone, however dark it might seem, that somehow either she or someone else would find a way out.'

'Oh God, but supposing...?' the Marquis began, but his Grandmother checked him.

'She will not kill herself,' she said, 'not yet at any rate.'

'I will kill him first,' the Marquis said violently, and they both knew of whom he was speaking.

But now in the darkness of his bed the Marquis thought how easy it was to talk, how difficult to act.

He could imagine the scandal there would be if he challenged Mr Cuddington to a duel and killed him. He had no stomach for pushing a man into the river when he could not swim, or hurling him off a cliff or smothering him as he lay asleep.

What other way was there but poison? But somehow he could not stoop to that.

And yet it seemed to him that it was narrowing down to a choice between Sylvina's life and Cuddington's.

He had half a mind to go now, rouse Sylvina and force her, if necessary by threats, to tell him what lay behind her fear. She was sleeping only a room away from him.

He had deliberately put her near to him in the old part of the house, where he felt she was under his protection, and had given Mr Cuddington one of the large, high-ceilinged, impressive chambers on the first floor overlooking the lake.

Even as he thought of such a plan he knew he could not frighten her more than she was frightened already.

Perhaps to question Clyde would prove his best chance of learning the truth. The boy was young and ingenuous, but despite his thoughtlessness there was no doubt he was fond of his sister.

That is what he would do tomorrow, the Marquis decided and in the same moment felt ashamed that he must go behind Sylvina's back, that he must intrigue about her, that he must discuss her with other people.

'Oh, my darling, why must you do this to me?' he asked in his heart.

He saw her little face turned up to his in the moonlight and felt that strange, inexplicable spell drawing them together when he had bent forward and touched her lips.

He was the first man – the first man who had ever kissed her! At least Cuddington would not be able to boast of that.

And then the mere thought of that thick, lecherous mouth kissing Sylvina made the Marquis clench his hands together again until his nails bit into the palms.

'Sylvina, oh, Sylvina, trust me!'

He felt as if his whole being went out towards her, as if he projected his love like a live flame fluttering between them.

'Sylvina, Sylvina.'

He whispered her name and turned restlessly from side to side on his pillow.

He knew that all night he would be haunted and bedevilled by her face, by the pain in her eyes and the tenderness of her lips.

He wanted her as he believed a man never wanted a woman before; at the same time he desired above all else to protect her and shelter her, to keep her safe and make her know that she need no longer be afraid because he would be standing between her and every terror.

As he tossed and turned the Marquis thought how he had never before known love.

He had thought love to be an amusement, a pleasure, a desire. This was agony!

This was an all-consuming flame, something which took away his pride and left him humble, something which made him know that he was very different from the person he had thought himself to be.

He knew now that his social position, his wealth, his title, his huge possessions were not of the least importance beside the happiness of one small elf-like girl.

What he wanted more than anything else in the world, more than his own hope of Heaven, was Sylvina's happiness.

Suddenly there was a sound which startled him.

The Marquis held himself rigid. Someone with hurried fumbling fingers was opening the door of his room.

# 10

The door opened and closed quickly.

Then as the Marquis raised himself a little on his pillows he realised that someone standing just inside the room was breathing in broken gasps like one who had been running hard and was very frightened.

He was about to speak when a small figure sped across the room, obviously finding the way by the last dying glow from the fire, and threw herself on the bed.

Then a voice almost incoherent with tears cried:

'Clyde! Oh, Clyde! He is in my room ... he touched me ... he has drunk too much wine ... and I cannot ... bear it ... I cannot!'

There was a pause, and the Marquis knew that Sylvina was gasping for breath as she went on:

'I left ... the candle burning ... as I thought ... perhaps ... you would come to say ... good night to ... me ... and I must have ... fallen asleep ... for when I awoke ... he was ... there! Oh, Clyde! It was ... horrible! He was looking ... down at ... me ... his face was near to ... mine ... and when I would have ... screamed h ... he put out ... his hand and ... covered my mouth. He held me ... down ... held me so I ... could not ... move ... and when I tried ... to struggle ... he said:

'"Now you see how helpless you are ... and how completely within ... my power! This will teach you ... not to look at me with contempt ... and disdain ... Miss High and Mighty, for you cannot ... escape."'

Sylvina's voice broke on a sob, but after a moment she went on:

'I writhed and ... twisted to get rid of ... him ... but he was too ... strong... Then he said ... and there was something ... bestial ... in the way he said it:

'"If you resist me when we are ... married I shall beat you... I shall beat you anyway because I am ... determined to break your ... spirit and make you ... humble and subservient as a woman should be to … her master. And every time you … refuse my … kisses, every time you … repulse me … then you will pay for it."'

Sylvina's voice was filled with an almost indescribable horror. Fighting with her tears she went on:

'He chuckled … a horrible sound … that was more … terrifying than if he had … cursed me. And then … Clyde, then … he said:

'"I shall beat you later, but now … I am going to kiss you."'

Sylvina drew a deep sobbing breath before she continued in a whisper:

'He took his hand from my mouth and … bent towards … me… I could move, Clyde, and I … hit him! I hit him with all my strength … between his eyes. I must have taken him … off guard and because he was so … drunk his feet slipped.

'For a moment he staggered against the bed and I was … free! Somehow I scrambled past … him, and even as he … reached out his arms … to stop me I was running down the passage to … you!'

She paused for breath.

'Clyde, he is there waiting … for me, and I cannot … not even to save you … I cannot marry him! He is foul … he is brutal … and I would rather … die than let him … touch me again.

'Save me, Clyde! For God's sake save me!

'Go to the Marquis ... tell him the truth! I know that he is ... just, I promise you he will not act harshly without ... thought... But even to ... save you from ... the Tower I cannot marry t ... that ... be ... beast.'

Sylvina's voice now broke utterly and she flung herself flat on the bed sobbing bitterly.

She was shaken by such a tempest of fear and horror that she was temporarily incapable of coherent thought...

After a little while she realised that her brother was moving about the room and she knew, even though her eyes were blinded with tears, that he had lit a candle.

'He ... must not ... he must not ... touch me ... again!' she moaned, and then with a sudden fear– 'But do not fight him! He is dangerous ... only prevent ... him ... please prevent him ... from touching ... me.'

'He will never touch you again,' a deep voice said.

For a moment Sylvina could not move.

Slowly as if in a dream she raised her head from the bed, the tears running down her face, her eyes wide with terror.

Standing by the bedside, clearly visible in the light of the candle, was not Clyde but the Marquis!

She gave a little cry, almost that of an animal that had been trapped, as a merciful darkness engulfed her...

She came back to consciousness from what seemed to her a long, long distance to find herself being carried closely and securely in the Marquis's arms.

It flashed through her mind that she was safe, that if he could hold her like this for ever she need never be afraid again.

Then she remembered what she had said and trembled.

He carried her through a doorway and into another room. She felt him set her down on a sofa and arrange soft cushions behind her back.

Lying very still, afraid to open her eyes, she felt him cover her with a fur rug, and she thought then that he had left her.

But peeping beneath her eyelashes she saw him at the far end of the room pouring something from a decanter into a glass.

He brought it to her side and she looked up at him with wide, dark, frightened eyes.

'Drink this,' he said.

She would have refused, but there was something authoritative in his voice which made her obey him.

She felt the brandy run like fire down her throat, and while she hated the taste of it she felt the darkness that was still somewhere behind her head recede and she was no longer faint.

The Marquis took the glass from her hand and stood looking down at her, thinking he had never seen a more woebegone little face or one more in need of his protection.

He had wrapped her, Sylvina realised now, in the cover from his bed.

It was of heavy white silk – she did not know it had been embroidered by loving hands with the same leaves that ornamented the posts of the bed itself.

She was only thankful that it covered the diaphanous transparency of her night-gown; and because she had cried so desperately the tears were wet on her cheeks and on the ends of her long eyelashes.

The Marquis put his hand into the pocket of his long brocade robe and took out a handkerchief. Then he set down the glass and going on one knee beside the sofa gently wiped away her tears.

His handkerchief was very soft. It smelt of lavender and some other sweet fragrance which reminded Sylvina of the woods and made her want to cry again.

'You look like a very small kitten which has been left out in the rain,' the Marquis said gently.

'You told me ... Clyde ... was in the ... second bedroom down ... the passage,' Sylvina said childishly.

'That is exactly where he is,' the Marquis answered, 'the second bedroom. I put you next to me because I thought I could protect you. I am deeply humiliated that you should have been insulted while you are a guest in my house.'

'But I ... went to the ... second door,' Sylvina persisted, as though somehow she must justify her action even to herself.

'That is where you made a mistake,' the Marquis explained. 'The first door next to yours is my Sitting Room, where you are now.'

He rose to his feet and sat down on the end of the sofa, facing her as she sat propped up against the cushions.

'And now, my foolish darling,' he said, 'suppose you tell me the truth.'

'But I ... cannot,' Sylvina protested. 'Can you not ... understand that I ... cannot tell ... you?'

'After I have heard so much?' the Marquis asked. 'Do you want me to question Clyde?'

'No, no,' she cried, her words coming quickly from between her lips.

She looked into his face searchingly and then capitulated:

'I will ... tell you ... but ... please ... please go further ... away... I cannot talk to ... you when you are so ... close to ... me.'

There was a gentleness in the Marquis's face that no woman had ever seen as he rose obediently from the sofa and went to stand against the mantelshelf.

The fire was burning low and he threw another log onto it. The flames shot up, bringing a touch of gold to Sylvina's fair hair which haloed her unhappy little face in the light of the candles.

She moved her hands free of the encircling silk bedspread and clasping them together said:

'If I tell you ... if I tell you ... the whole ... truth, will you ... promise ... to believe it?'

'You do not have to plead with me, Sylvina,' the Marquis replied. 'You know that if you tell me something that is true, then as far as you are concerned I shall believe it to be the truth.'

'Do you mean that? Do you really mean that ... Sir Justin?'

Her name for him slipped out, and he moved quickly from the fireside to cover her trembling hands with his.

'Look at me, Sylvina,' he said. 'You have a tale to tell. Could you not tell it, without being frightened, to Justin – the man you met in the woods, the man you said once you would trust wherever he might take you? Forget the Marquis of Alton, he isn't important.'

'But he ... is,' she interrupted.

'Not to us, Sylvina, not to us.'

She knew that because his hands covered hers he gave her a strength and a reassurance she had thought never to know again.

'I will tell you ... everything,' she whispered.

He released her hands and went to sit in

the big armchair opposite her on the other side of the fireplace.

The light was on her face and he thought he had never known a woman's eyes could be so variously expressive. At one moment they could seem full of sunlight, the next tragic to the point of despair.

'Where ... shall I ... start?' Sylvina asked nervously.

'At the beginning,' the Marquis answered.

'T ... that was when P ... Papa was k ... killed,' she said, stumbling a little over the words, 'and Bessie and I came back to London alone. We went to our house in Curzon Street which had always been our home when we were in England. It was then Clyde joined me and we discovered that we were p ... penniless.'

There was a little pause as if she remembered what a terrible shock it had been.

'Papa had been very improvident where money was concerned,' she went on after a moment, 'and after Mama died I do not think he cared much about anything. He just tried to forget. He did not want to sit at home alone and think.'

She was silent for a moment, and then she said miserably:

'I often wonder if I could have helped him then ... if I could have done anything to prevent his being so ... unhappy.'

'You were very young,' the Marquis said.

'I was seventeen when he died,' Sylvina answered, 'but I never wanted to be part of the social world which Papa enjoyed so much ... this is not very ... interesting to you ... but I am trying to explain.'

'I want you to explain everything to me,' the Marquis assured her, 'every little detail. Leave nothing out.'

'Clyde sold the house,' she continued, 'all Papa's silver and furniture and Mama's jewellery. Bessie and I found the little house in Chelsea. We bought it because it was cheap, but I liked it because there was a garden.'

'I thought that was why you had chosen it,' the Marquis commented.

'Sometimes I would forget I was in London,' Sylvina sighed. 'I kept only Mama's most personal things – her *Secretaire* on which she had always written her letters, her marquetry work-box, the table on which she had always stood her treasures which we had collected when we travelled. I tried to make a home for Clyde because Mama had loved him so much, much more, I think, than she loved anyone except Papa.'

There was something sad and desolate in Sylvina's voice which made the Marquis long to put his arms round her, but he knew that he must listen without interruption.

This was the moment of revelation for which he had been waiting.

'Clyde had to sell out of his Regiment,' Sylvina continued. 'He hated doing that because he was so proud of being a soldier, but it was obviously impossible for him to live on his pay, and he had to earn some money or we would have starved. He went to the Foreign Office, and as you know they took him because, as they said, Papa had served this country so faithfully and well.'

'That was the right thing to have done,' the Marquis approved.

'Clyde is clever really and serious about his career,' Sylvina said. 'He only seems thoughtless because he is young and he enjoys being gay, going to parties and meeting new people. He is like Papa in that. And it is hard for him to have so little money and not to be able to return hospitality. He minds that more than I can say.'

'And so you and Bessie kept house for Clyde,' the Marquis said as Sylvina paused.

A little ghost of a smile touched her lips.

'Bessie was wonderful. She had been Mama's Abigail for years and years, she loves Clyde and is so proud of him. She loves me too, and when Papa's sister, who was with us for a month or so, had to go to Harrogate, I did not miss her because I had Bessie. Then Bessie's sister fell ill and I was alone and … frightened.'

'How did you meet him?' the Marquis asked.

They both knew to whom he was referring.

Sylvina put her hand up to her forehead.

'I am being … stupid and skipping … bits
that are … important,' she said. 'After Clyde
had been six months at the Foreign Office
he was promoted. He came home to tell me,
very pleased with himself because he had
been commended for his work and had
been given a room on his own. I wanted so
much to see it, but he did not want to take
me there in the daytime. I believe really he
did not think I was smart enough.'

She saw the Marquis's expression and
added quickly:

'It was not Clyde's fault that I had no elegant gowns; we were still paying off Papa's
debts.'

'Yes, of course,' the Marquis said reassuringly.

'So Clyde said he would show me where
he worked after the building was closed for
the day,' Sylvina continued. 'I met him in
the Park. That was the afternoon I saw …
the ducks… Then we went into the Foreign
Office and down the long, empty corridors
to Clyde's room.'

She gave a little sigh.

'I suppose it was wrong of us to go really;
anyway, as it was, we were punished for it.
While Clyde was trying to decide which of
Papa's pictures would look best on the wall

over his desk, the door opened and ... Mr Cuddington came in.'

The Marquis saw Sylvina clench her fingers together.

'I knew ... as soon as I saw ... him...' she began and stopped.

'That he was bad, wicked and evil,' the Marquis finished.

'You remember that I told you that?' she asked.

'I remember every word you have ever said to me,' the Marquis replied simply.

'That is what I did ... feel about ... him,' she went on in her breathless, frightened little voice. 'There was something about ... him, something in the ... way he looked ... at me that made me know ... he was ... dangerous. He was pleasant enough ... very affable, Clyde thought him. And then the following day he came to ... call.'

'Were you alone?' the Marquis asked.

'No, he came home with Clyde,' Sylvina explained. 'When I saw him in the Drawing Room ... when I saw him look ... disparagingly at Mama's things ... I knew then I ... hated him.'

'And he came again?' the Marquis prompted as her voice died away into silence.

'The next day ... and the day ... after that,' Sylvina replied. 'And then I knew I could bear him no longer ... and when he called I told Bessie to say I was out, indisposed or not at home – anything so long as I did not have to speak with ... him!'

'How many times did he come?' the Marquis asked.

'I cannot remember,' Sylvina replied. 'I did not see him as Bessie kept him from entering the house. Then ... then ... a terrible thing ... happened...'

She put her hands up to her face as she spoke, and the Marquis saw that she was fighting for self-control.

'Tell me, my darling,' he said gently, 'I have to know.'

She took her hands away from her eyes and he saw that her face was drained of all colour, her eyes dark with apprehension.

'Mr Cuddington,' she said in a voice so low he could hardly hear, 'called Clyde into his office... He asked him whom ... else he had brought into ... the Foreign Office secretly when the place was ... closed! He asked him who were ... his friends to whom he had spoken about his ... work, and as Clyde became more and more bewildered ... not understanding why he should be cross-examined in such a way ... Mr Cuddington produced a ... book from his desk and ... opened it.'

'A book?' the Marquis queried.

'It was Clyde's ... bank-book,' Sylvina said in a very low voice.

The Marquis looked puzzled, and she

went on in frightened tones:

'There was an ... entry in ... it ... someone had paid into Clyde's ... bank the sum ... of two hundred ... pounds.'

Her head dropped forward again and she covered her eyes with her hands.

'You mean,' the Marquis said quietly, 'that Clyde had no knowledge of this money?'

'N ... none at all... Oh, Sir Justin ... believe me! I beg of ... you to believe ... me. He had no ... idea. He thought he was ... overspent, indeed he had been ... until this money in some ... mysterious manner ... appeared.'

'And how had Mr Cuddington obtained Clyde's bank-book?' the Marquis asked.

'Clyde did not know,' Sylvina answered. 'He went to the bank and they said the money had been paid in ... three days earlier. They did not know ... who it was, in fact, nobody had any memory of the ... transaction. But you can imagine what ... Mr Cuddington ... inferred from ... it.'

'He accused Clyde,' the Marquis suggested, 'of receiving money for information he had given the French?'

'Clyde would never do such a thing!' Sylvina cried hotly. 'He is loyal! He has served with the Army, and England means as much to him as it means to you.'

'And what did Mr Cuddington propose to do about this unaccountable sum of money?' the Marquis enquired.

'He said that if he did his duty he should hand Clyde over immediately to the ... Marquis of Alton ... but as he intended ... to marry ... me, he did not wish to have a brother-in-law who was branded as a ... spy and a ... traitor.'

'So that is how he did it,' the Marquis said grimly.

'When Clyde told me I thought ... I should go ... mad,' Sylvina said. 'I could not believe it possible that a man ... any man should make such a bargain ... especially one holding the position of Mr Cuddington. He came to see ... me and he spoke with ... terrifying frankness.

'"Your brother has behaved most reprehensibly," he said.

'"My brother has done nothing," I replied.

'"That will, of course, be for the Marquis of Alton to decide," Mr Cuddington answered, "unless, of course, I keep silent on this apparently debatable matter."'

'He then asked you to marry him?' the Marquis said.

'No, he told me I was ... to do so,' Sylvina corrected.

'"You will marry me," he said... "I will teach you to be a commendable wife. You will play hostess at my parties, you will grace my house. You and your brother are accepted by the *Beau Ton*, and that, my dear,

267

is the only asset you have.'"

Sylvina gave a little sob.

'I thought that was ... humiliation enough,' she said, 'but I was to endure much more. He taunted me with ... our poverty; he sneered at ... my clothes, the way we lived. He told me how different everything would be once I was his ... wife. And he made it very clear that if I did not ... consent, then he would take the book with its ... irrefutable evidence to ... you and Clyde must stand ... trial.'

The Marquis got to his feet.

'I will kill the swine with my bare hands,' he said violently.

'I have often thought that I would ... die rather than marry him,' Sylvina said, 'but that if I did so he would take his ... revenge on Clyde just the same. That is why I told you ... and I still tell you ... there is nothing that can be done ... nothing!'

'Except to clear Clyde and save you,' the Marquis said quietly.

She looked up at him, her face suddenly illuminated.

'You mean ... you mean that you believe that Clyde is ... innocent?' she asked. 'Oh, Sir Justin, I knew you would understand! You know he would not have accepted money from the enemy! How could Papa's son be a traitor?'

'I am sure he is not,' the Marquis said.

'Oh, my poor unhappy little love, why did you not trust me sooner? We might both of us have been saved so much suffering. I have never been so unutterably miserable as I have been this week, wondering if I had lost you for ever, half believing that in reality you hated me.'

'It was ... wrong of me to have said ... that,' Sylvina said, 'but I was so ... afraid when I learnt that ... you were the ... Marquis of Alton.'

'Are you still frightened of me?' he asked in a deep voice.

She looked up at him and her eyes seemed to dim the light from the candles.

'Not now,' she answered. 'You believe me, Sir Justin. That is all that matters.'

The Marquis deliberately looked away from the happiness in her face.

'We are not yet clear of all the difficulties,' he said soberly. 'With everyone searching feverishly for spies, expecting to find them under every bed, in every cupboard, up every chimney, the mere whisper that Clyde is untrustworthy, from whatever source it came, could ruin his career and remain a stigma for life.'

'Yes, I know,' Sylvina agreed. 'But, Sir Justin, you will find a way ... will you not?'

'I will do everything in my power to save Clyde,' the Marquis promised.

'And ... I will ... not have to ... marry ...

Mr Cuddington?' Sylvina asked, her voice trembling.

'I swear to you that that is something which will never happen,' the Marquis answered.

He saw the relief in her face and the fluttering of her hands and felt almost as if she held out her arms in invitation to him.

Their eyes met, and he drew a deep breath. She looked so lovely, with her face radiant, her eyes shining, her lips inviting his.

He had only to take one step forward to hold that slim, sweet, trembling body close to his heart.

He knew she wanted him to do that, she wanted to feel again, as he did, that ecstasy, that inexpressible rapture they had both known when he first kissed her.

It was with an almost superhuman effort that the Marquis turned away.

'You must go, my love,' he said abruptly. 'No one must be aware, as you well know, that you have been here in my room.'

The radiance on Sylvina's face was dimmed and she shivered.

'But suppose ... suppose he ... is waiting for ... me.'

'That I will first discover for certain,' the Marquis said.

He went to the door which led into the passage, opened it quietly, saw that the candles on the landing were extinguished and fetched one of the candles from the mantelshelf.

He went from the room and Sylvina, with a little sigh of relief, dropped back against the soft cushions.

It was as if a heavy weight that she had carried for so long had been lifted from her shoulders.

She knew that in a way nothing was yet solved, that Clyde was still in danger, but the mere fact that the Marquis now knew the truth and believed her was a joy beyond words.

She realised that indeed she was no longer afraid of him, and she thought perhaps it was because in his long blue brocade robe with its high collar and big velvet cuffs he looked so much younger.

The white frill of his night-shirt framed his chin, and the slippers that he wore were embroidered with his crest in 'petit point'.

'I love him,' she whispered to herself, and knew that the whole miserable nightmare of vowing that he would never mean anything to her again was over.

As he had said, it was fate. They could not escape each other.

The Marquis came back into the room carrying her night robe over his arm. He set down the candle and laid the robe down on the sofa.

'There is no one there,' he said. 'I have lit the candles, and now, my darling, you must go back to your own bedchamber. Lock the door, and I swear to you that no one will approach you tonight for I shall be here in this room with the door ajar.'

'Then I will not be frightened,' Sylvina said.

She reached out her hand towards her robe, blushed and looked at the Marquis.

'I will turn my back,' he said with a smile.

He walked to the mantelpiece to stand looking down into the warm embers of the fire.

'Now I am ready!' he heard her soft voice say behind him.

Her robe, made by Bessie, was of white wool and hung straight from her shoulders. It had a flat, round collar which Bessie had ornamented with little frills of lace.

With her fair hair tousled, her long dark eyelashes still wet from her tears, she looked like a small angel that had fallen out of Heaven by mistake.

'You are sure there is ... no one ... there?' Sylvina asked anxiously.

'I promise you the room is empty,' the Marquis answered. 'And you know that you can trust me to protect you.'

'I do trust you ... Sir Justin,' Sylvina replied breathlessly, 'and everything is quite ... quite different ... now.'

She dropped her eyes for a moment, and then she said hesitantly:

'I feel ... ashamed of making such a fuss over what must seem to you a very ... trivial episode when you are so vitally concerned with the 120,000 Frenchmen who may at this ... very moment be landing on the south coast.'

The Marquis seemed frozen to immobility.

'Who told you the number of men!' he asked, and his voice was like a pistol-shot. 'Was it Clyde?'

'No ... it was not ... Clyde,' Sylvina replied quickly.

'Then who?' the Marquis enquired.

She did not answer for a moment, and he said, his voice grim:

'Answer me, Sylvina – you must answer me.'

'You sound ... angry,' she protested. 'What have I ... done?'

'Just answer the question,' the Marquis said. 'Who told you that 120,000 men were to land on the south coast?'

'Must I ... answer that?' she enquired.

'I am afraid you must,' he said sternly.

Sylvina blushed.

'I ... overheard ... it.'

'Whom did you overhear?' the Marquis enquired.

She twisted her fingers together like a

273

child who had been caught out in some misdemeanour.

'I did not mean to ... listen,' she said. 'It sounds so ... ill-bred, but it was after ... you had come to see me in Queen's Walk and ... I was so ... happy. When you had gone I ran upstairs to my room, and hardly had I reached it ... when Bessie announced that the ... gentlemen were downstairs.'

Sylvina swallowed and went on:

'I meant to go straight into the Drawing Room, but I was afraid that Mr Cuddington would guess something ... had happened. My heart was beating and I felt so excited ... I was sure he would ... suspect.'

'And you heard the gentlemen talking inside the Drawing Room?' the Marquis prompted.

'Y ... yes,' Sylvina faltered.

The Marquis gripped her by the shoulders.

'Listen to me, Sylvina,' he said, 'this is of the utmost import. Tell me what they said. You have a good memory: try to recall every word – do you understand? – every word that you overheard.'

Sylvina shut her eyes and wrinkled her brow in an effort of concentration.

'I think it was the Comte I heard first,' she said. 'The sound of his voice made me re-member Paris and what a beautiful city it is.'

'He was talking French?' the Marquis asked.

Sylvina nodded.

'And Cuddington?'

'He spoke French too, fluently, but he made the language sound ugly instead of beautiful.'

'And what did he say?'

'The first words I remember hearing,' Sylvina began slowly, 'came from the Comte: "It is a bold stroke to enter that particular department," he said, "and because it is bold it will succeed."'

'Go on,' the Marquis encouraged her.

'And then I think he said,' Sylvina went on slowly:

'"When will the invasion start?"

'And Mr Cuddinton replied:

'"It could be any day now – if only the wind would drop. Everything is in readiness."

'"I heard the same in Paris," the Comte told him. "But you know more than I do."

'"Yes indeed," Mr Cuddington replied. "The plan is to transport 120,000 veterans. They will embark in 1,500 barges, and besides the barges there will be large sailing vessels more than 100 feet long, armed with twenty-four-pounders, and each carrying 150 men."

'"That is formidable!" the Comte exclaimed.

'"They will start from Boulogne, Wissant, Ambleteuse and Etaples," Mr Cuddington continued, "three hundred from Dunkirk,

Calais and Gravelines, three hundred from Nieuwpoort and Ostend and three hundred more with the Dutch army from Flushing.'

'"*C'est invincible!*" the Comte ejaculated.'

'"Can you imagine what they will do to the untried, untrained and mainly weaponless Volunteers?" Mr Cuddington asked.'

'"It will be a catastrophe!" the Comte exclaimed.'

Sylvina paused.

'It was then I went into the room,' she said. 'Strangely enough they were both ... smiling.'

The Marquis seemed to tighten his hold on her shoulders.

'Listen to me, Sylvina,' he said. 'Have you related what you have told me now to any other person?'

She shook her head.

'Then swear to me that you will not breathe a word of this to Clyde or to anyone else.'

'Of course not, if you ask it of me,' she answered.

'I not only ask it, I command it,' the Marquis said. 'Now listen, my love, our plans have to be changed. I must go to London.'

Sylvina gave a little cry.

'You are going ... away?'

'Only for a few hours,' he said, 'and no one must know I have gone. I will return in time for luncheon, but I want you to stay in your room. Send a message by Bessie that you have a headache. Mr Cuddington can be expecting nothing less after his behaviour tonight.'

The Marquis's voice sharpened as he mentioned the name of the Under-Secretary of State.

'You will come back?' Sylvina asked childishly.

'Nothing will keep me away,' the Marquis answered. 'Whatever you do, my darling, do not change your attitude to me. Behave with the same reserve, the same coldness – which hurt me so intolerably – you have shown up to now. When you are downstairs keep beside my Grandmother. You will travel back to London with Clyde, and perhaps tomorrow I shall have good news for you.'

'Good news?' Sylvina queried.

'The news that you and Clyde are free,' the Marquis said.

He took his hands from her shoulders and turned towards the door.

Sylvina did not move, and then as he looked round to see why she had not followed him she said in a very small voice:

'You are not ... angry with ... me ... Sir Justin?'

For a moment the Marquis looked puzzled, then with a very tender smile on his lips he walked back to stand looking down at her.

'Can you perhaps be wondering why I have not kissed you good night, my Dearest Heart? Why I have not taken you in my arms? Look at me, Sylvina. Do you think that I do not want to hold you close, that I do not want to kiss your lips, to know again that wonder and ecstasy that was ours for all too brief a moment before you cast me into the nearest thing to hell a man has ever experienced?'

He looked deep into her eyes, as he said softly:

'I love you! I love you as I have never loved a woman before and never will love again. But my innocent little sweetheart, if I have to protect you from other men, I also have to protect you from myself. Tonight, here in my own room, I am trying to behave as a gentleman should, and God knows it is hard when you look at me like that.'

'Then you do ... still ... love me?' Sylvina asked.

'One day very soon,' he replied, 'I will answer that question. I will hold you to me and kiss your mouth, your eyes, your hair, your neck until there is no longer any doubt in my mind, until you are sure – as I am sure – that we belong to each other and nothing and no one can ever keep us apart. But until then...'

The Marquis paused. Sylvina's face was lifted to his and her lips were parted.

He stared down at her and she saw a fire smouldering in his eyes and knew that he ached for her as she ached for him, but she was not afraid.

She seemed to sway towards him, and only years of self-discipline prevented the Marquis from sweeping her into his arms.

'God, how I love you – and want you!' he said hoarsely.

He reached out and took both Sylvina's hands in his and slowly turned them upwards.

Then he bent his head and kissed the palm of each little hand lingeringly, passionately, until her breath came quickly and she felt thrill after thrill ripple through her until she was quivering with the first awakening of desire.

'There, my darling, is my heart,' he said. 'Hold it secretly till I can tell the world it is yours for all eternity.'

# 11

In the Foreign Office Lord Hawkesbury glanced at the ormolu clock on the mantel-shelf and saw it was five minutes to ten o'clock. He rang for his secretary. When the man appeared he said curtly:

'Ask the Under-Secretary to be kind enough to attend me.'

'Very good, My Lord.'

A few moments later Mr Cuddington came into the office.

'You wanted me, My Lord?' he enquired.

'Yes, Under-Secretary,' Lord Hawkesbury said, 'I have a few problems here I would like to discuss with you. But first tell me if you enjoyed yourself at Alton Park.'

'Exceeding, My Lord. The Marquis is an excellent host and I found the house itself and its surroundings very agreeable.'

'Alton Park is indeed one of my favourite houses,' Lord Hawkesbury replied, 'and quite the most comfortable in my experience.'

'I must admit, My Lord,' Mr Cuddington said confidently, 'the Marquis becomes less formidable on acquaintance. In fact, he is so affable that I begin to wonder if he was the right person to be appointed to the post he now holds.'

'I think you need have no doubt on that point,' Lord Hawkesbury said drily. 'The Marquis has proved himself in the past to be highly efficient in everything he has ever undertaken. However, we have other matters to concern ourselves with this morning. I would like your opinion on this case.'

The further door of the office opened unexpectedly and Lord Hawkesbury paused.

'What is it?' he asked testily.

'The Marquis of Alton, My Lord, craves a few moments of your time.'

'Alton!' Lord Hawkesbury exclaimed with raised eyebrow. 'And just when we were speaking of him. Show His Lordship in.'

A few seconds later the Marquis came into the office. He was outstandingly elegant in a coat of dark blue superfine cloth, and Mr Cuddington noticed that he was wearing his cravat in a new style.

'Good morning, My Lord. Good morning, Cuddington.'

The Marquis walked up to Lord Hawkesbury's desk and said in a low voice:

'We cannot be overheard?'

'No, of course not,' Lord Hawkesbury replied. 'Is something amiss?'

'I have here a matter of tremendous import,' the Marquis replied.

Mr Cuddington started to rise to his feet as though he would tactfully withdraw, but he was stopped by a quick gesture of the Marquis's hand.

'No, no, Cuddington, I require your presence. What I have to impart to His Lordship is also for your ears.'

The Under-Secretary inclined his head. The Marquis, sitting down in a chair, drew a large envelope, which was heavily sealed, from his pocket and set it in front of Lord Hawkesbury.

'I have here, Secretary of State,' he said solemnly, 'a document so precious that only two other people know of its existence. They are the Earl St Vincent, First Lord of the Admiralty, and Lord Hobart, Secretary of State for War. It has been compiled by them, and while they each hold a copy, the only other one is to be left here in your charge.'

Lord Hawkesbury looked interested.

'And what does this valuable document contain?' he asked.

'It contains,' the Marquis answered, 'a complete and detailed plan of the disposition of all our troops and our Ships o' the Line. It shows the position of the Volunteers, our gun emplacements, supplies, Naval reinforcements and ammunition reserves. In fact, nothing has been omitted by Their Lordships which could be required immediately at the moment of invasion.'

'Then why should I have a copy?' Lord Hawkesbury asked.

'They have asked, My Lord,' the Marquis replied, 'that, when the Prime Minister or anyone else informs you that the invasion is actually taking place, you will break the seal and take this document to the Cabinet. Because of the leakage which we fear is taking place, it has been deemed advisable by the Earl St Vincent and Lord Hobart not to communicate, as is usual, with the Prime Minister himself or with his colleagues.

'As I have said, there are only three copies of this document, and they beg of you, My Lord, to keep it in the utmost secrecy, allowing no one save yourself to handle it until it is required. Then you can show it to the Prime Minister and members of the Cabinet and anyone else you think to be vitally connected with its contents.'

'I understand exactly,' Lord Hawkesbury said, 'and if I may say so, My Lord, I think it is a very wise precaution, if Mr Pitt is to be believed and there is indeed a traitor in our midst.'

'Personally I cannot credit that anyone at Cabinet level would behave in such a manner,' the Marquis said. 'Yet one can never be sure. And that is why, My Lord, I am asking you not to open this document in any circumstances except when the invasion has commenced.'

'You have my word on it,' Lord Hawkesbury said.

'And where will you keep it?' the Marquis enquired.

'Where all our most secret papers are kept,' Lord Hawkesbury replied, 'in a safe here in this office, to which only I and Mr Cuddington have keys. There is no question of anyone else in the whole building having access to it.'

'In which case it should be completely safe,' the Marquis said. 'The document has, as you can imagine, been compiled with the intention of repelling this invasion. That is why it is of the utmost importance that the position of the Ships o' the Line should not be known to anyone save the Earl St Vincent and Lord Hobart until the actual moment when they must move into battle.'

'I understand,' Lord Hawkesbury said.

'And as to the troops,' the Marquis went on, 'Your Lordship will understand that one thing we must avoid at all costs is an infiltration behind our lines of defence. That is why for anyone to get possession of this document would be utterly disastrous.'

'So long as it remains in my care, Alton,' Lord Hawkesbury assured him, 'there is no chance of that. I am ready to vouch at any time for the entire loyalty of my whole staff. Would you not agree with me, Cuddington?'

The Under-Secretary nodded.

'The majority of them have been with us many years, My Lord, and I can assure you that I always carry the key of this particular safe on my person. There is no question of it ever being purloined or borrowed, and I am sure I can say the same of yours.'

'You can indeed,' Lord Hawkesbury said. 'Now watch me, My Lord Marquis. I will lock up this document in your presence and there will, in fact, be no occasion for the safe to be opened until we hear news of an attempted landing – which pray Heaven will be never!'

Lord Hawkesbury rose as he spoke, and drawing the key from his pocket opened the safe set in the wall behind his chair.

It was made of thick steel, and having deposited the precious envelope inside, he swung the steel door to and invited Mr Cuddington to see that it was securely locked.

'There has never been a case of this type of safe being burgled,' Mr Cuddington said, a note of elation in his voice.

'Then you set my mind at rest,' the Marquis said, rising from his chair.

He bowed to Lord Hawkesbury and to Mr Cuddington.

'Good morning, gentlemen. I am afraid I shall not be in my office again today, I have various conferences to attend to elsewhere.'

Lord Hawkesbury glanced at the clock.

'And I must repair to the House of Lords,' he said. 'I regret, Under-Secretary, that the problems on which I wish to consult you must wait because I feel it unlikely I shall return here today. I have a meeting with the Prime Minister this afternoon and other appointments which will keep me busy until long after you have gone home. But I know I can leave the Foreign Office in your capable hands.'

'I will certainly do my best to deal with any difficulties which may arise in your absence, My Lord,' Mr Cuddington said servilely.

285

The Marquis left the room. The Secretary of State stayed behind to pick up various papers, then he too left.

He went down the steps to where his carriage was waiting and told the flunkey who showed him in to it to tell the coachman to drive to the House of Lords.

But when they were half across Parliament Square he changed his mind and ordered the coach to proceed immediately to Alton House in Berkeley Square.

He arrived to find, as he expected, the Marquis was already entertaining the Earl St Vincent and Lord Hobart.

Seated in the long library overlooking the garden at the back of the house, they each had a glass in their hands and raised them in salute as Lord Hawkesbury entered.

'I hear everything went according to plan,' the Earl St Vincent said in his deep voice.

'Alton played his part admirably,' Lord Hawkesbury said with a chuckle. 'Indeed, My Lord, if you are out of a job when this is all over, I suggest you take to the boards.'

'You did not do so badly yourself,' the Marquis replied. 'But do not let us be over-elated, gentlemen, we have yet to see if the rat will take the cheese.'

'I still cannot believe it possible that Cuddingtion is involved,' Lord Hawkesbury remarked, allowing the Marquis to pour him out a generous portion of cognac. 'I must admit to never really liking the fellow; but he is brilliant, there is no doubt about that.'

'It is always the same with these outsiders,' Lord Hobart snorted. 'They come up like a rocket and it goes to their heads. They want more and yet more. Power not only corrupts, it inflates a man who is not bred to take it.'

'In other words, they cannot take their oats,' the Earl St Vincent said scathingly. 'All I can say, Alton, is thank God you did not discover a traitor in the Admiralty. It would have been a humiliation from which the Navy would never have recovered.'

'Do not make me feel any worse about it than I do already,' Lord Hawkesbury begged. 'When I think of all the secret papers that swine has seen; when I remember how often I have related to him what has happened at Cabinet meetings, I feel like blowing a piece of lead through my skull.'

'It is not your fault,' the Marquis said soothingly. 'There is no blame attached to anyone where Cuddington is concerned. But what we must avoid now is a scandal.'

Lord Hobart sat upright.

'You are quite right, Alton,' he said. 'If this should become public it would seriously damage the morale of the troops. It is bad enough for a man to go into battle, in some cases only partially trained and in many cases inadequately armed, without feeling in addition that he has been stabbed in the back by those considered to be his superiors.'

'I agree with you,' the Earl St Vincent said. 'This treachery must be hushed up at all costs, and I am sure every member of the Cabinet will say the same when they know the truth.'

'Then let us hope our plans will succeed,' the Marquis said drily. 'You have, as I requested, Lord Hobart, a troop of Cavalry on every main road?'

'On the roads to Portsmouth, Brighton, Dover and Wapping,' Lord Hobart replied, 'and each troop is in the charge of an officer whom I considered completely trustworthy. When they apprehend this man there will be, if my orders are carried out, no gossip.'

'And if he eludes us?' the Marquis asked, looking at the Earl St Vincent.

'I have sent messengers at dawn this morning to alert the Admiral in charge of each one of our main harbours,' the Earl St Vincent replied. 'He in his turn will be in touch with coastguards, who will scrutinise every vessel leaving these shores. And even if this cur does not reach the coast, I shall find out in what ship he intended to travel, if I have to flog every rating in the Navy to discover the truth!'

'There is no reason to suppose it is the Navy which is involved,' the Marquis said quietly. 'You and I know full well, My Lord, that merchant ships from both sides exchange their flags in mid-channel.'

'Then this particular merchantman will not sail again,' the Earl St Vincent said grimly.

'And now, gentlemen,' the Marquis said, 'there is nothing for us to do but to wait, which is exceeding tiresome at the best of times. Shall we pass the hours recriminating and expressing the anxiety we each one of us feels, or shall we bestir ourselves to a game of cards?'

Lord Hawkesbury looked at the Marquis with a smile.

'You are a cool devil, are you not, Alton?' he asked. 'Does anything, however momentous, make you agitated or, as my children would put it more colloquially, in a flip-flutter?'

'You flatter me,' the Marquis replied. 'I assure you, My Lord, I am often deeply agitated, and this particular problem certainly comes into that category.'

'Then I have never seen you show signs of it,' Lord Hawkesbury retorted.

The Marquis rang the bell, and servants brought in a card-table and presented a cold collation to the gentlemen for their delectation.

'Damn it all,' the Earl St Vincent ejaculated, 'I have no stomach for food at this moment.'

Nevertheless like the other guests he partook of the *pâté* sandwiches, lark and oyster pie and slices of Boar's head. It was only the Marquis who appeared to be uninterested in either food or drink.

They played cards quietly with little conversation, and the only sound was the clink of golden guineas passing from purse to table and the flip of the cards as they were shuffled by expert fingers.

Then after nearly two hours had passed there was the sound of voices outside in the Hall.

The Marquis sprang to his feet, pushing back his chair, and opened the door of the Library.

Outside a dirty, ragged little man was arguing with the footmen.

'Come in, Jeb,' the Marquis said sharply.

The man obeyed him. He was thin and undersized and had a broken nose which gave him a somewhat grotesque appearance, but his eyes were sharp and shrewd.

He waited until the Marquis had shut the door before he said:

"'E's bolted, Guv!'

'He has gone?'

It sounded as though the four men at the table spoke with one voice.

'Tell me from the beginning,' the Marquis said authoritatively.

'I did as ye tells me, M'Lord,' Jeb said, twisting his battered hat round in his hands as he spoke. 'I stands about near the steps and sees 'is Nibs come swanking up in 'is curricle. I think's 'e'd be akeeping it, but no, 'e tells the coachman to go 'ome. Then 'e goes inside. I looks around, thinking it queer-like, 'cos if 'e was aleaving 'e'd 'ave no vehicle in which to travel. I then sees under the trees out of the sun Bill Daws with 'is britsy adrawn by two of 'is fastest 'orses.'

'Who is Bill Daws?' Lord Hobart asked sharply.

'He holds the record from London to Brighton,' the Marquis answered curtly, 'owns a livery-stable, and without exception is the best tooler of horseflesh in the whole country. Go on, Jeb.'

'I knows Bill,' Jeb said, 'so I sidles up to 'im all casual-like and says:

"'Them be mighty fine cattle ye be adriving. Whose record are ye out to beat today?"

"'Me own," Bill answers.

"'Now let me see," I says, "'is Royal 'ighness does London to Brighton in four hours and thirty minutes and ye does it in four and twenty. But ye don't like to spoil the pride o' Princes, and so ye keeps yer yapper shut.'

"'Not that record!" Bill answers. "London to Dover takes me three hours and twenty-five minutes last month. If I can't drop ten minutes off it with these nags and two I have stabled 'alfway, then Oi'll sell 'em all for 'orsemeat."

'"Yer'll do it," I says, "there be no one like ye when it comes to making the flesh fly over the miles, be there, Bill?"

'"E grins at me and I was athinking 'e might be athrowing me a copper or two to drink 'is 'ealth when there comes a call from the steps and 'e whips up 'is 'orses and off 'e goes.'

'Dover, so that is where Cuddington is going!' the Earl St Vincent exclaimed. 'I wonder where exactly he means to disembark?'

'You have not finished yet, Jeb, have you?' the Marquis interrupted.

'No, Guv,' Jeb replied. 'I nips on behind just as ye tells me to make certain sure 'e doesn't change 'is direction. I tells you, M'Lord, it's dangerous atravelling between the wheels when Bill is atooling the 'orses. 'Sides, I might 'ave been seen for the cover of the britsy were down.'

'What is this vehicle he calls a britsy?' Lord Hobart enquired.

'He means a Side Light Britcha,' the Marquis explained. 'It is one of those new vehicles built for speed, with the driver sitting up in front and two seats for passengers behind. They are damn fast, I can assure you. Go on, Jeb.'

'I be 'oping Yer Lordship'll see fit ter reward me for risking life and limb,' Jeb said in a whining voice.

'I wish first to hear the end of the story,' the Marquis said sharply. 'You actually saw him onto the Dover road?'

'Yes indeed, M'Lord, though we'd 'ave been there a sight sooner if 'e'd not stopped in Chelsea to pick up 'is fancy mort.'

The Marquis was very still.

'Chelsea?' he said in a voice which seemed to echo round the room like an explosion.

'Yes, M'Lord, fair took me by surprise it did,' Jeb said. 'Bill pulls up at a 'ouse in Queen's Walk, and 'is Nibs hops out. I only had time to scramble away from the carriage or 'e'd 'ave seen me.'

'What happened?' the Marquis asked in a voice so ominous that everyone else in the room was silent.

'A few seconds later out 'er comes,' Jeb said. 'Prettiest bit o'...'

'She came willingly?' the Marquis interrupted.

'So 'elp me bob!' Jeb replied. ''Urrying down the steps awearing a blue travelling cloak with the 'ood pulled over the 'ead.'

'She did not protest or cry out?' the Marquis insisted.

'No, Guv, strike me dead if I bean't telling yer the truth!' the small man said, worried now by the harshness of the Marquis's voice and the frown between his eyes.

''Er runs across the pavement and gets into the carriage as if she were as eager to be off as 'e were.'

'She did not speak to him?' the Marquis insisted after a moment's pause.

'Take me dying oath, M'Lord.'

It seemed as though the Marquis was turned to stone.

The men sitting at the table watching him realised that something gravely untoward had happened and were also silent.

And then, as if he realised that he must do something to relieve the tension, Jeb said hesitantly:

''Er did say somenat, Guv.'

'What was it?'

'It bean't to 'im, it were to the old female who comes to the door as 'er were aleaving.'

'What did she say?' the Marquis demanded. 'Tell me exactly what she said or I will throttle it out of you.'

He took a step back towards the little man, who had backed away from him apprehensively.

''Er says, M'Lord, and I be sure I were 'earing right:

'"Don't worry, dear, maybe Clyde" – I thinks that be the name– "ain't hurt as badly as we fear."

'That's what 'er said, Guv, I ain't a bamming yer, them were 'er very words.'

'So that is how he persuaded her!'

The Marquis pulled open the door of the Library and walked into the Hall.

'Have the fastest horse in my stable saddled immediately,' he said. 'Mer – no, Thunderer, and order my travelling carriage with four horses and an extra groom to proceed down the Dover road until they find me. I shall ride across country. Is that understood?'

The flunkey ran to obey his bidding.

The Marquis came back into the room, threw a purse to Jeb as he passed, and going to the table at the far end of the room took out his duelling pistols and started to prime them, completely disregarding the three men watching him with startled eyes.

Finally as he thrust first one and then the other into his pockets, Lord Hobart asked:

'What are you going to do, Alton?'

'Kill that scum,' the Marquis replied shortly.

Lord Hobart sat back in his chair.

'You have my full and unqualified approval.'

'And mine,' the Earl St Vincent said.

Only Lord Hawkesbury looked across the room at the Marquis with worried eyes.

'Be careful, Alton! There is nothing more dangerous than a cornered rat.'

His warning fell upon deaf ears for already the Marquis had left the room and was picking up his tall hat and riding-whip from the Hall.

Sylvina had come down to breakfast so happy with her thoughts that it was some time before she realised that her brother was unusually silent.

All the way back from Alton Park the previous afternoon he had talked incessantly of the Marquis, his admiration for him, and his desire to imitate him in every way.

'Did you see the fit of his coat, Syl?' he asked. 'I must find out if he patronises Weston or Stultz. There was not a wrinkle! It looked as though he were poured into it, and yet he is the least affected man I have ever met. And his cravats! If I could achieve just one of mine in even a near imitation of his, I think I would die happy.'

He talked on and on, and Sylvina realised that with his youthful impetuousness Clyde had found a new hero.

'You should see him ride,' he continued, 'he seems part of the horse. I know he has magnificent horseflesh, but he shows them off, Syl, and I believe he would look the same on any old screw. That is horsemanship for you! I want above all things to watch him drive a four-in-hand. They say he can turn a corner closer and neater than any man in the whole Corinthian set.'

Sylvina had been only too content to sit and listen to this spate of admiration for the man whose very name made her quiver with joy and happiness.

'Oh, Sir Justin! Sir Justin!' she murmured in her heart. 'I have found you again. Nothing in the whole world matters save that you ... love me.'

She thought of how he had kissed the palms of her hands, putting his heart into her keeping, and she hugged the secret of it, as he had meant her to do, within her breast.

When she went to bed she was too happy to sleep, she could only press her lips against her own palms and pretend that they touched his.

Now surprisingly this morning Clyde was silent.

'What ails you, dear?' she asked at length. 'I can see that you have not slept well.'

Her brother rose from the table and walked towards the window.

'I was thinking last night when I got back,' he said in a low voice, 'that I have been behaving like a coward, Syl. It is not for a man to shelter behind a female.'

'But, Clyde...' Sylvina began, only to be silenced by his raised hand.

'I have made up my mind,' he said. 'I am going to do what the Marquis would if he were in my shoes; I am going to make a clean breast of it, Syl. I am going to tell him the truth – and hope to God he believes me.'

Sylvina clasped her hands together.

Just for a moment she contemplated telling her brother that his sacrifice might be unnecessary. The Marquis was pledged to save them both, and he already knew that the dilemma in which Clyde had found himself arose from no fault of his own.

Then she remembered she had promised the Marquis that she would not speak of what had happened to anyone, and how indeed could she comfort Clyde without telling him how she had gone to the wrong bedroom when she had fled from the attentions of Mr Cuddington?

'If the Marquis is in the office today,' Clyde said in a slightly unsteady voice, 'I will request that I may see His Lordship. Perhaps after luncheon would be the best time. If not, it will definitely be tomorrow. Do not argue with me, Syl, I have made up my mind.'

He looked at her as if for the first time and saw there were tears in her eyes.

'It is all right,' he said, 'you are not to be unhappy about it. I will take what punishment is coming to me, and I hope I behave like a man.'

'Oh, Clyde, I am so proud of you!' she cried.

'No reason to be,' he said embarrassed. 'I should have done this ages ago. It was only when I got to Alton Park, met the Marquis and realised what a contrast he was to that common swine Cuddington that I realised I had let him terrorise me into behaving like a cad. Papa would have been ashamed of me, and Mama also. You should not have let me do it, Syl.'

'I was so frightened for you,' she said.

'I am ashamed of myself,' Clyde said, 'and that's a fact. Oh well, I had better repair to the office. It is too early for heroics.'

He walked across the room, put his arm round his sister and gave her a hug.

Then before she could say any more to him he had gone from the room. As she heard him slam the front door behind him she clasped her hands together and said a little prayer of thankfulness.

'Thank you, God, thank you!'

She knew now that she had been deeply hurt, without hardly realising it, by the knowledge that Clyde was prepared to sacrifice her and ignore her suffering so that he could be safe.

Now he was facing up to his problems like a man, and she thought with a sudden burst of joy it was all due to the Marquis.

How wonderful he was, how good and upright in every thing that mattered!

She sat for a long time in the Dining Room, too happy to notice the passing of time. Bessie did not disturb her.

After a time she went upstairs, put on her hat and took Columbus out into the sunshine. When she came back she was suddenly aware of all the household duties she had forgotten.

'I am sorry, Bessie,' she said, meeting the old maid in the narrow hallway. 'I have been sadly neglectful this morning but you must forgive me.'

'I will forgive you anything to see the happiness on your face, Miss Sylvina,' Bessie answered. 'What has occurred that you are smiling after all these weeks of the dismals?'

Sylvina laid her cheek against the old woman's face.

'I cannot tell you yet, Bessie,' she said, 'but I am happy, so happy again. I can hardly believe it is true.'

'Then that is all I want to hear, Miss Sylvina,' Bessie said. 'You deserve happiness, indeed you do.'

'Everything is going to be all right,' Sylvina said. 'I promise you, Bessie, everything is going to be all right.'

Even as she spoke there came a sudden rat-tat at the door. Bessie moved to open it, and as she did so Mr Cuddington burst in.

'You!' Sylvina ejaculated, stepping back a pace almost without realising she was doing it.

'Come quickly,' he said, 'there has been an accident. You must come to Clyde at once. He is injured and asking for you!'

'What has happened?' Sylvina cried. 'How

is he hurt?'

'I will tell you about it as I take you to him,' Mr Cuddington answered. 'Have you a cloak?'

'I have it somewhere,' Sylvina said vaguely, picking up her hat.

'I said a cloak,' Mr Cuddington rebuked her. 'I am in an open carriage and the wind is cold.'

Bessie looked at him in astonishment because it was a warm day, but she fetched from the hall-cupboard Sylvina's travelling cloak.

In dark blue wool with a hood edged with marabou, it was not an expensive garment but extremely becoming. She slipped it over Sylvina's shoulders even as she hurried forward.

Mr Cuddington opened the door and stepped out first. As he did so Sylvina remembered how deeply Bessie adored Clyde and turned back.

She put her arms round the old woman.

'Do not worry, dear, maybe Clyde is not hurt as badly as we fear.'

Then she ran down the steps, across the pavement and into the carriage. They set off, the horses travelling at what seemed to Sylvina an unprecedented speed.

Mr Cuddington did not speak, and after a short while she realised they were leaving the houses behind and were out in the country.

Then turning to the man beside her she asked:

'Where can we be going? Clyde left for Whitehall! Tell me please what occurred.'

He glanced down at her white, strained face with a smile on his lips.

'You can ease your mind,' he said, 'there is no accident. Clyde, as far as I know, is safely in his office.'

'In his office!' Sylvina repeated incredulously. 'Then why, why am I here?'

'Because I wanted you,' he said roughly.

'But where are you taking me?'

'I am taking you to France.'

'To France? Are you crazed?' Sylvina asked. 'We cannot go to France, we are at war!'

'Nevertheless you and I are crossing the Channel,' Mr Cuddington replied.

She stared at him apprehensively as though he had taken leave of his senses.

'Why ... why are you saying this?' she asked.

'Because I have a communication for the leader of the French which will delight him, and which will ensure that you and I, my dear, will return to England with the victorious invaders as virtual King and Queen of this island.'

'You are ... mad!' Sylvina half whispered in a frightened voice.

'No indeed, I am entirely sane,' Mr Cuddington retorted. 'Do you realise that we will live together at Buckingham Palace? And I have decided something that will please you, my dear. Our country home will be Alton Park. A fine place, and one where we can entertain to advantage.'

'But Alton Park be ... belongs ... to the M ... Marquis,' Sylvina stammered, too bewildered to realise what she was saying.

'The Marquis will die,' Mr Cuddington snapped, 'with all the other members of the Government whose lives have already been declared forfeit by Napoleon Bonaparte.'

'Let me down!' Sylvina cried. 'I cannot go on talking to you like this! I do not know what has occurred or why you should be making such a jest of serious things; but if Clyde is not injured then I wish to return home.'

'You will return home when it suits me,' Mr Cuddington replied. 'And our home, will be a very different place to the small, squalid building you have just left. Do you not understand? I shall be the most important man in Britain! I shall represent Bonaparte; and as he has done in other countries, he will make me a nobleman and maybe he will even make me royal.'

His voice was triumphant.

'But whatever my actual title,' he continued, 'I shall have power – power over the people who have despised me, power over those who have sneered and scoffed, who have thought me clever but not quite distinguished enough to grace their dining-tables.'

'So ... you are a ... traitor,' Sylvina said accusingly.

'Yes, a traitor,' Mr Cuddington boasted, 'and one whom they could not unmask. Now in a short time, perhaps tomorrow, they will learn to their cost that I was not a man to be ignored or treated with disdain.'

'I only hope you get your deserts, Sir,' Sylvina said bitterly. 'But at least do not involve me in your treachery. I am English and proud of it. My father served our country all his life, and my brother was in the Army. Do you think I can look at you without loathing, without despising you and everything you stand for?'

Mr Cuddington laughed and put out his arm.

Sylvina tried to shrink from him into the corner of the carriage, but there was very little space between them, and the swaying caused by the speed at which they were travelling made it very difficult to avoid his encircling arms.

In fact, it was impossible. She was further handicapped by the cape which covered her shoulders, and though she fought and twisted against him, in a few seconds he had pulled her close to him, laughing at her struggles.

'So you still despise me!' he exclaimed. 'Well, at least I shall not tire of you easily. But I shall tame you. As I told you the other night. I shall make you humble and subservient, even though you may find it a painful process.'

'Let me ... go!' Sylvina pleaded, suddenly afraid as she had never been afraid in her life before.

He understood that she was referring to something more momentous than the fact that he held her in his arms.

'You will come with me to France,' he said, 'but we will not be married there. The British people enjoy a wedding almost as much as a Coronation.'

'Do you really think I would ... marry you, a man who would betray his own country, his own people?' Sylvina asked bitterly.

'I think after tonight you will have little choice,' he replied.

He looked down at her and the lust in his eyes made her shrink from him as far as she could. Then he took her chin in his hands and turned her face up to his.

'So small, so ineffectual, and yet so desirable,' he said.

She felt herself sicken at the passion in his voice, and then his lips, hot and possessive, were on hers and she felt as if she would die from the shame of it.

He kissed her roughly, brutally, until she

could no longer breathe. She felt as if he was drawing her down into a dark river of slimy degradation from which she would never be clean again.

She felt him slip his hand beneath her cloak and fumble at her breast, tearing the thin gauze of her gown as he did so. She struggled frantically even while she knew it was useless.

When he finally took his lips from hers she was half swooning. He looked down at her pale, terrified face and chuckled.

'You see how helpless you are,' he jeered. 'Do you really think you can oppose me? But in time to come you will admire and revere me for all I shall achieve.'

'I ... I ... loathe ... y ... you,' Sylvina managed to stammer between trembling lips.

He laughed and would have kissed her again, but some instinct as he turned his head made him glance back over the open hood in the direction from which they had come.

It was then he released her, taking his arms from her and muttering almost beneath his breath:

'It cannot be – it is too soon for them to have discovered anything.'

'What is it?' Sylvina asked, a sudden hope rising irresistibly within her.

He turned and snarled at her almost like a wild animal.

'Did the Marquis call on you this morning? Is there anyone likely to have known that we had left London together?'

'No ... no, I do not think ... so,' Sylvina answered, at the same time there was a sudden light in her eyes.

As Mr Cuddington turned his head again she raised herself on the seat to look back.

She saw, as she prayed almost without hope to see, a figure riding towards them through the dust, someone she recognised instantly by the breadth of his shoulders, the angle of his top-hat and his superb horsemanship.

'It is the Marquis!' she ejaculated before she could prevent herself.

'Yes, the Marquis,' Mr Cuddington said grimly, 'and alone.'

It was then she realised that Mr Cuddington had drawn a pistol from his coat-pocket and was priming it.

'What are you ... going to ... do?' Sylvina cried desperately, knowing the answer.

'Kill him,' he replied. 'He is due, anyway, for extermination. He merely gets his deserts before the others.'

'But you cannot ... you cannot shoot down a ... man in ... cold blood,' she protested.

'Are you so interested as to whether he lives or dies?' Mr Cuddington asked. 'I had thought otherwise, but perhaps I was mistaken. If what now I suspicion is true, it will amuse me to hold you tonight naked in my arms and know you are mourning an effete aristocrat lying dead in his blood on the highway.'

'I always knew you were ... wicked and evil,' Sylvina whispered. 'I knew it the first time I met ... you. And now I know you are worse ... you are a ... devil in ... human form.'

And then in a kind of terror which seemed to creep over her like the tentacles of an octopus, freezing the very blood in her veins, she remembered how in her prediction for the Marquis she had seen for him both danger and the spilling of blood.

'Oh God, help him!' she prayed aloud.

Then to Mr Cuddington she cried:

'You cannot do this! I beg you to spare him! I will be to you anything you wish, but spare his life!'

Mr Cuddington merely laughed, and she knew that in some horrible way her words merely inflamed the lust within him to kill.

The Marquis was drawing nearer, and now Mr Cuddington turned and knelt on the seat, steadying himself against the open hood, pointing his pistol towards the Marquis.

He was not an easy target: it had not rained for over a week and the dust was rising off the dry road in such thick clouds that the Marquis could be seen one moment and the next was entirely obliterated from sight.

And yet all the time he was drawing nearer and nearer.

Bill Daws was driving superbly, but the Marquis's horse, with its Arab blood, could overhaul anything that a livery-stable could produce.

Sylvina knew it was only a matter of seconds before he drew level with the carriage and called upon the driver to halt.

She wanted to scream that there was danger, that he must save himself, but her voice was strangled in her throat and though she opened her lips no sound came forth.

Then, when she could hear the thunder of his horse's hooves and saw the Marquis's face quite clearly emerging from the dust, Mr Cuddington rose high on his knees and raised his pistol to bring it down towards him.

With a despairing effort to save the man she loved, Sylvina threw herself against his assailant.

She tried to force his arm upwards, and small and weak though she was her action took Mr Cuddington by surprise.

Though she did not stop him from pulling the trigger, she succeeded in jolting his arm so that the shot aimed at the Marquis's chest harmlessly pierced his high hat and blew it from his head.

As the report ran out deafeningly, the Marquis fired in return and with superb marksmanship shot Mr Cuddington through the heart.

The Under-Secretary gave a hoarse cry and throwing up his arms toppled backwards into the carriage to lie sprawled on the floor as blood began to flood crimson over his white shirt.

With difficulty Bill Daws drew his frightened team of horses to a standstill.

The Marquis, riding round to the side of the carriage on which Sylvina was sitting, saw her trembling in the corner, her eyes staring wide and frightened at the body at her feet.

The Marquis dismounted, slipped his horse's reins over one of the carriage lamps and opening the door drew her gently into his arms.

'It is all right, my darling,' he said. 'You are safe.'

She gave a little sob which seemed to come from the very depths of her being and hid her face against his shoulder.

'I ... thought he ... would ... kill you,' she murmured.

'He might have done if you had not saved me,' the Marquis answered.

He lifted her clear of the coach and set her down on her feet, but he still held her close as he saw riding towards them down the road a troop of Cavalry.

The officer dismounted, came towards the Marquis and saluted smartly.

'Major Wyndham at your service, My Lord.'

The Marquis smiled at him.

'So it's you, Freddie,' he said. 'There is no one I would rather see at this particular moment.'

'In one of your usual hot spots it appears, Justin,' Major Wyndham remarked with a grin. 'By Gad, it seems like old times to be coming to your rescue in the nick of time.'

'I have already rescued myself, thank you, Freddie,' the Marquis retorted, 'which, as I will have you know, I have managed to do on other occasions.'

Major Wyndham glanced towards the body of Mr Cuddington.

'You've certainly made a tidy job of it,' he said casually. 'What do you want me to do with the body?'

'Now listen, Freddie, and this is serious,' the Marquis said. 'First of all, there is a sealed packet – or he may have opened it – in his pocket. Destroy it personally, let no one else have so much as a glance at it. It contains a lot of moonshine, but even so it might cause trouble in the wrong hands. Do you understand?'

'Of course I understand,' Freddie Wyndham answered aggressively. 'Do you take me

311

for a turnip-head?'

'I take you for a damn good officer and someone with discretion, which is what I asked for,' the Marquis answered. 'Then question this chap who is driving and discover exactly where he was taking the swine, who, incidentally, was a traitor who had given his allegiance to Bonaparte. He was to cross the Channel as soon as he reached the coast.'

'With the lady?' Major Wyndham asked.

'With the lady,' the Marquis said grimly.

'Then you wish to apprehend the ship on which they were to embark?' Major Wyndham asked.

'Exactly,' the Marquis approved. 'I will say one thing for you, Freddie, you always were quick on the uptake. Send several of your fastest riders to notify the Navy or the coast-guards, whichever is the nearest, and they will do the rest.'

'Can I not go with them?' Major Wyndham asked. 'I do not want to miss all the fun.'

'No, send a subaltern,' the Marquis said. 'There are more important things for you to do.'

'And what may they be?' Major Wyndham enquired.

'Take this body with all speed to your camp,' the Marquis said. 'Cover him with a blanket, a flag or anything you have handy, and take him immediately to your Commanding Officer's quarters. There he is to be put in a coffin and the lid nailed down. Do you understand, Freddie? No one must see he has been shot.

'The Commanding officer will tell the Regimental Surgeon that the Under-Secretary of State for Foreign Affairs has died of a heart attack when on his way to inspect the camp. The Surgeon will agree.

'You will then escort the body to London deferentially and with proper military honours, from where Lord Hobart and Lord Hawkesbury will take over.'

'Good God, Justin, you really have thought out the Cheltenham theatricals this time, have you not?' Major Wyndham ejaculated.

'It is of the utmost importance from a national point of view that there should be no scandal,' the Marquis said briefly. 'You can trust your men?'

Major Wyndham grinned.

'I'll make the penalties too high for them to chatter!'

'Then I will leave it to you,' the Marquis said. 'And be as quick as you can, Freddie. The sooner all this is cleared up the better for everyone.'

'I can understand that,' Major Wyndham said soberly.

He glanced curiously towards Sylvina, whose face was still hidden against the

Marquis's shoulder.

The Marquis also looked down at her.

'And one more thing,' he said. 'I will now take this lady out of sight of this carnage. Leave one of your men to hold my horse and to let me know as soon as my carriage arrives, which will not be too far behind. He can join you later.'

'I will do that,' Major Wyndham promised, 'and – my very best wishes, Justin.'

The Marquis raised his eyebrows and his friend added quietly:

'I have never seen you look so happy before.'

The Marquis did not answer but he smiled and lifting Sylvina up in his arms carried her into a wood which bordered the highway, the branches of the trees casting a shadow over the open carriage with its motionless occupant.

The Marquis walked until he was out of sight and sound of those he had left behind, and then he set Sylvina down on her feet, knowing that while she lay still with her face turned against his shoulders she was aware of what was happening.

The hood of her cloak had fallen back from her fair hair and holding her hands tightly in his he stood looking at her as if he had never seen her before. Her cheeks were pale but her eyes were shining.

'It is all over, my darling one,' he told her

softly, 'the nightmare is finished. There are no more ogres, dragons, bogeys or anything to frighten you.'

'Then I am ... free,' she said with a little catch in her breath.

'Not free,' he answered, 'for I cannot let you go.'

She made a little movement as if she wished to be in his arms again.

'Oh my darling, my little love,' the Marquis said unsteadily. 'I have been so afraid for you, so terrified that I would not be able to save you.'

'He might have ... killed ... you,' Sylvina murmured almost beneath her breath.

'Forget it,' the Marquis commanded. 'The only question now, my dearest dear, is how soon will you marry me? Tonight? Tomorrow? I swear I cannot wait for you any longer.'

She made an impulsive gesture towards him, and her cloak fell to the ground so that the Marquis saw that she was wearing the green gown she had been wearing the first time they met.

He swept her into his arms, holding her so fiercely she could hardly breathe.

'Do not make me wait too long,' he pleaded.

She raised her face to his but there was a shadow in her eyes.

'I want to ... belong to ... you,' she

whispered, 'you know I want it beyond ... anything in the ... world. But ... you are so ... important, of such ... consequence ... I am ... afraid of ... losing ... you.'

She hid her face against him and the Marquis touched her fair hair with gentle fingers.

Was there any other woman in the whole length and breadth of the land, he wondered, who would find his rank and vast possessions a liability?

'You will never lose me, darling,' he promised, 'but I have something to suggest to you. I have finished the task Mr Pitt asked of me. I think that with honour I can now resign from my post at the Foreign Office. I believe that this war is not going to be a quick or an easy one, and what will be more vital to the country than anything else will be food.'

He paused and his voice was very tender as he continued:

'Could you contemplate helping a certain farmer called Justin to put into cultivation two thousand acres of land at Alton Park this year, and more next year? It may not be very gay living in the country, but there will be our dogs, our horses, and perhaps in time – our children.'

Sylvina drew in a deep breath and looked up at him.

'Oh, Sir Justin!' she cried, and her face

was radiant, 'could ... we do ... that?'

'There is only one thing which could prevent it,' the Marquis answered.

'And what is ... that?' Sylvina asked a little apprehensively.

'If you did not love me enough,' he replied. 'Do you realise, my precious one, that you have told me how much you hated me, you have told me that you are grateful to me, but you have never yet told me that you love me.'

He thought he had never seen her look more beautiful as she lifted her face to his, her eyes wide and excited but with a depth of emotion in them which was inexpressible.

Once again they were joined by that strange magic which had drawn them together the night in the park when their lips had met irresistibly.

Then just as the Marquis sought her mouth he felt her stiffen and she whispered:

'Listen ... oh, Sir Justin ... do you ... hear it?'

Somewhere far away in the wood a bird was singing.

'It is a ... bluebird,' Sylvina breathed, 'a bluebird singing of ... our love. I am sure of it.'

After all he had been through in the past weeks, the Marquis thought, so long as he could hold this small, exquisite creature in his arms and know that his heart was behaving in a most peculiar and erratic fashion, he was prepared to believe in anything – even bluebirds.

'Yes, my darling,' he said softly, 'it is a bluebird singing for us. And now will you tell me what I want to hear?'

Then Sylvina threw her arms around his neck and drew his head down to hers.

'I love ... you, Sir Justin,' she cried, 'I love ... you, and there is ... nothing left ... but love.'

The publishers hope that this book has given you enjoyable reading. Large Print Books are especially designed to be as easy to see and hold as possible. If you wish a complete list of our books please ask at your local library or write directly to:

**Dales Large Print Books**
Magna House, Long Preston,
Skipton, North Yorkshire.
BD23 4ND

This Large Print Book, for people
who cannot read normal print,
is published under the auspices of

# THE ULVERSCROFT FOUNDATION